"I don't let strange men pick me up in parks," Lisa said frostily.

"I could ask you where you *do* let strange men pick you up," he returned. "Or argue that I'm not all that strange. Instead, I think I'll play the gentleman and introduce myself. I'm Sam Ravenal."

Lisa looked pointedly at his extended hand, her own remaining eloquently in her lap. "I'm afraid you're laboring under a misconception, Mr. Ravenal. A gentleman is someone who takes a hint graciously. Not someone who insists on staying where he isn't wanted."

"The truth is, you look like you could use a friend."

"You, for instance?"

"I'm available."

"I'm sure. Let's be honest, *pal*, this has nothing to do with *friendship*. You gave it your best shot, I declined, end of story."

His eyes glittered. "You think that was my best shot? Hell, that wasn't even close. If I were trying to pick you up—which I most definitely am not—I wouldn't come on to you with some clichéd line like asking for the time."

"Oh, really? How would you come on to me?"

He smiled that lazy, circling-hawk smile. "Irresistibly."

Dear Reader,

Each and every month, to meet your sophisticated standards, to satisfy your taste for substantial, memorable, emotion-packed stories of life and love, of dreams and possibilities, Silhouette brings you six extremely **Special Edition**s.

Now these exclusive editions are wearing a brand-new wrapper, a more sophisticated look—our way of marking Silhouette **Special Edition**'s continually renewed commitment to bring you the very best, the brightest and the most up-to-date in romance writing.

Reach for all six freshly packaged Silhouette **Special Editions** each month—the insides are every bit as delicious as the outsides—and savor a bounty of meaty, soul-satisfying romantic novels by authors who are already your favorites and those who are about to become so.

And don't forget the two Silhouette *Classics* at your bookseller's every month—the most beloved Silhouette **Special Editions** and Silhouette *Intimate Moments* of yesteryear, reissued by popular demand.

Today's bestsellers, tomorrow's *Classics*—that's Silhouette **Special Edition**. And now, we're looking more special than ever!

From all the authors and editors of Silhouette **Special Edition**,

Warmest wishes,

Leslie Kazanjian
Senior Editor

PATRICIA
COUGHLIN
The Bargain

Silhouette Special Edition

Published by Silhouette Books New York

America's Publisher of Contemporary Romance

SILHOUETTE BOOKS
300 East 42nd St., New York, N.Y. 10017

ISBN: 0-373-09485-X

First Silhouette Books printing October 1988

All the characters in this book are fictitious. Any
resemblance to actual persons, living or dead, is
purely coincidental.

®: Trademark used under license and
registered in the United States Patent and
Trademark Office and in other countries.

Printed in the U.S.A.

Books by Patricia Coughlin

Silhouette Special Edition

Shady Lady #438
The Bargain #485

PATRICIA COUGHLIN,

also known to romance fans as Liz Grady, lives in
Rhode Island with her husband and two sons. A former schoolteacher, she says she started writing after
her second son was born to fill her hours at home.
Having always read romances, she decided to try pen-
ning her own. Though she was duly astounded by the
difficulty of her new hobby, her hard work paid off,
and she accomplished the rare feat of having her very
first manuscript published. For now, writing has replaced quilting, embroidery and other pastimes, and
with a dozen published novels under her belt, the author hopes to be happily writing romances for a long
time to come.

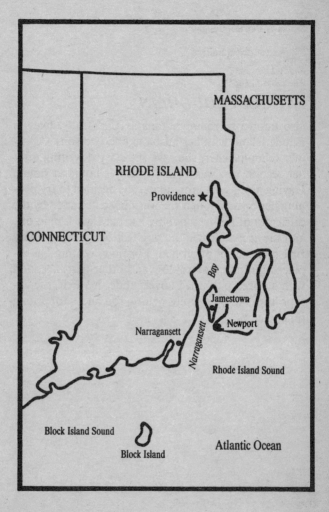

Chapter One

The torn screen on the back door snagged Lisa's sweater as she stepped outside, ending the tentative truce between her and her temporary home. Whoever had said old houses oozed charm obviously had never had to deal with one that oozed quite as much charm as this one—two hundred-plus years of it. Of course, as the lady from the Jamestown Historical Society had pointed out, necessary repairs and tasteful renovations *had* been made since the house was built in the early 1700s. Why, Lisa would be willing to wager the screen door holding her prisoner wasn't a day over seventy-five.

As her fingers impatiently plucked at the strands of jade-green yarn entwined with the jagged ends of rusted wire, she felt her sketchbook slip from beneath her arm.

"Damn," she muttered, instinctively making a grab for it. Too late. Helpless, she watched the loose sketch she had been working on earlier slip from the covers and float between the warped wooden floor planks, to be lost forever to the black hole beneath the porch. She wasn't about to brave those damp, spiderwebbed depths, even to recover something of much greater value than a preliminary sketch. Still, she'd spent over an hour getting the basic concept down, and she hated losing the piece, especially since her futile rescue attempt had resulted in a small tear in one of her favorite sweaters.

Once disentangled, Lisa briefly considered wearing the sweater to the park, hole and all. It wasn't as if anyone were likely to notice. In the week she'd been here, she had exchanged only brief greetings with a couple of neighbors, and no one at the small park down the street ever accorded her more than a nod. That isolation made the park the perfect place to work. Still, the habit of looking presentable had become so deeply ingrained that Lisa knew if she didn't change, the rip would drive her crazy, making it impossible to concentrate on her work. Sighing, she went back upstairs to slip on her taupe cotton pullover. It was equally comfortable for sketching and went just as well with the black slacks she was wearing.

Actually, thanks to a liberal dose of black in her wardrobe, everything she owned went well together, making it easy to look good with a minimum of thought and effort. Additionally, the contrast of black with her ivory skin and shoulder-length pale gold hair helped create the aura of aloof sophistication she cherished. It was her armor.

After years of being held hostage by male response to her appearance, she had recently, at age twenty-eight, discovered that the power of beauty could be twofold. Used correctly, it was as effective at holding men at bay as it was at attracting them. Men who wouldn't have hesitated to come on to her back in the days she'd hidden behind baggy clothes and a squeaky clean face could now be stopped dead in their tracks with the arch of one perfectly shaped eyebrow. Whether it was actually the sophisticated clothes and make-up that made her appear unapproachable or simply the cool self-confidence that looking flawless gave her, Lisa wasn't sure. She only knew that the trick worked, and, like the celebrities in that famous commercial, she never left home without it.

This time she moved cautiously past the screen door with its grinning slash and wire teeth. She even remembered to avoid the loose wooden step and managed to traverse the entire walk without once getting a narrow heel caught between the bricks. Turning toward the park as she reached the sidewalk, she couldn't resist a triumphant sneer at the plaque proudly proclaiming the hazardous white clapboard structure the Jonathan Bennett House. Then, feeling a little ridiculous, she wiped the expression from her face. Though at times it felt as if she were residing within the jaws of death, it was, after all, only a house.

Only a house, she reminded herself, ignoring the odd inner tug the building produced in her at unexpected moments. Just because its last name was Bennett and so was hers didn't mean there was some deep spiritual connection between her and that hulk of dried timber and chipped paint. She didn't even feel all that attached to the name Bennett, for Pete's sake. It was simply something to scribble on the line when they asked for last names first. No matter what the lady from the historical society and the local neighborhood association wanted to believe, she hadn't come here as a long-lost heir hell-bent on saving the family homestead. She was here because, at the moment, she needed the money she was being paid to be here.

As soon as she had this proposal together for the Boston-based greeting card company that had expressed interest in her work and had her advance check in hand, it would be goodbye Jamestown, Rhode Island, and hello to the nice, neat, wonderfully modern apartment awaiting her back in Chicago. As for the Jonathan Bennett House... Lisa shot it a disparaging glance over her shoulder. She would gladly relinquish it—lock, stock and yellowed lace doily—to the bats or the wrecking ball, whichever laid claim to it first.

As far as she was concerned, the only redeeming feature of the Bennett house was its location—only a few blocks from Jamestown Harbor and the picturesque little park overlooking it. For some reason she found it impossible to concentrate in the house. Creativity and mustiness must be incompatible, she had decided, refusing to acknowledge, much less explore, any other possibility for her uneasiness. Many evenings she worked outdoors, in the grassy back-yard that rolled gently down to the oceanside cliffs. But her favorite daytime workplace was the park, with its shaded benches, salt-scented breezes and, most important, that precious commodity she had begun to fear had been sucked from her life along with a lot of other fine things: inspiration.

Approaching the stone wall that surrounded the park, Lisa hoped that her inspiration wouldn't pick today to take a day off. She was nearly finished with the general part of the proposal. Next she would draw up sample cards appropriate for specific occasions, say, five each for birthdays, anniversaries, weddings. Finally she would transfer everything from sketch pad to elegant folded parchment to approximate finished greeting cards, and she would be ready to take the bundle to Boston and go crazy waiting to hear if PaperThoughts liked the concept enough to buy it. The package might even be ready as early as next week if things went smoothly—and if she could just figure out what intangible element was naggingly missing from the drawings.

Holding her breath, Lisa headed straight for her usual bench, glancing neither left nor right and telling herself that if she didn't look until she sat down, they would be there. It was crazy, of course, but when it came to courting the Muses, Lisa didn't deem any superstition too absurd to indulge. She waited until she was comfortably seated on the bench, her pencils neatly arranged beside her, her sketchbook propped open on one bent knee, before looking around, and sure enough, like magic, they were there. All three of them: the Sea Gull Queen, the Sweeper and the

Whittler. Her Muses, her inspiration. The cornerstones of the world she was creating on paper.

Lisa had struggled with and discarded several ideas before suddenly realizing that what she was searching for—a whimsical, manageable microcosm of life—had been right there in front of her. That day she had worked until dark, and for the first time in months her pencil had flown effortlessly, transforming the park into the fictional town of Wayward.

The residents of Wayward—slightly scruffy, quick-witted characters uninhibited enough to say all the things people wished they could say but usually resorted to letting a greeting card say for them—were fashioned after the park regulars, with a talking sea gull and clam thrown in here and there. Though Lisa took pains to enhance reality to make the creations her own, she had already sketched each of her "models" so many times that she could probably do it with her eyes closed. Still, until this proposal sold and she had her confidence back full force, she treasured the security of being able to verify a particular facial expression or the slope of a shoulder as she worked.

Selecting a broad-tipped pencil, she decided to begin with a sketch featuring the Sea Gull Queen, knowing she was usually the first to disappear each day. In reality, the Sea Gull Queen was a stooped, gray-haired lady who perched on the edge of her bench and regally dispensed bread crumbs to the gulls who pranced before her. She clucked and cooed at the birds as they took turns swooping and diving.

The Sweeper Lisa had viewed only from a distance as he spent his day keeping the scarred gray boards of the dock below clean. Her imagination supplied the details of his whiskered, weathered face, also providing the pipe and yellow slicker that rendered him the ultimate old salt. If the Sea Gull Queen's "voice" was one of slightly zany benevolence, the Sweeper's was pure cynicism.

Tempering the two of them was the Whittler. He was the most intriguing character of all, and he had gradually taken command of the world she was creating. Looking down, she saw that it had happened again. The Sea Gull Queen had become a bit player in the sketch that was supposed to star her, and the focus was on the Whittler. Lisa had gotten so good at drawing him she could suggest his long, easy stride with only a few strokes of her pencil. She stared at the drawing in her lap for a few seconds before penciling in lines that elevated the Sea Gull Queen's expression from jovial to rapturous as she watched the Whittler walk by. As any red-blooded woman's would, Lisa thought derisively.

On impulse she scrawled a greeting across the bottom of the sketch: *You charm-bag, you.* Without consciously thinking about it, she simply knew that that's what the Sea Gull Queen would be thinking of the Whittler.

Peeling the new sketch loose, she stuck it behind the others she had completed and put the pad aside to treat herself to a well-earned stretch. Automatically she found her gaze wandering toward the flesh-and-blood prototype for her Whittler. He was sitting with his back propped against the sun-warmed stone wall, his long legs negligently stretched out in front of him. Oh, yes, she had him down pat all right. From his lean, angular frame to the thick dark hair that curled a little too long over the collar of his denim shirt, he was hers. Artistically speaking, of course. She had no other possessive urges toward him whatsoever.

On paper the Whittler was often sardonic but basically cooperative, malleable, responsive to her whims, submissive to her will. Everything Lisa had learned in life told her the man himself was not like that at all. For one thing, he simply looked too darn easygoing to be easygoing. For another, what was he doing here? He looked about thirty years too young to be retired and close to twenty years too old to be ducking the truant officer. What sort of able-bodied man spent his days whittling by the seashore? One who traveled to the beat of a different, if somewhat unambitious, drummer—that's what kind. And one who didn't particularly care what the rest of the world thought about it. That alone ruled out the chance of his being malleable, and it shed a rather dim light on responsive and submissive, as well.

What he appeared to be, Lisa concluded, eyeing him through the camouflage of her oversize sunglasses, was cocky. Cockiness—pure and simple and not to be confused with mere self-assurance—was suggested by that lazy swagger she had struggled to capture with her pencil, and in the tilt of his head as he coolly appraised whatever his project for the day happened to be. But where it really showed was in his smile.

Lisa had seen it only a couple of times, but it was burned into her consciousness. It didn't flash into existence as a happy grin might. No, the Whittler's smile spread across his face slow and easy, the way a hawk circled its prey. It lifted the edges of his chiseled mouth and transformed a face that was basically good-looking into a sinfully tempting one. Now that she thought it over, it was actually more of a smirk masquerading as a smile. It marked the man wearing it as a fast-talking, rule-bending...charm-bag. And it was the equivalent of a giant CAUTION sign to any woman smart enough to interpret it correctly. Lisa had recently had a crash course in how to get smart in a hurry.

To her horror, as she sat there speculating about the Whittler, he looked up and gazed directly back at her in a way that said, sunglasses be damned, he knew exactly what she was staring at so intently. Then he smiled, and it was like an unspoken challenge zinging her from thirty feet away.

Lisa instinctively grabbed her sketchbook and pretended to work. Damn. That had been so obvious. She should have slowly swung her gaze back the length of the horizon, stopping absorbedly along the way to make it clear to the man that he held about as much interest for her as the haul of fish being unloaded nearby. Then she could have executed a delicate yawn and reached for her pencil. Unfortunately, it was too late for any of that now.

Resisting the urge to peek and see if he was still watching, she began to rough in the outline of the Sweeper with vigorous pencil strokes. The body flowed like rote, but his face refused to come together, and eraser particles soon roughened the paper. No matter how she concentrated, the cheeks kept turning out too lean, the jaw too stubborn, the whole thing too like the man who, Lisa knew from the annoying tingling of her spine, was still staring at her. Impatiently she tugged the completed sketches from the back of the book and riffled through them. She had drawn the expression she was striving for at least a dozen times, and she could do it again, dammit.

She was still searching for an earlier sketch to refresh her memory of the Sweeper when a shadow fell across the pages. It disturbed her to note it wasn't a chill, but sudden heat she felt as she looked up into the Whittler's eyes.

Green. His eyes were as green as the patch of spring grass beneath his feet. Rogue's eyes, naturally homing in on a woman as if she were the only thing on God's planet that mattered . . . for the moment. Her instincts had been dead right about him.

"Excuse me," he said, his voice deep and every bit as seductive as Lisa had known it would be. "I was wondering if I might bother you for the time."

"Sorry. I never wear a watch when I'm working."

"I see." But instead of wandering off in response to her expertly cool dismissal, he hunkered down directly in front of her and nodded toward her left wrist. "Then I can only assume you're not."

"Not?"

"Working."

Irritably Lisa glanced down at the slender gold watch she had forgotten she was wearing. She gave a slightly uncomfortable shrug. "I *usually* never wear a watch when I'm working. I'd forgotten that I put it on today because I wanted to be home by two to catch a movie on . . . on TV," she concluded, annoyed with herself for making explanations.

"So?"

"So what?"

"So could I bother you for the time?" he asked again, still wearing that flagrantly challenging smile she decided she detested.

Unable to think of any civil reason to refuse his request, Lisa glanced at her watch. "Twelve forty-five."

"What movie?" he asked without a pause.

"None of your business."

"Never heard of it. Supposed to be good?"

His playful manner made no attempt to disguise the fact that he was flirting with her, and Lisa stiffened in response. "I told you the time," she said, "but now you really are bothering me. I'd like to get back to work."

He stood, but before she had time to exhale with relief, he flopped down beside her on the bench. Too close beside her. Glancing quickly to the other side, Lisa realized that if she slid away from him even so much as a few inches, she would end up fanny first on the ground.

"What kind of work do you do?" he asked, peering over her shoulder at the sketches she was clutching.

"Let me tell you what I don't do," she countered in her frostiest tone, one guaranteed to make the most obstinate of admirers turn tail and run. "I don't let strange men pick me up in parks."

"I could ask where you *do* let strange men pick you up," he returned with lazy unconcern. "Or argue that I'm not all that strange. Instead, I think I'll play the gentleman and introduce myself. I'm Sam Ravenal."

Lisa looked pointedly at his extended hand rather than simply ignore it, her own remaining eloquently in her lap. "I'm afraid you're laboring under a misconception, Mr. Ravenal. A gentleman is someone who takes a hint graciously. Not someone who insists on staying where he clearly isn't wanted."

"How about a gentleman being someone who comes through when he's needed?" he shot back, apparently immune to insult. "Let's be honest, shall we...shall we...?"

Lisa arched an eyebrow at his feeble attempt to elicit her name.

"Let's be honest, shall we, *pal*?" he finally capitulated. "I've been watching you sit here all alone, day after day, trying to pass the time by drawing. And I said to myself, that is not a happy woman. The truth is, you look like you could use a friend."

"You, for instance?" Lisa's tone was a chilly blend of hostility and lofty amusement. Her expression could have withered a full-blown rose.

"I'm available."

"I'm sure. Let's be honest, *pal*, this has nothing to do with friendship and everything to do with scoring. You gave it your best shot, I declined, end of story."

His eyes seemed to get greener, glittering with indignation. Lisa couldn't decide whether his outrage was real or feigned. "You think that was my best shot? Hell, that wasn't even close. If I were trying to pick you up—which I most definitely am not—I wouldn't come on to you with some clichéd line like asking for the time."

"Oh, really?"

"Really."

"How would you come on to me?" she was startled to hear herself ask.

He smiled that lazy, circling hawk smile. "Irresistibly."

She let her gaze drift over him, taking in the relentlessly cocky expression and five feet ten or so inches of very nicely maintained male body, and smiled smugly. "Yes, well, we'll never know, will we? Since you aren't coming on to me."

"Right. No offense, of course, but you just aren't my type."

Her smile grew smugger. "I see."

Lisa knew she was virtually every man's type—not because she thought so highly of herself, but simply because she had learned from experience that most men's standards weren't terribly tough when it came to heeding basic bodily urges. The any-port-in-a-storm philosophy. Of course, in all candor, she knew she was hardly just *any* port. She was slender, curvy in all the right places and blessed with a very attractive face. When she wore makeup that emphasized her blue eyes and high cheekbones, that face could even be very dramatic. She was wearing such makeup now, and that a man dressed in a faded denim shirt and jeans, a man who literally whittled his time away, should dismiss her as "not his type" was almost laughable.

And annoying.

"Don't feel bad about it," he urged magnanimously.

"I'd say *relieved* is a more accurate description of the way I'm feeling," snapped Lisa.

He leaned back against the bench and rested one ankle on a knee. "There's no need to get testy."

"There's every need. I very much want to get back to work, and I'm not at all interested in you, in your type of woman or in continuing this conversation."

To underscore her position she began rearranging the papers in her hand.

"It seems to me you have to be at least a little interested," he remarked. Lisa felt a twinge of alarm. "Otherwise, why would you sit here drawing me day after day?"

"Drawing you? You think that's what I've been doing?" Lisa scoffed even as she frantically tried to shove the sketches back into the book. "Believe me, it's not."

How much had he already seen? Was it a copyright infringement to draw someone without his permission? she worried. She refused to consider splitting royalties with him. She'd rather turn her Whittler into a basket weaver and give him a scowl and a potbelly. Damn. Just when everything had been going so well.

"No? Well, I was taught that a gentleman never calls a lady a liar," Sam Ravenal intoned solemnly, casually extracting a particularly incriminating drawing from her pile, despite her efforts to hang on to it. "But this sure looks like me . . . unless you happen to know another guy who needs a haircut and whittles for a hobby?"

"Hobby?" echoed Lisa, making an unsuccessful lunge for her sketch. "And here I was convinced it was your vocation."

"No. But as long as you're interested enough to wonder, I'm a marine archaeologist by vocation. I happen to be between projects at the moment, so I have plenty of time for whittling. Actually, it isn't even a hobby, it's more like a necessity. Model shipbuilding is my real hobby, and I whittle to make the pieces I can't buy. Plastic offends me," he announced with the sort of disdain Lisa reserved for slimy insects and her ex-husband.

He pulled a tiny piece of wood from his pocket. It was as smooth and pale as the inside of an eggshell and carved to a cuplike roundness on both ends. "This, for example, is a fitting for the deck of my model of the sloop *Black Star*. At least, that was the new name given her by the pirate who appropriated her from the French. She sank somewhere off the coast out there in 1712." He gazed out over the blue-gray ocean with a curiously entranced expression before turning back to Lisa. "Ever hear of it?"

She shook her head with open impatience.

"She caught fire before she went down. Some say the people along the coast got word that the infamous pirate Captain Alexander Brandon was heading for Newport with the *Black Star*, loaded with booty, in tow and that they lured her aground during a storm by lighting false beacons, plundered her, then set her afire. Of course, there are just as many who claim the captain himself was responsible, that he sank her in shallow water with a fortune aboard, fully intending to reclaim it later."

Lisa frowned. In spite of herself she found her curiosity aroused by the story from the past. "Why would he do a thing like that? Whatever was on board the ship was already his."

Sam's smile was wry. "More or less. It seems the disreputable Captain Brandon had been doing some dirty work for a group of respectable Newport businessmen. If you want the pirates cleaned out of the shipping lanes, who better to hire to do it than another pirate? They finagled permission from the king to make it all nice and legal, and theoretically they were all to share equally in whatever spoils Brandon seized.''

"Theoretically?"

"Right. And it might have worked that way...if he hadn't struck a private bargain with the leader of this group of upstanding citizens. Evidently Brandon had developed a yen for the man's very proper daughter, and along with the financial reward, he wanted permission to do more than worship her from afar.''

"I didn't think pirates asked permission," Lisa commented in amusement. "I was under the impression they just took what they wanted.''

"Yes, well, old Alex was trying to break with that tradition. He'd made a fortune plying his craft and was ready to settle down on solid land and take a stab at respectability. With his chosen lady at his side, he planned to raise a family that would have all the advantages and social position stolen gold doubloons could buy. Unfortunately, becoming a pirate's wife wasn't exactly what the lady's father had in mind for her.''

"I'm sure what the lady had in mind—"

"Would hardly have mattered at the time," Sam interjected. "Don't glare at me, pal. I had nothing to do with creating the eighteenth-century custom of male supremacy.''

"Maybe not, but you probably approve of it," she concluded.

"Actually, I prefer a woman who can think for herself and take care of herself if she has to—not that I think she should always have to.''

"How did we get back on the subject of your type of woman?" Lisa demanded. "I want to know what happened to the pirate and this poor, powerless pawn of a woman.''

"*Powerless* is hardly the image this woman left behind," Sam informed her with a dry chuckle. "Not only did she have this hardened sea captain jumping through hoops and taking wild risks to be near her, but her father was evidently reluctant to incur her wrath by outright forbidding her to associate with a man he clearly thought unworthy of her. Instead, he developed this elaborate plot to get rid of Brandon permanently—and increase his share of the profits at the same time.''

"What sort of plot?''

"A classic double cross. The day after the *Black Star* went down, Brandon anchored his own sloop somewhere offshore and met with this woman's father at their home here in Jamestown. Mind you, a pirate didn't stay alive long unless he had brains to go along with his brawn, and Brandon no doubt suspected a double cross was in store for him. That's why he may have taken the precaution the night before of hiding the spoils in the only sure way he knew—by sinking them.''

"Why did he bother to come back at all if he suspected a double cross?''

Slanting her a condescending look, Sam demanded, "Aren't you listening? He came back for love, of course.''

"I don't know, it sounds more like lust to me.''

He shrugged. "Either one can screw up an otherwise well-planned operation. Brandon was arrested and shipped off to Boston for a quick trial before the governor of the Colonies, during which his letters of marque from the king and other documents that would have legitimized his privateering were declared nonexistent. He was sentenced to the gallows for treachery at sea.''

"That's awful!'' gasped Lisa. She knew well what it felt like to be used and cast aside, and she felt a rush of sympathy for the long-dead pirate. "What about this supposedly crafty woman of his? Didn't she speak up in his defense?''

''No, it seems that in the end she was just as willing as everyone else to believe the worst of a man who was, after all, a thieving, bloodthirsty rogue. Her father evidently convinced her that not only had Brandon intended to cheat his backers out of their profits, but that his only interest in marrying her was to put a veneer of respectability on his future.''

''So they hanged him,'' Lisa concluded softly.

''Not by a long shot,'' countered Sam.

Startled, Lisa whipped her head around to find him wearing a smug smile worthy of any pirate. ''What do you mean, not by a long shot?''

''Brandon was no stranger to jails. He escaped, collected his lady right out from under her scheming old man's nose and probably lived to a ripe old age on some South Sea island.''

''You mean he kidnapped her?'' Lisa asked, eyes wide, imagination whirling.

''Either that or she went willingly,'' Sam replied with another shrug.

''I hardly think a woman like that, if she believed what she did of him, would have gone traipsing off willingly,'' she argued.

A smirk edged his mouth. ''A woman like what? We've already established that lust can make a person take unreasonable risks.''

''I still say she wouldn't have gone willingly,'' insisted Lisa, her sympathies now split between the wronged pirate and the **poor** woman he thought he could commandeer as if she were a ship that caught his eye.

''What difference does it make? The final result was the same. And, willing or not, I'm sure Alex was angry enough by the time he got to her that he'd lost whatever small taste he had for saying please.''

Lisa stopped just as she was about to launch into a heated argument that it made a great deal of difference. This was crazy. The whole thing had happened centuries ago. It was hardly worth haggling over with a stranger.

"And the treasure aboard the *Black Star*?" she inquired lightly. "Did Brandon take the time to snatch that up, too, as he made his great escape?"

"Good question." Sam gazed out over the smoky-blue Atlantic. "To this day there are some who insist they've seen a strange light out there that resembles a ship. Legend has it that the devil uses light to mark the spot for when his pirate cohort returns to claim what's his."

"Is that what you believe?" Lisa inquired carefully. Something in his expression suggested he just might.

"Hell, no." He laughed, and the wistfulness, or whatever it had been, disappeared from his face. "I'm a scientist, remember? I believe the light radiates from the movement of schools of menhaden—they're oily, phosphorescent fish—below the surface. But phosphorescent fish make for lousy legend."

"I guess they do."

With the story tied up as neatly as history would permit, Lisa's earlier discomfiture began to reassert itself. How could she have allowed this man to distract her so easily? Irritated anew with him and with herself, she restlessly began to straighten her sketches. At the same time she struggled to come up with a foolproof way to get rid of him. By the time all the papers were neatly aligned in the book, she had concluded that there wasn't one. Sam Ravenal might make his living studying old ships rather than hijacking them, but she sensed he was every bit as intractable as Captain Alexander Brandon had ever been. The only way she was going to be rid of him was to leave.

"Knocking off early today?" he asked as she got to her feet. His arms were stretched nonchalantly along the back of the bench, and his green eyes laughingly proclaimed that

he recognized her departure for precisely what it was: a retreat.

"I told you I wanted to get home in time to watch a
movie."

"At two."

"I'm a slow walker."

"Me, too. Want some company?"

"No," she replied emphatically. "I enjoyed your story
today, Mr. Ravenal, but I'm afraid I have a lot of work to
get done and not much time to do it. In the future I'd really
appreciate not being interrupted."

"You never did tell me what kind of work you do."

She smiled coolly. "No. I didn't. Goodbye, Mr. Ravenal."

"Call me Sam," he urged, but Lisa had already started
walking away.

Damn Sam Ravenal. She didn't want to call him anything. She just wanted him to leave her alone. But thanks to
his being impervious to insult, she was probably going to
have to find a new place to work. She tried not to dwell on
how that might affect her productivity.

Why couldn't he have reacted to her Ice Bitch routine the
way he was supposed to? The way every other man she'd
ever had to use it on had responded? Some might be a little
slower than others to get the message, but eventually they all
grew a little red around the Adam's apple, looked ready to
curse her and took a hike.

It occurred to Lisa as she walked home that Sam Ravenal
might not have reacted on cue because she had slipped up in
her tactics, given conflicting signals. After all, for a few
moments she *had* gotten utterly caught up in his storytell-
ing. There was also the unsettling possibility that he hadn't
reacted as if she'd wounded his fragile ego because she
hadn't. Maybe he'd been telling the truth when he said she
wasn't his type. The notion should thrill her. Hadn't she insisted for years that she wished just once she could meet a

man who saw her as a person, a potential friend, instead of a potential conquest?

The disturbing truth was it didn't thrill her at all, and Lisa wasn't sure why. Maybe because she hadn't envisioned the man who would find her so bland to be so attractive himself. Like it or not, Sam Ravenal had created a little flutter of interest inside her. Nothing she couldn't easily control, of course, but the fact that she didn't seem to stir any corresponding flutter in him was a bit disconcerting.

Lisa hated the irrational insecurity that prompted her to stop before the hall mirror just inside the front door. She looked exactly as she always did—no pencil smudges on her nose, no recently erupted warts anywhere. So what was the man's problem? Even more interesting, if she wasn't his type, what was? And why did she even care?

Telling herself she *didn't* care, Lisa headed for the kitchen to see what was on hand for lunch. Salad had just won by default when the doorbell rang. Even that had a rusty, unused echo to it, she thought as she went to open the door. It never occurred to her until the moment she saw him standing there that it might be Sam.

"How—"

"I followed you," he explained before she could finish asking. There wasn't a trace of sheepishness in his admission. "You left in such a hurry you forgot this."

Lisa took the sketch he held out without glancing at it. "You could have reminded me."

"Then I wouldn't have had any excuse to follow you."

"Oh, somehow I think you would have come up with one," she countered, feeling the situation tip into her control. After all, if he weren't interested, why would he have bothered following her all the way home?

"Probably," he agreed. "I don't have a lot of self-control when I'm curious, and I was very curious when you left."

"About where I lived?"

"About you. And now I'm doubly glad I followed you here."

"Because you think you're going to have a chance to satisfy your curiosity?"

"Or to arouse yours. You're sure you never heard of the *Black Star* or Alexander Brandon until today?" he asked.

"Very sure," replied Lisa, determined not to be sidetracked again.

"That's strange."

Silence.

The pendulum on the grandfather clock behind her dragged back and forth.

Somewhere behind Sam, the first bumblebee she'd heard this spring was buzzing a furious path through the crocus patch.

Finally Lisa couldn't resist any longer.

"Why is that strange?" she asked, trying to sound as if she were merely placating him.

"Because Captain Brandon's woman—" He broke off with an accommodating smirk. "Correction, because the woman Captain Brandon kidnapped lived right here in your house."

Chapter Two

That's impossible." The words were very nearly a gasp. Unthinkingly Lisa pushed the door open a little wider and frowned at Sam Ravenal. "She couldn't have lived here."

"Why not?"

"Because...because this house has been in my family for generations—ever since it was built, in fact."

My, my, chided a sardonic voice inside her. Until a few weeks ago she'd had no idea there was a long line of Bennetts, let alone a Jonathan Bennett House, yet here she was, dismissing out of hand the very suggestion that any Bennett ever could have been involved with pirates or scandals.

"I'd say all that proves is that you're related to Elizabeth Bennett."

"Elizabeth Bennett?"

"Elizabeth Bennett was the woman's name. As soon as I saw the plaque on the corner here," he explained, indicating the brass nameplate bestowed by the historical society,

"I knew for sure this had to be the house. Her father was—"

"Jonathan Bennett," Lisa finished for him, her expression dreamy. No matter that the manner in which Alexander Brandon had gone about capturing his woman offended her modern sense of equality, the story itself appealed to the strong romantic streak in Lisa. Discovering she had a blood tie to the woman involved somehow intensified her emotional response.

Sam's deep voice intruded on her thoughts. "How does that make you feel? Knowing that one of your ancestors was half of such a legendary love affair?"

"Unlucky," Lisa retorted, automatically hiding her feelings behind a quip. "For all I know, foolish romanticism may well be a latent genetic defect, handed down for generations from a woman crazy enough to let herself fall for a pirate."

"Foolish romanticism? You say it like it's one word."

"It might as well be."

"I see. Besides being uninterested in making new friends, you also disapprove of romance."

"I didn't say I wasn't interested in making friends. Only that I'm not interested in you."

"Did anyone ever tell you that you have a winning personality?"

"No."

"I can see why. Look, just because I put you into a rotten mood is no reason to go around slandering your ancestors."

"I thought you were the one doing that."

Sam shook his head. "Not me. I happen to think Elizabeth must have been some woman to drive a hard case like Alex Brandon to such lengths. And even if you don't appreciate her romantic soul, think of the other qualities you might have inherited from a woman like Elizabeth. Courage. Passion. Determination."

Lisa smirked. "Bad taste in men?"

"That could be corrected," Sam quickly countered. "You could, for instance, admit that your first impression of me was wrong and let yourself get to know me."

"I thought you weren't coming on to me," Lisa challenged. "That I wasn't your type."

"I wasn't, and you're not. That doesn't mean we can't be friends. In fact, it probably means we *can* be friends, without anything hot and heavy getting in the way. After all, I'm a scientist, cold and clinical, and you're an admitted anti-romantic. It's a non-match made in heaven." He gave her a minute to wrestle with that, then added quietly, "Besides, I meant what I said back at the park. You do look like you could use a friend. And to tell you the truth, I could use one myself."

Lisa eyed him skeptically. "Why? You're hardly what I'd call shy and retiring."

"Maybe not, but I am a stranger around here."

"Then I'm afraid you picked the wrong person as a potential friend. I'm not from around here, either. In fact, I'm only going to be here a few weeks. If I'm lucky," she couldn't help adding.

His head tilted in an assessing pose she had captured in one of her drawings. "But I thought you said your family—"

"It's a long story," Lisa interrupted, folding her arms in a way that announced it was also a story she didn't plan to share with him.

Acknowledging her silence with a shrug, he pressed his argument. "I'd say the fact that we're both strangers here makes us even better candidates to be friends. We can go sight-seeing together. I mean, if you have to get lost, you might as well have someone to do it with."

His smile made it almost impossible not to smile back, but Lisa kept her expression as firm and discouraging as she could manage. "I'm afraid I don't have time for sight-seeing, much less getting lost. I meant what I said earlier, too: my work keeps me pretty busy."

"You can't work all the time," he pointed out. "And how many sights to see can there be on an island this small?"

It always startled Lisa to hear Jamestown referred to as an island, but that's exactly what it was—a small island connected to the neighboring resorts of Newport and Narragansett by massive suspension bridges. Small or not, however, it was an area rich in history and natural beauty, and Lisa knew exploring it could easily take more time than she cared to squander.

As if reading imminent refusal in her expression, Sam moved directly into the doorway, stealing from her even the scant protection provided by the torn screen door.

"Listen, sunken ships might be my area of expertise, but I'm not completely obtuse when it comes to reading people...even if it might seem that way to you at the moment," he allowed in the face of the skepticism expressed by her quickly raised eyebrows. "I can interpret signals, and I get the message loud and clear that you're not looking for a man in your life right now. You want to know how that makes me feel? Relieved. The fact is, I'm not looking for a woman, either. That doesn't mean it wouldn't be nice to have somebody to share a pizza with or just talk to once in a while. No strings. No pressure. What do you say?"

Lisa took a deep breath and said nothing. It was a tempting offer. It had been a long time since her life had permitted anything as uncomplicated as simple friendship. Somehow all her college friends had gotten swept aside, lost, during her marriage to Ron. Ignoring the lingering bitterness she refused to wallow in, she concentrated on the situation at hand. Nothing in Sam Ravenal's manner at the moment suggested that he had anything more than friendship in mind. Had she jumped to that conclusion earlier simply because he was a man and she a woman? And why was she feeling a perverse twinge of resentment that he saw her only in such a platonic way?

He'd been right about her not wanting a romantic involvement, but did that mean she had to avoid the entire

male half of the population? Or that she couldn't trust herself to keep things under control around a man? Her behavior certainly suggested that, and she didn't like what *that*
suggested about her attitude or her self-control.

"If it would help to ease your mind any, I could show you
some ID," Sam volunteered. In a flash he had his wallet out
of his pocket and had begun pulling various items from it.
"American Express card—at the very least that should
prove I'm financially solvent. Social Security card, ticket
stubs from a Boston Red Sox game—what could be more
American? Here's my license—"

"Proof that you've had all your shots?" Lisa couldn't
resist interjecting.

Sam glanced up from the fan of cards in his hand and
appeared surprised to see her grinning broadly. "Proof that
I can be trusted behind the wheel of a car—a much more
pertinent factor in this situation. The shots would only
matter if I were going to bite you," he pointed out, "which
we've already agreed I'm not."

"So we have," murmured Lisa. Nevertheless, his unwa-
vering green gaze sent a ripple of awareness through her, and
his sense of humor reminded her how good it felt to smile.
For that alone she owed Sam Ravenal more than a slammed
door.

"Just friends?" she demanded.

"You've got it."

"Well, then. I can't offer you pizza," she began tentatively, "but if you'll settle for salad and maybe..." She
mentally reviewed the meager contents of the refrigerator.
"*Maybe* a grilled cheese sandwich, you're invited to stay for
lunch."

"Sounds great," Sam accepted even before the satisfied
smile had fully formed on his wide mouth.

Probably afraid that if he hesitated she'd change her
mind, Lisa decided. Ignoring the niggling notion that
changing her mind would probably be the smartest thing she

could do, she held the door open wide for him to step inside.

"Uh...do you think..."

His hesitant tone made her halt midway to the kitchen and turn back.

"Do you think that, seeing as how we've agreed to be friends and all, you could suggest something I could call you that's a little more personal than *pal*? I mean, if I'm being too pushy..."

"All right, all right, the sarcasm's not necessary. My name is Lisa. Lisa Bennett."

"Pretty name," he said, extending his right hand to her for the second time that day.

This time Lisa met it with her own. Their handshake was brief, almost perfunctory, but it seemed to seal something between them. And it left Lisa's senses vibrant with the feel of him. His skin was warm and smooth except for a rough line of calluses at the base of his fingers. His hand was big enough to give her the sensation of being very small, even though at five-seven she hardly thought of herself as petite. There was an element of latent power in Sam Ravenal that had nothing to do with size or with the strength of his handshake.

"I guess somebody really liked green," he observed as he followed her into the kitchen at the back of the house.

Lisa glanced with disdain at the walls and cabinets, all painted the same murky shade of green. "Yes, bile must have been a popular color choice for kitchens back in the forties or fifties. The *eighteen* forties," she added dryly.

"Maybe it didn't age well. It might have been a lighter shade originally."

Lisa snapped her fingers. "You know, you've got something. Pale bile would be so much more appealing."

"If you hate it that much, why don't you do something about it? Anyone can swing a paintbrush."

"I won't be here long enough," Lisa explained, pulling butter, cheese and the container of salad from the refriger-

ator and crossing her fingers that she had four slices of
bread left. She did.

"Besides, painting the walls would probably make the
floor and countertop look even shabbier," she continued,
referring to the ancient yellowed linoleum that covered both
the floor and the kitchen's single narrow counter. "And if
they were new, the room would cry for a new light fixture."
She indicated the fluorescent ring overhead with the tip of
the knife she was using to butter the bread. "Then those
rooster print curtains would probably just slink out of here
on their own from sheer embarrassment and have to be replaced. That would leave me with that tacky kitchen set to
contend with."

"Not much for antiques, huh?" There was unmistakable
amusement in his query.

Lisa glanced up from unwrapping the cheese. "Antiques
I can take or leave. That…" She frowned at the gray-toned
kitchen set with its pitted metal top and scarred chairs.
"That I wouldn't even bother to dust."

"I noticed."

"I don't eat in this room," she explained sheepishly, as if
that somehow justified its condition. "In fact, I spend as
little time in here as possible."

"I can understand why. It's a bit … oppressive."

"Exactly."

She put the frying pan with the sandwiches on the stove
and turned on the burner. Nothing. Well, why should today be any different from every other day since she'd been
here? Reaching for a match from the box on the shelf above
the stove, she added, "Oppressive and frustrating. I mean,
the house is basically clean enough, and there are no leaks
or danger spots—that is, if you don't count that deadly
porch step—but everything about this place is just so damn
old and uncooperative."

She kept talking as she attempted—and failed—to light
the gas pilot. Twice. Then Sam was behind her, reaching
over her shoulder to take the third match from her fingers.

He flicked it with the tip of his thumbnail and held it to the stove far longer than Lisa would have dared. Flames soon danced in a blue circle around the burner, and Lisa suddenly knew what it felt like to be trapped between a hot place and hell. Sam's shoulder brushing against hers ignited in her a heated awareness of him, which she suspected could be every bit as dangerous as the fire in front of her.

"See that?" Sam asked, still standing close beside her as he slid the pan over the flames. "You're too skittish. Don't be afraid of it, Lisa. It can't hurt you."

"It can't?" she countered, wondering if they could possibly be talking about the same thing.

"Not if you don't let it burn out of control."

She stared down at the sandwiches, which were beginning to sizzle in the pan. "Right. I just have to stay in control. That's all."

"That's all there is to it."

She turned her head, startled to find his face so close to her own. She was suddenly taken by the outrageously wayward impulse to run her tongue across the trace of dark stubble shadowing his lean cheek. Just thinking about it made staying in control seem as much within the realm of possibility as did swimming the Strait of Gibraltar.

"Pour the drinks," she ordered.

Without questioning her brusqueness, Sam obligingly ambled toward the refrigerator. "What are we drinking?"

"Whatever's there. Orange juice, I think, and there should be a few cans of Diet Coke buried somewhere."

"Or we could settle for this."

Lisa paused in the process of tossing the salad and glanced at the nearly full bottle of expensive white wine he was holding aloft. She had splurged on it one night last week when her work was going particularly badly, then had decided it probably wasn't a good idea to start drinking alone and had relegated the bottle to the bottom shelf of the refrigerator. At least today she wouldn't be drinking alone.

But alcohol at midday on top of her already unsettled feelings still did not strike her as a particularly wise choice.

"To toast our new friendship?" Sam suggested, smiling innocently.

Somehow Lisa felt as if she were being asked not to choose between Diet Coke and Chablis, but whether or not she was capable of remaining in control of this situation.

She smiled at him over the salad. "Why not?"

Immediately her common sense listed several dozen good reasons, which she promised herself she would keep firmly in mind. Eschewing the plain water glasses she had been using, Sam explored the cupboards Lisa hadn't been able to reach and located delicate stemware. Unwrapping two from the plastic wrap they had been stored in, he poured the wine while she finished the salad.

After they fixed their plates in the kitchen, Lisa led the way to a tiny room tucked at the back of the house. She imagined it had originally been a study or perhaps a first-floor bedroom used in case of illness. When she had arrived, it was empty except for a desk and two cane chairs. That fact, coupled with its spectacular view of the ocean, promptly made her decide to make it her own for as long as she was there.

It had cost her several days and a few aches and pains to rescue it from the musty grayness that gripped the rest of the house. Here she had relented and gone to the trouble of applying fresh paint, pale rose on the walls and ceiling and glossy white for the woodwork. She'd also polished the hardwood floor and stripped the curtains from the windows to expose the natural beauty framed in their tiny panes. Finally she'd roamed the rest of the house, choosing just the right furniture—a couple of easy chairs upholstered in navy-and-rose chintz, several mismatched mahogany tables and a pair of beautiful crystal lamps. The result was a comfortable sitting room with a vaguely French country feeling, well worth all her efforts.

Lisa had decided it was also worth whatever flak she might have to take from Mr. William Fredericks, Esq., when he saw it. Fredericks obviously took his role as executor of the estate very seriously and had made it clear that she was to check with him before altering the Jonathan Bennett House in any way. However, Lisa knew he might have said no, and there was no way she could have lived in the house as is, no matter how temporarily. Now, as Sam followed her into the haven she'd created, she listened with pride to the surprise and approval in his reaction and was even happier she'd taken matters into her own hands.

"Wow." Putting his plate and wineglass down on a small table beside one of the chairs, he did a full three-hundred-and-sixty-degree inspection. "Is this really the same house?" he asked, openly incredulous.

"I didn't do much really. I told you I don't plan on being here long. It just goes to show that, with a little elbow grease, anything is possible."

Lisa's tone was offhand, but inside she was beaming. She'd also forgotten that part of the satisfaction and fun of accomplishing something was sharing it with someone, seeing your success reflected in another's reaction. Sam had been right. She did need a friend.

"It goes to show a hell of a lot more than that. It also proves that you're one talented lady. I mean it," he insisted when she settled into her chair with a self-effacing shrug. "I can imagine what this room looked like before you got hold of it—probably a close relative of the kitchen. Now it's something special. You have a great eye for color and proportion. But then, I guess that goes along with being an artist. Are these yours?" he asked, moving to take a closer look at the ebony-framed drawings she'd hung on the wall between the windows. They were among the few touches of home she'd brought with her.

"Yes. But I wouldn't call myself a real artist, exactly. Maybe a graphic artist. A commercial artist, really." Lisa knew she was babbling the way she always did when she was forced to watch someone examine her work.

"These are . . ." Sam paused. Lisa leaned forward in her seat, her breath sealed behind tightly closed lips. "Familiar. I've seen these drawings somewhere before. I remember them because, even though the faces are sketchy, they manage to express a lot of emotion."

"Thank you," she murmured. Nothing he might have said about her work could have pleased her more. "You probably have seen them before, or similar drawings of mine. They were part of a line of greeting cards I designed."

Sam's eyes grew bright with recognition. "Of course. Maxine's . . . what were they called? Maxine's Musings, right? I've seen them everywhere."

"They were very successful." Lisa wondered if the sudden tightness in her voice was as obvious to Sam as it was to her. "Maxine was a great character to work with, sort of glib and sort of neurotic—something to appeal to everyone. We were even able to branch out into other products—mugs, beach towels, that sort of thing."

Sam whistled between his teeth, taking one last look at the drawings before sitting and reaching for half of his sandwich. "That stuff must have made you a fortune. No wonder you aren't going to waste time spit-shining this old place. I'll bet you have your eye on something a little less lived-in."

Strangely, his personal remarks about her income didn't bother her—maybe because he was so far from the truth.

"Hardly," she replied. "Maxine's Musings made a fortune all right, but not for me. The profits from all sales were neatly tied up by the man who owned the company that printed the original series of cards."

The corners of Sam's mouth tipped down sympathetically. "You mean he ripped off your idea?"

"Actually, it was more a case of my giving it to him." Suddenly not hungry, she pushed her plate aside and reached for her wine. "What was the expression you used?

Oh, yes, a classic double cross. Well, in this case, I not only smiled while I got screwed," she said with uncharacteristic coarseness, "but I paid for the privilege." She met his puzzled gaze over the rim of her raised glass. "The owner of the card company, Ron Trebek, was also my husband. Ex-husband now." She took a long sip.

Sam responded with a softer version of his earlier whistle. "Lisa, that's really rough. Divorce itself must be shattering enough, but when it's that complicated, tied in with your career..." He broke off, shaking his head. "How long ago did all this happen?"

Lisa couldn't prevent a mirthless laugh. "Hindsight being what it is, I can see that it obviously started happening the moment I met Ron."

Sam pushed his own plate aside, his sandwich unfinished. Neither of them had touched the salad. "How did you meet the guy?" he asked.

Maybe it was because she'd been living with the Whittler night and day for a week now, and because her intelligent, irreverent creation and Sam Ravenal had indeed turned out to be uncannily alike. Maybe it was because she needed a friend to talk to even more than Sam or she had guessed. Whatever the reason, and in spite of the fact that they'd just met, it felt natural to tell Sam about things she had never discussed with anyone else.

Leaning forward to rest her elbows on her knees, Lisa propped her chin on her clasped hands and thought about her and Ron and about how it had all started so promisingly for the two of them.

"We met because of business," she finally began. "I had come up with the character of Maxine for some posters I did for a class reunion at the school where I was teaching at the time. Some of the other teachers suggested that my drawings and slogans would make great greeting cards. Somehow I let them talk me into approaching a card company with my ideas."

"Your husband's card company?"

"Right. It was a small operation, but I'd done some research and learned that the smaller firms were more apt to take on an offbeat idea then the bigger, more traditional card publishers. What I didn't know was that Ron was struggling just to keep his head above water financially. He needed something or someone to bail him out."

"And there you were, bucket in hand."

"I'm afraid so. He was more than enthusiastic about my proposal, and I was so thrilled I was willing to believe anything he said. You know that old saying, 'Those who can, do, and those who can't, teach'?"

Sam nodded.

"Well, that was my opinion of myself. I'd been labeled *competent* in enough college art classes to convince me that that's what I was: barely competent. Suddenly, Ron's enthusiasm changed all that."

Lisa noted how the muscles in Sam's face tensed in a sympathetic frown as he waited for her to continue. If he'd pressed or prodded, she might have retreated, but he didn't say a word. Clearly, he understood that cutting through the layers of memory got more painful as she went deeper.

"It wasn't only my work Ron seemed to like, it was me, too. Me. He made me feel like a combination of Michelangelo and Cleopatra. He was sweet and charming. I saw stars." Her wistful tone sharpened into a harsh laugh. "While he obviously saw a pigeon ready to be plucked. We were married only a few months after we met, and once the first cards I'd designed took off, I was busy just keeping up with the demand for new material. It seemed natural for Ron to handle financial matters, and he always insisted the smart thing to do was for us to plow all the profits right back into the company. *His* company, as it turned out."

Wincing slightly, Sam asked, "And you went along with that?"

"He was my husband," Lisa responded, her voice riddled with self-disgust. "I assumed...I thought..." Her eyes flickered shut briefly. "What I thought doesn't really matter now. Of course I knew Ron and I weren't as close as married couples should be, as close as I wanted us to be, but I kept telling myself that was because we were both so busy trying to get ahead, that soon there would be time for each other, time for a family. About a year ago I finally had to face what I'd been avoiding: the fact that what Ron wasn't getting from me he was getting plenty of somewhere else.''

"It's hard to imagine any man cheating on a woman like you."

Delivered in Sam's deep, self-confident voice, the remark wasn't mere lip service. It was a statement of fact, with an intensity Lisa absorbed right through her skin. It brought color to her cheeks, and her heart began to pound erratically. And suddenly she wasn't at all sure she could handle friendship with Sam Ravenal.

Chapter Three

Well, I definitely didn't imagine this," Lisa assured Sam, hoping he would assume it was the memories she was dredging up and not him that had her clenching her fingers uneasily. "I ran into him and his...his mistress coming out of a restaurant on one of the many evenings he was supposedly working late.

"It was all very civil," she went on, the humiliating words now racing from her mouth. "He admitted that he'd been seeing her for some time and had every intention of continuing to do so. It seems she couldn't draw a straight line to save her soul—never mind his precious company—but she sure had everything else he ever wanted in a woman."

"So you left the bastard."

Smiling a little at the rasp of satisfaction in his tone, Lisa nodded. "It took me a few months to come to terms with it emotionally, and I was almost feeling human again when the lawyer I had hired called and dropped the next bombshell. He'd just come from a meeting with Ron's attorney to work out the financial aspects of the divorce and been informed that out of the sheer goodness of his heart, Ron was willing to give me a small cash settlement. Everything else—all investments, all past and future profits from my work, even the condo we were living in—were the sole property of the company, and *that* was the sole property of a dummy corporation Ron had set up, with himself as head. It was all very legal and very clever and very well documented by papers I had been gullible enough to sign without so much as reading them.''

"I don't care what the hell you signed," Sam declared, rising from the chair in agitation. He paced the room as restlessly as a newly caged leopard, then stopped a few feet away and turned to face her. "There had to be some grounds for you to sue the swindler. Sounds to me like you needed a new lawyer."

"Oh, the lawyer I hired explained that I could sue. He said I might even win. But he also warned me that it would take years before I ever saw a penny of what was rightfully mine...if I ever did. He explained how Ron could shift funds around, file bankruptcy and claim he was unable to pay whatever the courts might eventually award me. I decided it wasn't worth the effort."

"I can't believe you're so damn calm about this."

"Not calm," she corrected. "Philosophical."

"Screw philosophy. And never mind the money involved. That guy deserved years of aggravation and harassment in court for what he did to you."

"I won't argue with that," Lisa agreed, lifting her wineglass to toast his opinion. "But *I* didn't deserve it. And that's exactly what it would have been—long years of aggravation and hostility. I had to make a decision. Did I want to fight to make Ron pay, invest yet more of my heart and soul in that man, and maybe risk being consumed by bitterness? Or did I want to cut my losses, make a fresh start and trust fate to deal with Ron? I opted for a fresh start."

Lisa settled back in her chair and couldn't help smiling at the angry frustration still darkening Sam's face. Gradually it eased, turning to bewilderment and finally a sort of amazed admiration.

"You're really something," he told her.

"Not really. I talk a good game, but sometimes I still have moments . . . hours . . . days of rage."

"I'd say you're entitled. You're also entitled to be as gun-shy around men as you are."

"It's not a case of being gun-shy," she protested. "I simply don't see the point of wasting time when there's no possibility of a man fitting into my future—at least not the kind of man who might interest me."

"What kind of man is that?"

Lisa didn't even have to think about it. "Someone so secure, so self-assured and so fabulously successful that I'd never for an instant have to worry that he wanted me for any other reason than that I'm me. And since I plan to be pretty secure and successful myself this time around, the prospects are limited."

Sam threw himself back into his chair, hitched one leg over the arm and regarded her with wry amusement. "I hear there's still an unmarried prince or two in England who might qualify."

"Too young."

"Iacocca?"

"Too old."

"That settles that."

"*C'est la vie.*"

"Not much of one, though."

"Well, if I have to settle, I'll settle for security and success and pass on the romance."

"I have a feeling another woman once made that same decision in this same house and had trouble making it stick."

"Luckily for me I'm not Elizabeth, this isn't 1700, and there's no pirate so hot for my body that he's willing to risk the gallows to have it."

Sam slanted her a speculative look. "At least none that we know of."

"I'm not worried."

"I can see that. You seem pretty confident about the success in your future."

"I am. That's one thing I suppose I owe to Ron. He made me see that my ideas are worth developing and that, while my style might be unconventional, I have the talent to make them work. I did it once, and I can do it again."

"Is that what you're working on now? A new idea for greeting cards?"

"Yes. And that's why I'm living in this place. Once I indulged in the satisfaction of telling Ron what he could do with his cash settlement, my resources were severely limited." She grimaced. "To put it bluntly, I was down to one more month's rent in my checking account when I got the offer to live here, all expenses covered. And on top of that, I'm getting money to do it, which pays for my apartment back in Chicago."

"What are you doing? House-sitting?"

"More like house saving," Lisa explained with a laugh. "It's really a wacky situation. I told you this house has been in the Bennett family forever. Well, it seems the last Bennett to live here was a woman named Miriam Bennett. She died a few months ago and left this outrageous will."

"Leaving everything to you?" Sam guessed.

"Oh, no. She didn't even know I existed. You see, she thought she was the last in this boringly long line of Bennetts, and she was determined that no one who wasn't family should ever live in this house. So she drew up a will instructing that it be torn down, the foundation filled in and the land deeded to the town of Jamestown as a permanent public right-of-way to the ocean."

"That's the craziest thing I ever heard. No matter how you feel about this house, it's a piece of history. They can't just tear it down."

"They might have to. Evidently a will is binding as long as the author is competent and the contents don't violate public policy. I got all this legal stuff from the attorney who contacted me."

"Then that's it. From the sounds of it, Miriam Bennett couldn't have been close to competent."

"Wrong. The will was drawn up years ago and witnessed by a very well respected attorney who's now deceased. Everyone involved agrees he never would have signed it if there had been any question of Miriam Bennett's state of mind."

"You're telling me the town might have to destroy a house that's listed on the National Historic Register because of some old lady's whim?"

"Evidently. Being listed on the register is prestigious rather than protective, unless federal funds are needed to demolish the house, which they wouldn't be in this case. Wait," Lisa urged as Sam opened his mouth to speak. "You haven't heard the whole thing. Her will also specifies that everything stays in the house when it goes down. I think 'destroyed rather than sold' is the way it's stated. Furniture, clothes, old books, whatever treasures might be stored away in the attic—the whole shooting match."

"And they say she wasn't loony." Sam's eyes were narrowed, his mouth a hard line of disgust.

"It must be an antique-lover's idea of a nightmare."

He turned that look of distaste on Lisa. "But not yours, I take it?"

"It does seems like a huge waste, but . . ." She trailed off with a shrug, unwilling to tell him that she didn't like to think, much less talk, about the strange feelings the house stirred in her. Feelings that puzzled her as much at that moment as when she lay in that creaky old bed upstairs each night and felt the unfamiliar sense that she was a part of something much bigger and more significant than she had ever imagined.

"Doesn't it even bother you that in a very short time this might be all gone?" Sam demanded with a sweep of his hand. "You said yourself it's been your family's home for generations."

"Yes, well..." Lisa shifted uncomfortably in her chair. "That was a little pretentious of me. The truth is, I never knew any Bennetts... not even my own father when he was alive. I have about as much connection to this house as you do."

Lisa stared out the window, aware of Sam's inquisitive gaze resting on her for several moments before he spoke.

"You said a minute ago that Miriam thought she was the last surviving Bennett," he said. "So where does Lisa Bennett come in?"

"My father was Miriam's nephew, the only child of her only brother. He and my mother were divorced when I was a baby, and for reasons of his own he never even told his aunt I existed. My mother said it was probably because he didn't want to risk sharing any inheritance that might come his way. For that matter, he never even told my mother about his illustrious background or about how someone who could trace his roots back to pre-Revolutionary America had ended up a traveling salesman."

Lisa's attempt to smile was doomed. There was little cause to smile about the brief, ill-fated union of the two people who had brought her into the world and then left her to drift through it with no father and a resentful mother.

"Anyway," she continued, pushing aside thoughts that could only bring her pain and confusion, "after Miriam died, the neighbors banded together and hired a lawyer to try to block the will. Evidently they weren't smitten with the prospect of having a paved lot here and lots of strangers roaming what has traditionally been a private beach. I understand that it was this lawyer who suggested that, since Miriam's will opens with a statement of her belief that she had no heirs, finding a legal heir might void the entire thing.''

Sam nodded slowly, as if the pieces of the weird puzzle were beginning to slip into place. "And you're the heir they came up with.''

"Right. The lawyer for the neighborhood group delved a little deeper into my father's affairs, and voilà!" With a self-deprecating wave of her hand, she went on. "I'm a stroke of luck, according to Mr. Fredericks, the attorney for the estate. Of course, he warned me that my legal claim to the house is by no means clear. As if I'd want it," she muttered. "But my existence at least throws the matter into legal limbo, buying the historical society and the other state agencies involved time to work out a solution.''

"And so you'll be living here until they do.''

"Not on your life!" Lisa exclaimed. "I told Fredericks and the neighbors' attorney, Mr. Tillinghast, up front that I'm doing this because I need the money, period. Actually, I didn't see why I couldn't just phone in my existence, but Tillinghast insisted that my being here, even temporarily, strengthened the case for saving the house. It also makes filing all the necessary legal papers easier. I agreed to come with the understanding that as soon as I sell my new proposal, it's back to Chicago and a stove that works, windows that stay open without sticks propping them up, hot showers—''

Sam interrupted her rapturous litany. "What about your heritage?''

"I'd gladly trade it for a long hot shower. I hate taking baths.''

"Don't you even want to know more about these people you're descended from?''

"Nope," she returned without giving herself time to think. She didn't want to think about it. "Ignorance is bliss and all that. I've survived this long without knowing whether I came from a line of patriots or pickpockets. Why complicate matters now?''

Sam reached for his wineglass and took a swallow. His eyes were narrow green slits, regarding her critically, as if gauging the truth of what she said was a matter of earth-shaking proportions.

"So you really are in this purely for the money?"

"Purely," Lisa confirmed without a twinge.

"And once you have another source of income, you're gone?"

"Uh-huh."

"When will that be?"

Lisa sighed and ran her fingers through her hair. "I wish I knew. For a while there everything I put on paper looked wrong. But this past week has been more promising. Granted, what I'm working on is still rough around the edges, but it's coming. And I've been in touch with a small avant-garde card publisher in Boston who's agreed to take a look at it."

Sam seemed to be carefully weighing his next words as he took another gulp of wine. He put the glass down and looked at her. "I know I'm not exactly what you'd call avant-garde, and I admit I don't know much about cards except that I always send one to my mother on her birth-day, but if you have no objections, I'd like to take a look at your project, too."

His request added to the excitement that coursed through Lisa whenever she thought about her work in progress. Part of her had to fight to keep from leaping up and running to the kitchen for her sketchbook. Another, more cautious part of her, however, was reluctant to put herself in such a vul-nerable position. What if Sam recognized how much he dominated her sketches? What if he thought the whole idea was ridiculous? Or worse, that it was a great idea but she was doing a miserable job of bringing it to life?

"Look, I already saw enough to know that you based some of your drawings on me and those other characters who hang around the park," Sam reminded her. "And speaking for myself, I don't mind. In fact, I'm flattered."

"So flattered that I'll soon be hearing from your attorney about the little matter of financial compensation?"

Lisa had lifted her chin and squared her shoulders as she fired the question at him. If Sam was surprised or offended, he didn't show it. He met her defensiveness with a steady gaze, his expression calm, unsmiling. "That won't ever happen."

Lisa believed him, just like that. For no better reason than that he had said it. She already felt certain that lying wasn't one of the ways Sam went about getting what he wanted. Without another word she went to find the sketchbook. Sam followed, fetching the wine bottle and refilling both glasses. She waited until he was seated once more to hand him the book. As he settled back and propped it open on his bent knee, her stomach twisted into nervous knots and her fingernails bit crescent-shaped dents in her palms.

She sat on her hands before she drew blood, but inside her, butterflies still circled. It irked her that, thanks to Sam, the sketches were in such total disarray she couldn't tell which one he was looking at when. Hours seemed to pass before he'd worked his way through the top few pages and a smile appeared on his lips.

"These are great. Really great." He flicked her a glance, his mouth curved in that cocky grin. "Charm-bag?"

Lisa made a sheepish gesture with her hands. "That's just..."

Sam flipped to the next page, rescuing her. "Whoa...I love this one."

He tipped the paper so she could see he was talking about her rendering of a rather cavalier clam, complete with sunglasses propped on his shell and glittering chains around his nonexistent neck. "Who are you calling shellfish?" he was demanding of the lady clam by his side.

"You don't think it's..." Lisa bit her lip. "A little silly?"

"Not silly enough," Sam countered decisively. "I'm no artist, but maybe they ought to have legs. You know, skinny ones, with knobby knees—"

"Clams don't have legs," Lisa interrupted.

"They don't talk or wear sunglasses, either," Sam pointed out. "That doesn't seem to have hampered your creativity."

"You're right. Legs, huh?" Head tilted to one side, she eyed the drawing thoughtfully.

"Got a pencil?" he asked.

"Always." Laughing, she pulled one from the pocket of her slacks and handed it to him.

He glanced around for something to lean on, then moved to sit on the floor beside one of the small tables. Just before the pencil tip touched the paper, he looked questioningly at her. "Do you mind?"

"No, go right ahead," she urged, amazing herself. Usually she couldn't bear to have her drawings out of order, never mind subjected to an amateur's whims.

He made a few labored marks with the pencil, lifted his head to examine the result, then added a couple more strokes. Turning to Lisa, he ordered, "Don't laugh when you see it."

"I won't," she promised.

"You already are. Inside. I can tell."

She clicked her tongue. "You artists are so sensitive. Just let me see it."

He angled the paper toward her. Lisa slid to the floor by his side to get a better look and let loose a whoop of laughter.

"You call those legs?" she exclaimed. "Give me the pencil."

He handed it over, muttering under his breath, "Everybody's a critic."

It took Lisa only seconds to alter Sam's squiggly lines. "There. Now, *those* are clam's legs."

Sam brought his head close to hers to take a look. Their shoulders touched.

"Now they need arms," he pronounced.

"And lounge chairs."

Sam snorted in derision. "Don't you think that's going a tad too far?"

"Well, they look stupid just plunked there in the sand now that they have legs," she insisted.

"This must be how materialistic societies get their start," he mused. "Legs require lounge chairs. Arms require Gucci purses."

"A designer beach bag! Perfect!"

Sam's sound of disgust ruffled the wisps of hair at her temple. "If she's getting a fancy beach bag," he said, "I think you ought to go whole hog and give the guy a beat box. And a can of beer."

"Who said the beach bag was for her?" Lisa demanded, quickly making the additions he'd suggested. Her excitement mounted as she examined the result. It looked good. She pushed the paper toward Sam. "There. What do you think?"

"Perfect. Now he reminds me of Joe Cool in the *Peanuts* comic strip."

"Clam Cool," Lisa retorted, giggling.

Sam's groan of laughter mingled with hers. "Clam Cool. A hero is born."

"But now he makes all my other characters look...stark."

"Minimalistic."

"Dull."

"Then let's get cracking and liven them up. Let me see that one of the sea gull again."

They spent the rest of the afternoon embellishing the citizens of Wayward. At least half a dozen times something Sam said inspired a new idea, and Lisa roughed it in on paper so she wouldn't forget. By the time they'd worked their way through the entire pile of sketches they had emptied the wine bottle, and Lisa's jaw ached from laughing.

"I can't draw one more lounging clam or limping gull," she declared, tossing the pencil down. "If I do I'll laugh, and it hurts just to smile."

"That's proof that you don't use those muscles enough. Laughter's the best exercise."

Lisa glanced sideways to see him stretching his arms overhead and found she couldn't look away. Her own muscles were stiff from sitting so long, but she hadn't even noticed. She seldom noticed anything when she was engrossed in work. She was not, however, engrossed now. Except in the sight of his shoulders flexing. His arms beneath the rolled-up sleeves of his shirt looked sun-browned and hard with the kind of muscles she didn't think you got from whittling. How rigorous was a marine archaeologist's life? she wondered, realizing that for all their talking she knew very little about him.

"Medicine," she murmured distractedly.

Sam tilted his head to glance quizzically at her from behind deliciously curved biceps. "What?"

"Medicine," repeated Lisa, shaking off the spell his body had cast on her. "You said, 'Laughter's the best exercise.' It's, 'Laughter is the best medicine.'"

"Either way, I'm beginning to sound like a damn greeting card myself," he grumbled, glancing at her watch. "Not surprising. Do you know we've been at this for hours? You missed your movie."

"I forgot all about it," she admitted. "And I'm glad. You've been a real help, Sam. These sketches are much better now. They're...richer somehow. They have the fullness they were missing. Thank you."

"You did all the work."

"Then thanks for the inspiration."

"No problem." He leaned back on his palms, grinning that cocky, challenging, very male grin. "Inspiration comes naturally to us charm-bags."

Lisa felt the power of his appeal in the pit of her stomach, and behind her knees, and in the heightened sensitivity of every inch of her skin. She turned away from him and began straightening the already perfectly aligned pile of sketches.

Swinging around again, she began, "Look..."

"Well..."

Sam laughed and waved his hand for her to continue. "You first."

"I was going to say that I know lunch wasn't very impressive—I do better when I take time to shop for groceries—but I can order a pizza for dinner. That is, I mean, if you don't have other plans." Lord, she was babbling! She never babbled around men! What was happening to her trademark aplomb?

"Actually," Sam replied, straightening, "I do have plans. Maybe some other time."

"Sure. Some other time."

A strange heat washed through Lisa, part embarrassment, part disappointment. Distantly she heard his offer to help her clean up, and together they gathered the glasses and plates and carried them back to the kitchen.

Lisa automatically warned him to watch out for the top step as he opened the outside door, and then he was gone. Without a word said about calling. Or about getting together again.

Of course not, Lisa thought ironically. Friends didn't make parting promises. No strings. No pressure.

She automatically fastened the heavy bolt behind him and stood in the darkening kitchen with her back pressed against the door. She ought to move, turn on a light, do something, but she was afraid. She was afraid that the slightest movement would crack the floodgates, and she would be crushed under a wave of what she'd managed to hold at bay all these long months. Loneliness. Why was she feeling this way now? Why after all this time alone? Why tonight?

Lisa's eyes closed. "Fool," she whispered, standing alone in the big, empty house. "Oh, you fool."

The phone was ringing as Sam approached his boat. He swung himself over the rail and hurried down the stairs to the cabin, filled with an irrational hope that it was Lisa calling him. A totally irrational hope, considering that he had carefully avoided mentioning anything that would enable her to contact him or find out more about him than he chose to reveal.

"Hello."

"So, how'd it go?" *the familiar male voice on the other end demanded without preamble.*

Wishing he'd walked slower and missed this call, Sam carried the phone the few steps to his desk and sat down. "How did what go?"

"I thought today was the day you were finally going to make contact. For sure. No cold feet. No excuses."

"So?"

A pained huff filtered through the wires. "So did you talk to her, or didn't you?"

"I did," *Sam answered, puzzled by a sudden gnawing reluctance to discuss Lisa with anyone, even a friend.*

"And was I right, or was I right?"

"About what?"

"About Lisa Bennett. Gorgeous but bitchy, right? A real ice cube."

"I don't know," *Sam countered, telling himself that the quickest way out of this was to agree, but somehow unable to.*

"Don't know? Did you spend five minutes with her?"

"The whole afternoon, actually."

"And you still don't know? Were you awake at the time? Sober?"

"Both. I agree that she's gorgeous, but a bitch? I'm not sure yet."

"Give me a break, will you? I hadn't even introduced myself when she arched her eyebrows and gave me a look that nearly froze my tongue to the roof of my mouth."

Sam had to laugh at the picture that presented.

"Didn't she give you that haughty arched-brows look?" *the other man demanded.*

"Yes," admitted Sam, "and for a second I felt like slinking away, but then later—"

He stopped himself, thinking of how different and far from haughty Lisa's expression had been while they talked and while they worked on her sketches. In her work and in her eyes he'd seen flashes of humor and vulnerability that didn't mesh with his first impression of her, or with a great many things she'd said. How could he explain to someone else what he didn't even understand himself?

"Later what?" prodded the voice on the telephone.

"Forget it."

"Sure . . . just as long as you didn't forget it. You did remember that you were supposed to get this whole mess cleared up with her today?"

"I'd hardly describe it as a mess."

"You would if it were your professional reputation at stake."

"You haven't done anything unethical," Sam reminded him. "And I'd never ask you to, friend or not."

"Maybe it wasn't unethical if you go strictly by the letter of the law."

"Isn't that your business?"

"Let's just say I'll feel better when you come clean about this. And you gave me your word you would."

"I will," Sam assured him, matching his suddenly serious tone. "As soon as I'm sure that telling her won't hinder things."

"What things?"

"My project. She made a few remarks that suggest she has a mercenary streak as wide as the Golden Gate Bridge."

"See? Like I said, a heart of ice."

"Maybe," Sam allowed. "Anyway, I'll figure out some way to see that she doesn't complicate matters, and then I'll tell her."

"And when will that be?"
"Soon."
"How soon?"
"Soon," Sam repeated and hung up.

Chapter Four

Loneliness Lisa could take. She could even live with the self-recrimination over having lowered her guard with Sam in the first place. What she couldn't afford was to let any of it sabotage her concentration the way it was this afternoon.

The Sea Gull Queen was holding court nearby, a bright red scarf topping off her habitual gray housedress and slippers. On the docks below, the Sweeper was engaged in a comical battle with a coil of rope. Lisa knew his endeavors would be wonderful grist for a frustration theme. But the message paths between her brain and her fingers gripping the pencil seemed to be blocked. It was hard to produce anything worthwhile when you kept lifting your head every minute or so to see if a particular man was approaching.

Not that she cared if Sam showed up, she reminded herself over and over, hoping it would sink in.

With a sigh Lisa flipped her sketchbook closed, abandoning even the pretense of working. Sam's offer of friendship had been so tempting, so reassuring. Unfortunately, it wasn't going to work. She was attuned enough to her feelings to know that the little flutters of excitement in the pit of her belly when he came close had nothing to do with burgeoning friendship. And she was honest enough to admit that she probably couldn't learn to suppress them. Nor could she risk letting her feelings for Sam follow nature's course.

For one thing, she hadn't been kidding about the conditions the next man she ever became involved with would have to meet. And Sam didn't even come close. Clearly he wasn't fabulously successful or wealthy. As far as she could tell, he wasn't even gainfully employed. All right, so she also wanted a man with self-assurance, and he had enough for an entire pro football team. That didn't change the fact that he wasn't looking to get involved. He was looking for friendship, period. Unrequited love was definitely not on her agenda.

Walking home, Lisa decided it was for the best that Sam had stayed away from the park today. It had given her time to compile all these reasons for keeping him at a safe distance. In fact, she thought as she climbed the steps and unlocked the door, it was too bad he hadn't stayed away yesterday, too, instead of stirring her curiosity about this old house and disturbing its sleeping ghosts with his tales from the past.

Ever since Roger Tillinghast had first approached her with the crazy news that she was the last survivor in a long line of Bennetts, Lisa had been fighting a gut-level desire to know more about the blood relatives who had lived here before her. While she was growing up, family had meant only her mother, and that had meant arguments and power plays and the pain she was always left with no matter who ostensibly won the battle. Her marriage to Ron had been proof that she wasn't any luckier at picking relatives than she had been at birth. The word *family* had come to have decidedly unpleasant connotations, and so far that had offset her natural curiosity about her past.

Sam had upset that delicate balance. Alone in the house last night, she had found the strange feeling she'd been trying to ignore since her arrival stronger than ever. It wasn't frightening; rather, it was more like a warm, pleasant sensation of being connected. To what, Lisa wasn't sure. Thinking it over as she started upstairs to change into something more comfortable, she was caught up in it once again.

The wooden bannister was smooth beneath her fingers, worn to a marblelike patina from years of use, and she wondered how many hands had been part of that process. Aged, gnarled hands, like eighty-seven-year-old Miriam's might have been just before she died. The soft hands of children and hands callused from hard work outdoors. That is, if any Bennett had ever made a living with manual labor. Something in Lisa burned to know what had filled the days of the people who'd climbed these stairs countless times before her.

How many young brides had nervously gripped this bannister as they descended the narrow treads? Had they left this house eager to get away or filled with happy memories that would tie them to it for a lifetime? Had any of them paused on the top landing to gather their long white lace skirts and ponder the life that lay ahead of them? Certainly Miss Miriam Bennett never had. Nor Elizabeth Bennett. A wedding day surrounded by her family and friends was just one of the things Alexander Brandon had stolen from Elizabeth.

Lisa reached the top of the stairs and started down the narrow, windowless hall to the bedroom she'd chosen to use. She had purposely avoided the room that had been Miriam's, because it was the one most full of life. Her silver hairbrush and mirror were still on her dresser, her shoes neatly arranged in pairs on the floor of the tiny closet. Lisa had not wanted to face all those reminders of the maiden aunt she'd never met. She had assumed she would be safer from her own curiosity in the small room at the end of the hall. Thanks to Sam, however, she'd discovered it was not only the last woman to live in this house who captivated her imagination, but one of the very first.

After pulling her sweater off over her head, Lisa rummaged through her suitcase and came up with a teal-blue cotton shirt. She had hung a few things in the closet, but storing clothes in the bureau drawers smacked too much of the feeling of permanency she was determined to avoid. She traded her slacks for a pair of jeans and looked around for the comfortably worn moccasins she wouldn't be caught dead in outside her own backyard. She planned to work later to make up for the time she had lost today, and jeans were the only sensible choice for sitting on the grass down by the cliffs. Before she worked or fixed dinner, however, she wanted a nap. She needed to clear her head of thoughts of Elizabeth and Miriam and all other Bennetts. And of Sam.

Easier said than done. Lying in the ancient wrought iron bed, covered with a comfortably worn and faded quilt, surrounded by antique lilac-sprigged wallpaper only intensified the dreamy spell cast by the house, or Sam, or both. Had this been Elizabeth's room? she wondered. That question led her to thoughts of what Elizabeth's life had been like with Alexander Brandon. It was exciting to picture her on an unspoiled island, living a life of freedom and passion with the man who'd been strong enough to force her to admit she loved him beyond all reason.

Lisa closed her eyes, and suddenly her head was filled with a tangle of thoughts of the past and images of Sam: the spare angles of his face, the soap-and-water scent of him, the rock hardness of his arm when it pressed against hers.

Lisa abruptly swung her feet to the floor. She'd rather do without a nap than surrender another moment of this day to thoughts of Sam Ravenal. After heating a can of soup for dinner and doing the dishes, she carried her sketchbook to her favorite spot at the top of the bluffs out back.

The lush lawn was a brilliant, unblemished green and still held a trace of heat from the sun. It merged on both sides with the neighboring lawns, which in turn merged with the next. There were no walls or fences as far as Lisa could see in either direction. Except for the towering grove on her left, which were nearly as tall as the house, there weren't even any trees to block the view. The grass carpet ended at the ten-foot-high bluffs that stretched for miles along the coastline. Beyond was a narrow beach accessible only through the backyards of the homes on this side of the street. For now, at least. If Miriam had her way, there would soon be a patch of pavement where the house behind Lisa was standing. A shudder of anger passed through her at the thought.

Swell. All she needed now—to add to the befuddling presence of Sam in her life—was to get emotionally involved with a lost cause. The fate of the Jonathan Bennett House was out of her hands. And a good thing that it was. Her hands were already full to overflowing trying to finish this proposal.

With a determined frown she picked up her pencil and got to work. It was an effort to focus on the page before her instead of on the daydreams hovering at her mind's edge, but she managed to produce a halfway decent rendering of a ship riding a storm-torn sea, an utterly confident Whittler at her helm. She was just contemplating a slogan—"Long time no sea" perhaps?—when she heard a branch snap nearby, then a whisper of sound behind her. Footsteps. Turning quickly, she felt her heartbeat pick up speed until she noticed that the legs approaching through the grove of trees were not clad in worn denim but in nylon stockings. So, it wasn't Sam. And to Lisa's absolute disgust, her heart not only slowed, it sank.

Listlessly she glanced higher to discover that the legs belonged to a plump, silver-haired woman. She was wearing a gray skirt and a navy cardigan sweater over a white blouse, and she was headed straight toward Lisa with a purposeful gleam in her eye. Irritated with any interruption that wasn't Sam, Lisa had to force herself to return the woman's friendly smile.

"Hello there," she called to Lisa as she drew closer. "I'm Helen Van Egan. I live right next door, in the dark blue house." She waved her arm in the general direction of the Federal-blue colonial behind her.

Lisa had wondered who, if anyone, lived in that house. Despite the sandbox in one corner of the big backyard and a tire swing hanging from a tree limb, she hadn't seen any sign of life over there since she'd arrived. Now her curiosity was renewed. Helen Van Egan looked spry but certainly nowhere near young enough to have children in the sandbox set.

Getting to her feet, Lisa stuck her sketchbook under her arm and held out her right hand. "Hi. I'm Lisa Bennett."

"I know." The older woman nodded and held Lisa's hand tightly as she inspected her face. "Miss Bennett's great-niece. Yes, I can see the resemblance around the eyes a little. Although, heaven knows, you're prettier than Miriam Bennett ever dreamed of being. Not that I knew her when she was your age, you understand. I moved here...let's see, thirty-three years ago. That would mean Miss Bennett was in her fifties then, and she was already a little prunish around the eyes and mouth." She laughed and rolled her eyes. "Look who's talking, huh? I should live to see fifty again."

Lisa smiled. She liked Helen Van Egan's uninhibited laugh. It sounded natural, a perfect complement to the fine laugh lines that added richness to her skin.

"Do you really think my eyes look like hers?" Lisa asked on impulse. "Miriam's, I mean."

"Miss Bennett's, you mean," the other woman corrected with a good-natured grin. "No one, but no one, ever called Miriam Bennett anything but *Miss*. And, heavens, yes, your eyes are like hers. Bennett eyes if ever I saw them."

More questions bubbled inside Lisa. Her initial annoyance at being disturbed had vanished with the realization that she had finally encountered someone with firsthand knowledge of the Bennetts. Thirty-three years, Helen Van

Egan had lived next door. Lisa felt a rush of anticipation as the woman continued her close scrutiny of her face.

"Truth be told, I'd say your eyes are the exact same shade of deep blue that your great-grandmother's were."

"My great-grandmother," Lisa repeated softly, experimentally. She couldn't even begin to visualize such a person.

"Yes, your great-grandmother," Helen Van Egan went on. "Miss Bennett's mother. She was in her seventies when we moved here, and she wasn't one to socialize any more than her daughter was, but I always remember her snow-white hair pulled tight on top of her head and those eyes like dark sapphires. Striking. And so are yours. Of course, you're much too young to remember her."

"Actually, I never met any of my father's family," Lisa revealed, keeping to herself the irony that that included her father, as well.

Recognition brightened the other woman's eyes. "That's right, I remember hearing something about this whole thing being a big surprise to you. What a shame—that you never got to meet your relatives, I mean." She reached out and patted Lisa's hand. "Well, no matter, we're all certainly glad you finally did learn of your birthright and that you're here now."

"Thank you," Lisa returned, feeling a little uncomfortable with the way her neighbor described the situation. She wondered if Mr. Tillinghast had bothered to tell the neighborhood group who had hired him that Lisa's involvement in this endeavor to save the house was to be short-lived. Ignoring the trace of guilt she felt as she looked into Helen Van Egan's friendly eyes, she added, "I only hope it all works out for the best."

"It just has to." Helen shook her head, her smile pulling into a tight pucker of disapproval. "Not that anyone around here was what you'd call friendly with Miss Bennett—she'd nip any of that right in the bud. But we all did what we could to be good neighbors. Many a time I sent my boys over to shovel her walk when they were still living at home, or to see if she needed anything from the store in bad weather. And all that time not one of us had any idea what she had planned. She made that awful will years ago, you know. Right after her mother died and left the house to her. Such a waste," she murmured, shaking her head again as she gazed past Lisa to the house. With a sudden smile she swung her attention back to Lisa.

"Will you listen to me rattle on?" she exclaimed. "I really came over here to invite you to join me for a cup of tea. I would have been over sooner, but I was visiting my son in Florida. Just got back yesterday. I hope you've been made to feel welcome by the others around here."

The unmistakable question lurking beneath the remark made Lisa surmise that Helen Van Egan was something of a social organizer in the neighborhood, now checking to see how things had been handled in her absence.

"I've been fine, Mrs. Van Egan," Lisa assured her.

"It's Helen. All that Miss and Mrs. stuff between neighbors is for the birds."

"All right, Helen," Lisa responded, silently wondering whether she qualified as a genuine neighbor. "You're the first one I've had a chance to meet."

Helen sniffed.

"But that's probably more my fault than anyone else's," Lisa hastily added. "I keep pretty busy with my work."

"So I see. Well, you needn't worry that I'll be a bothersome old busybody interrupting you all the time. What is it my sons were forever telling me? Oh, yes, they needed space." She chuckled. "It's just nice to be able to wave and say hello and share a cup of tea now and then. You come along, Lisa. I put the tea to steep before I came over, so I hope you like it good and strong. I have scones fresh from the bakery to go with it. And strawberry jam. My own from last season. Have you ever made jam?"

Replying that she hadn't, Lisa decided she had little choice but to follow Helen's drill-sergeant lead home. A

small table on the screened back porch had been set for two,
with fresh flowers from the garden, lace-edged napkins and
brightly flowered teacups made of china as delicate as egg-
shells. This sort of tea party had been the stuff of Lisa's
childhood dreams, and she was enchanted. She and Helen
talked easily between bites of warm buttered scones. She
learned that Helen was a widow with two sons and that the
swing and sandbox were put to good use whenever her
grandchildren visited.

Only when the conversation swung in Lisa's direction did
her defenses slip efficiently into place. She liked Helen, it
was true, but Sam was still the only person in a long time to
whom she'd revealed anything remotely personal. She
formed her answers to Helen's inquiries carefully, explaining as little as was politely possible about herself. When
Helen expressed an interest in her work, Lisa seized the opportunity to discuss a topic far more pleasant than her past.
She told her about her current proposal and then tactfully
explained that the opportunity to work was actually her
main reason for deciding to come and live in the Bennett
house temporarily. The older woman seemed oblivious to
the emphasis she placed on the word *temporarily*.

"I suppose the peace and solitude in that big house is
wonderful for an artist," Helen observed, looking du-
bious.

"It helps," agreed Lisa.

"You're not scared there by yourself?"

"Not at all."

"The lights and telephone are in working order?"

"Perfect."

Helen smiled. "Good. Well, remember, I'm only a holler
away if you need anything."

"Thanks. But I'm pretty well settled in now. Mr. Tillinghast arranged everything for me before I arrived."

Helen's brow wrinkled. "Mr. Tillinghast?"

"Right, the lawyer who contacted me in the first place,"
she said to refresh Helen's memory. "He was the one who

explained about the will and the house and how anxious all the neighbors were to save it."

She nodded. "Of course, the attorney. That man is an avenging angel. And so are you, my dear. None of us wants to see that beautiful house destroyed. Why, we held a big neighborhood meeting right here in my parlor when we first found out what it was that Miss Bennett wanted done. We knew we had to put a stop to it somehow, but of course we don't—"

She broke off, squinting at something through the screen. It was getting dark, but Lisa followed her gaze and was able to see shadows moving in back of her house next door.

"Who on earth . . . ?" she began to ask.

Helen was already out of her chair and stalking toward the porch door.

Yanking it open, she muttered, "Those darn kids." She stopped on the top step and shouted, "All right, I see you over there! Joshua, Peter . . . and you, too, Daniel Markham. Now, vamoose, all of you, before I have to call and tell your mothers what you've been up to. You've no business being on someone else's property, let alone playing dirty tricks on a poor woman living all alone."

Not a word was said in reply, but Lisa, who had moved to stand behind Helen, could see the small dark shadows skulking to the far side of her yard and then darting out of sight.

"Who were they?" she asked as Helen stepped back inside.

The older woman's smile was broad with delight. "Boys from the next street over—and not one of them any worse than my own were at that age. They were having a swell time smashing chokecherries against the back of your house, making a fine mess."

Lisa looked puzzled. "I've never heard of chokecherries. What are they?"

"I'm sure chokecherry isn't the official name, but I've always heard them called that because they have so much pit and so little meat that the birds choke when they try to eat them.''

"How horrible.''

"What's really horrible is that you have trees full of them in your yard, and the neighborhood kids have made a tradition out of pelting your house with them.''

"Brats," Lisa muttered.

Helen laughed. "Not really. It's a natural reaction to the way Miss Bennett treated the kids around here.''

"And how was that?''

After a moment's deliberation, Helen replied, "Firmly," leaving Lisa no doubt that she was being charitable and could easily have used a much harsher word. "She would stand guard in her window when they passed on their way to or from school, just waiting for one of them to step foot on her property. Then she'd be out there in a flash to order them off in that haughty tone of hers. How she hated when they climbed those trees—as any kid worth his salt is bound to do. I think she just hated kids, period. In the summer I'd see her go out with the hose and make them wash the sidewalk after they'd dripped a Popsicle on it. And once after a big snowstorm, I heard her shouting at them to get off her walk and go play in their own snow.''

Lisa smiled sadly at the image.

"But you know the oddest thing of all?" Helen asked.

Lisa shook her head.

"The thing no one can figure out is that, for all she seemed to despise children—and animals, too, for that matter—she divided the cash in her estate between a charity for homeless children and the Animal Rescue League. How do you figure that?''

"I don't know. Do you think Mir—Miss Bennett might have been senile?''

"If she was, then she was senile for as long as anyone around here can remember. No, I tend to think she was just very set in her ways and had her own reasons for doing whatever she did. Including putting her name to that bitter, twisted will."

Lisa stared at the dark outline of the Bennett house against the reddish-black night sky. "And I suppose we'll never know what those reasons were."

"Probably not. But, God willing, we can do something to keep her from getting her way this last time. And we all have you to thank for that, Lisa."

Again Lisa felt uncomfortable wearing the cloak of heroine when her role was actually that of a mercenary. "I hope so," she murmured. "Although sometimes I wonder if anyone has the right to circumvent her will. It was her house after all, and—"

"Gibberish," Helen interrupted. "No one has the right to reach back from the grave and steal things of importance from the living. And in this world of throwaway and prefab everything, the Jonathan Bennett House is certainly something of importance. To this neighborhood—to the whole town, really—and to you. You're a Bennett just as she was, Lisa, and you have as much right to that house now as any who lived in it before you."

"No, you're wrong, Helen. Until a few weeks ago Bennett was only a name to me, no better or worse than any other. Even now I can't truly say that my feelings about the house or my past are anything deeper than curiosity."

Helen regarded her quizzically for a few seconds, then gave a nod that seemed to rival the Presidential Seal for authority. "The feelings will come, Lisa. Whatever else the Bennetts were or were not, they had a strong sense of family. They had to in order to hold on to that land and house for generations, through good times and hard, when lesser people lost everything they owned or else traded it in for something newer and flashier. The Bennetts had a sense of family that you can't buy or teach or wish away. It was just in them, and it's in you. You mark my words, Lisa Bennett."

"Maybe," Lisa conceded out of politeness. "I appreciate the vote of confidence, at least...and the tea, but I really should be going."

"It was a pleasure having you," Helen said as she held the door open. "A house needs a dose of young people in it now and again. Especially that one," she added with a meaningful nod at the house next door.

Lisa had to agree. The laughter and exuberance synonymous with youth were high on the list of things the Bennett house needed, along with fresh paint and wallpaper, a sander applied to the floors, and bits and pieces of molding and trim that had disappeared or been damaged through the years. And it all ought to be done with care to preserve the structure's authenticity. Even Lisa, who was no history buff, knew that. She also knew it would have to be done by someone with genuine dedication, whose love for the house was deep enough to offset the hours of research and hard work its restoration would entail.

That certainly wasn't she. Maybe she didn't hate the old place as much as she'd originally thought, but she certainly didn't love it. She would never allow herself to. After divorcing Ron she had made up her mind that she would never again tie her heartstrings to any person, place or thing. It might be nice someday to share her day-to-day life with someone, but only within the strict confines she'd established.

She and her imagined partner would have to be equals in every way, and remain so, each free to walk away at any time and still be whole. Others might deem that a rather cold-hearted approach to life, but others didn't have her track record. Knowing such a relationship was the perfect blueprint for her happiness, she had no intention of compromising it for any man—and certainly not for a drafty old wreck of a house!

Halfway across the yard she remembered she'd left a case of pencils down by the bluffs, where she'd been sitting earlier. The red glow in the sky signaled that it wasn't likely to rain, but even the night dampness would soften them. She quickly detoured to retrieve them, shivering as the cool breeze off the ocean sliced through her thin cotton shirt. Slipping the case into her pocket, she started to turn toward the house when the glint of the full moon on the water caught her eye. She stood absolutely still, staring out over the waves that glimmered and rippled like a black satin sheet. Something universal and timeless in the sight and in the bite of salt air held her there in spite of the cold.

He collected his lady right out from under her old man's nose.

Sam's words ran through her head. *Collected*, indeed. It had been kidnapping, pure and simple. Lisa's mouth immediately curved into a wry smile at her own choice of words. Maybe she was prone to romantic fantasy, but she'd wager there had been nothing *simple* about Elizabeth's abduction or *pure* about its aftermath. The daughter of a wealthy businessman, Elizabeth Bennett had probably been pampered and spoiled and totally unaware of how dangerous a man she'd picked to flirt with. How exciting the risks of such an affair must have seemed to her at first, and how quickly it had all spun out of her control.

Had she been frightened when he came for her that fabled night, or had she been reckless enough to welcome the adventuresome reprieve Alex offered from the staid, proper life that would have been hers otherwise? One thing Lisa was absolutely sure of was that it had happened at night ... and that he had carried her off by ship. He was a pirate, after all. She wished Sam had mentioned what time of year it had been. Perhaps it had been a night like this, cool and windy, only darker because at that time the Bennett house would have stood alone here.

She glanced up at the darkened window of her room, wondering again whether it had been Elizabeth's. Maybe Alex had surprised her in her bed, still flushed and disoriented from sleep. With the gallows already hanging over his head, he'd had little to lose if caught prowling about the

Bennetts' house in the night. Had Elizabeth been tossing and turning over her pirate's fate or sleeping soundly when his hand touched her in the darkness?

Lisa jumped and gave an alarmed cry as something warm and solid touched her shoulder. This time there had been no sound to warn her that someone was approaching, and as she whirled around, visions of bats and other creepy night creatures flashed in her head. Sensing that her frightened leap had brought her dangerously close to the edge of the cliff, she thrust her hands out to balance herself. Then she realized that was already being taken care of for her, that she was in no danger of hurtling over the rocky ledge to the beach below. Sam was there.

The hand he'd placed on her shoulder, scaring her out of her wits, had curled around her neck, and his other was now planted securely at her waist, steadying her.

"Sam!" she whispered on a long, shuddering breath. Then, accusingly, she said, "You scared me to death."

"Hardly." His voice was soft, low pitched, a soothing caress to her reeling senses. His hand at her neck shifted slightly so that his thumb was pressed to the pulse point at the base of her throat. "You feel very much alive. In fact, your heart's pounding."

Lisa slapped his hand away. "Your heart would be pounding, too, if someone had sneaked up behind you in the dark and grabbed you."

"That wasn't grabbing. You want to see grabbing?"

She didn't. She was already far too conscious of his hand resting in the curve of her waist. He was right. Her heart was pounding, and it didn't show any signs of slowing, even though Lisa told herself the moment of danger was clearly past.

"No. I don't want to see grabbing," she retorted in her most dismissive tone. "And while we're at it, you can remove your other hand now."

He glanced down as if unaware it was even there, as if the nice warm tingle Lisa was feeling wasn't reciprocal.

"Of course," he murmured, "as long as you'll move a safe distance from the edge."

Even as Lisa stepped forward he took her by the elbow and steered her a few feet back on the lawn, somehow ending up standing just as close to her as before. True, he was no longer touching her, but Lisa still felt ... corralled. To make things worse, the ratty way she was dressed and her lack of make up made her feel even more vulnerable.

"That's better," Sam pronounced almost distractedly, his attention already wandering to the sparkling black ocean that had so captivated Lisa. "You see it, too, don't you?"

"See what?" Lisa asked, following the direction of his gaze.

"The light. The *Black Star*," Sam replied.

Looking again, she did indeed see an eerie white light that seemed to hover beneath the surface some distance out.

"No, I don't see anything," she lied without quite knowing why. She kept facing straight ahead, but she knew Sam had turned his head to look at her.

"Liar." The quiet accusation held more amusement than scorn. "You see it. I think maybe you don't want to see it. Maybe you're afraid to admit it. But you see it."

"Ha! You're pretty opinionated, you know that, Ravenal? First you know what I need and who I need, and you spend most of yesterday telling me what I should do about my house and my work and my ex-husband, and now, now—" she was picking up speed and volume as she went along "—now you know what I want and don't want and what I'm afraid of and even, wonder of wonders, what I can and can't see. I know what I can see, and I can't see what isn't there. So there."

She finally closed her mouth, feeling slightly stupid, and nervously folded her arms across her chest, which made her feel even more stupid, like a child pouting after an outburst. She half expected Sam to laugh and point out that she was acting like a jerk. The mere fact that he had the decency not to made her feel even worse for lashing out at him that way. Before she had a chance to formulate a graceful apology, he spoke.

"All right. If you don't see it, you don't see it. You're probably not looking in the right place. Let's see if I can help."

Lisa didn't have time to think, much less protest, before he was standing close behind her, his chest pressed to her stiff back, his hands on her shoulders turning her a little to the left. With one hand he reached around and gripped her chin, gently directing her gaze. He might as well have been gripping her throat, because she couldn't seem to draw enough air to keep from feeling light-headed.

"All right, all right, I see it," she admitted, stepping away from him.

Sam released her instantly, easily, leaving Lisa torn. Her relief was pierced by the slight wish that he wasn't quite so obliging, quite so damn *friendly, period.* How was it possible that he could touch her so casually, stand so close to her, gaze so intently into her eyes and feel none of the attraction other men felt for her? None of the attraction that Lisa was feeling for him? She would love to blame his indifference on the way she was dressed, but in her heart she knew that Sam's reaction would be the same even if she'd been wearing a diamond tiara and a sequined gown.

The truth was that Sam didn't seem to pay enough attention to her to notice what she was wearing. Unlike Lisa, who couldn't seem to look anywhere but at him, he was serenely staring out over the water. Standing next to her, his hands thrust into the back pockets of the black jeans he was wearing with an old black crewneck sweater, he seemed to her to be one with the night—dark, elusive, mysterious.

"It's really something, isn't it?" he remarked without turning his head.

Lisa knew he was talking about the eerie white light. "Yes, it's something," she agreed, then added dryly, "and I know exactly what: a school of menhaden moving under the water."

That brought his attention back to her. He looked at her, releasing that slow, devastating smile before laughing out loud. "Maybe," he allowed.

"Maybe?"

He cocked his head. "Maybe. And maybe not."

"I thought you were a scientist. What happened to all that methodical logic you spouted yesterday?"

"I'm also a realist. I accept the fact that not everything in the universe has a scientific explanation."

"I don't know, Ravenal, that sounds more like romanticism than realism to me."

"Maybe it is. Maybe it's being here, in this place, at night." He briefly glanced over his shoulder at the house. "It has to make you wonder what really happened that night."

She'd been wondering exactly that, but some instinct warned her against sharing the fantasy with Sam. She feigned a blank look. "What night?"

Sam regarded her with a slightly condescending smile, indicating that he knew she knew very well what night he was referring to.

"There was a party going on at the time," he said, "a celebration of the first safe arrival of a merchant ship through the sea-lanes Brandon had secured for them. From here the house must have seemed to glow with candlelight, while inside Bennett and his wealthy business associates from Newport stood around drinking their black-market French champagne. No doubt they raised more than one toast to the executioner who was about to rid their lives of the untidy detail Brandon had become."

"Somehow I'd imagined him stealing into Elizabeth's room while everyone was asleep," Lisa murmured. Even before she met Sam's smug expression, she realized she had just confirmed for him that she hadn't dismissed his romantic tale as completely as she'd pretended. "I mean, it seemed the most logical approach."

"Logic had nothing to do with it," Sam asserted quietly. "I'm sure Alex would have had no compunctions about confronting the lady in her bedchamber, or about crashing her father's celebration if need be. But as it turned out, Elizabeth made it easy for him. She was right out here, and all he had to do was scoop her up and bring her to his waiting ship."

His arms were folded across his chest, his gaze trained on the ocean, his manner so richly satisfied you might think he'd done the swashbuckling deed himself.

Again Lisa was startled at how close her fantasy had been to the "reality" Sam was describing, but she made her smile a scornful challenge. "How do you know she was out here?"

He slanted her another condescending look. "It's part of the legend. The boy who was assigned to care for the guests' horses saw the whole thing. He didn't recognize Brandon, but he described him well enough, and he explained how Brandon carried her off in his arms."

"Dragged her off, you mean."

He shot her a look. "The boy said carried. Besides, you don't have to drag a woman who wants to go."

"You don't have to carry her, either."

"Maybe he didn't want her to fall down the bluff...the same way I didn't want you to fall a few minutes ago. Some forms of masculine protection are timeless, and natural, Lisa, no matter how independent a woman is."

"And some legends get embellished in the retelling. Poor Elizabeth was probably screaming her head off as he *carried* her off into the sunset."

"The sun had already set. And there were no reports of any screams. Face it, Lisa, she went willingly. In fact, I think she knew Alex was coming. Why else would a woman be walking out here all alone at night?"

"Trying to escape the heat from all those candles?" Lisa suggested sarcastically. "I don't know. There were probably dozens of reasons for her being out here alone. Look at me," she argued with a wave of her arm. "It's night, I'm a woman, and I was out here all alone."

"And look how vulnerable you were to a stranger coming up behind you in the dark," Sam shot back. "An eighteenth-century woman wouldn't have taken a risk like that."

"I hardly think it's a risk to go for a walk in your own backyard."

"No?" Sam grinned. "Listen, pal, you're just lucky you're not the object of some pirate's obsession."

Lisa looked into his eyes. In the darkness they were as inky as the sea. His hair was in disarray from the wind, and his mouth had eased into a faint twist Lisa found decidedly erotic. "Yeah, *pal*. Lucky me."

She suddenly felt cold inside and out and wrapped her arms around herself, shivering. "I'm going to have to go in," she told Sam. "I'm freezing."

Part of her wanted to invite him in, and part of her warned that to do so was asking for trouble. The wimpy part of her was simply afraid if she did ask, he would decline. During the short walk to the back door, she devised a string of ways to prolong his visit but passed on all of them. She couldn't suggest he stay awhile without setting herself up for rejection, which she flat out refused to do. Pausing with her hand on the doorknob, she decided the only thing to do was to thrust the whole thing into his lap.

"Was there a reason you stopped by tonight?" she asked, pleased to hit exactly the right note of nonchalance. "I mean, besides the chance to argue your version of history?"

"That was merely a bonus," Sam replied. "What I really came for—" he paused, propping the screen door wider with his shoulder, which brought them face-to-face "—was to measure your step."

Lisa didn't know what had made her catch her breath in anticipation, but it certainly wasn't that. The nonchalance was gone from her tone and her expression, obliterated by a fiery irritation she wasn't sure was more appropriately directed at him or herself.

"My step?" she snapped.

Sam nodded. "Right. The broken one you mentioned to me yesterday. That's a real safety hazard, you know."

"I know. Why do you think I mentioned it?"

"Well, you won't have to worry after tomorrow. I'm going to fix it for you. That's why I had to get a measurement, so I could pick up the wood first thing in the morning."

"That's very thoughtful, but you really don't have to bother."

"It's no bother," Sam returned, his tone more matter-of-fact than gracious. "It's just a job."

"And a big one from the looks of it. Judging from the condition of the wood, you'd probably end up building a complete new set of stairs." Lisa ended her examination of the rickety steps to meet Sam's gaze, pleased out of all proportion by his offer to help. And encouraged. Certainly this gesture was a little more than *friendly, period.* "As I said, I appreciate the offer, but it's too much work. This isn't even really my house."

"I know. That's why I checked it all out with Mr. Fredericks this afternoon. You mentioned he was the executor for Miriam Bennett's estate, so I figured he'd be the one to ask. I mentioned the steps and those loose vents I happened to notice at the roofline, and he agreed it was worth whatever he had to pay me to take care it."

Lisa's eyes had narrowed in bewilderment, but now the facts were slowly sinking in.

"That's what you meant when you said it was a job?" she demanded. "That Fredericks has hired you to fix the stairs?"

Sam nodded, smiling with obvious pleasure over the prospect. "And the vents and whatever else needs fixing around here."

Such as her head, Lisa thought with disgust. So his offer wasn't even a friendly one. It was totally mercenary. Talk about stupid.

"But why?" she demanded. "Why bother to fix the place up only to tear it down?"

Sam's mouth twisted. "Maybe because some people around here aren't as happily resigned to that prospect as you are. And on the slim chance that they can preserve the house, it would be a shame to have it threatened again by a lawsuit because someone tripped and broke his neck on these stairs."

"That makes sense," conceded Lisa. "And you don't have to make it sound like I'm happy the house is going to be destroyed. I'm not."

"Right," he countered, "you're neutral. Anyway, Fredericks did say it all depended on whether or not you had any objections to having me around. You don't, do you?"

The question was clearly rhetorical. It was apparent from his relaxed manner that Sam assumed she wouldn't think twice about having him underfoot, a constant, potent distraction.

"Do you?" he prodded when she hesitated.

Lisa had objections galore but none she was willing to own up to. "I thought you were a marine archaeologist," she blurted.

"I am. But I told you, I'm currently between projects. That also means I'm between paychecks," he explained without embarrassment. "I can handle whatever needs to be done around here, if that's what's worrying you. I'm real good with my hands."

Lisa could believe that, and the flush it brought to her face made her thankful the porch light was off.

"I thought you'd be pleased about it," Sam told her in a suddenly subdued tone.

"I am."

She wasn't, but no matter how much having him so close so often was going to complicate her life, she wasn't heartless enough to deny him after he'd admitted needing the money.

"C'mon, Lisa," he urged, his tone cajoling and husky with amusement. "It'll be fun. You'll get to play lady of the manor."

"And you'll get to play my hired hand?"

"You got it. I know that's not as dramatic a scenario as pirate and captive wench, but you're a creative woman. Who knows," he continued in a sexy drawl Lisa knew was totally unconscious, "maybe you'll be lucky and get an idea or two out of this."

Lisa was already getting ideas, and none of them was suitable for the kind of greeting cards she created. Already she was fantasizing, wondering whether the coming days would be warm enough for him to work with his shirt off.

Feeling a little naughty and more than a little worried, she managed to return his smile. "Yeah. Lucky me."

Sam figured he had returned to the boat late enough to miss any nagging calls, and he was almost asleep when the shrill ringing of the phone just above his head dragged him back toward consciousness.

He rolled onto his stomach and groped for the receiver in the darkness. "Yeah?"

"It's me."

With a resigned sigh, Sam muttered, "Surprise, surprise."

"Well, have you told our charming houseguest what you're up to yet?"

His reply was muffled as he pressed his face into the pillow.

"What the hell did you say?" demanded the voice on the phone.

"I said, sort of," Sam repeated, shifting onto his back.

"Define sort of for me. No, never mind. You're stalling, I can tell. You didn't tell her a damn thing. She still thinks—"

"*Objection,*" Sam groaned. "*You're leading the witness.*"

"*Overruled,*" snapped the increasingly impatient voice on the other end. "*C'mon, Sam. Why don't you just—*"

"*I don't just,*" Sam interrupted once more, "*because it's not that simple. This thing with Lisa is more complicated than I anticipated.*"

"*You're making it complicated. Just tell her, for God's sake.*"

"*I want to get to know her better before I confide in her. I want her to trust me.*"

"*Ha! Keep dreaming, buddy.*"

Sam didn't join in his laughter, and he knew the reason was that his friend's retort had hit home. Was it already too late for Lisa to ever trust him? Not for the first time that day, he wished he could back up and start over with her.

"*Listen, you're wasting your time,*" the other man continued. "*Our icy blond beauty Lisa Bennett isn't the type to trust any man all that much.*"

Sam curbed the impulse to confide how much he was beginning to hope that wasn't so. Judging from all she'd told him, Lisa was a hard case where men were concerned, and not without cause. Yet the way she'd looked tonight, with her hair all soft and loose and her face scrubbed, it was hard to think of her as being anything but guileless and vulnerable. And it was even harder to remember the boundaries of his self-assigned role as her friend.

"*You're probably right,*" conceded Sam, mostly because he wanted to go to sleep. "*But, please, give me another couple of days to handle this my way. It's important to me.*"

"*And my career's important to me.*"

"*A couple of days, that's all. I plan to be spending a lot of time with Lisa, and I'll find some tactful way to slip in the truth.*" Sam hoped he sounded more confident than he felt about that. "*At the same time it will give me the chance I wanted to have a look around inside the place...all nice and legal.*"

"It'd better be. And just what makes you think this woman is willing to spend all this time with you?"

"Easy," Sam said ruefully. "She has no choice. Oh, yeah, I almost forgot to fill you in.... I told her that your eminent colleague William Fredericks hired me to do some repairs on the Bennett house."

A sharp, horrified intake of breath came before the words. "You told her what? You can't go around—"

"Sleep tight," Sam muttered, tumbling the receiver back into place. He closed his eyes, thought better of it, and quickly reached down and disconnected the phone line from the wall jack.

Chapter Five

The very real possibility that Sam had been angling for a job all along did not escape Lisa. She entertained the thought often during the next week, along with other, more explicit thoughts of Sam. There was simply no way to avoid it. The man was so... ever-present.

The idea that he'd set her up right from the start and had employed their barely existing friendship to influence Mr. Fredericks's decision to hire him filled Lisa with the familiar feeling of having been used. Yet she found it difficult to maintain her resentment in concert with all the other, nicer feelings Sam evoked. Not to mention the fact that, whatever his motives, the repairs he was accomplishing were making her life considerably easier.

As promised, he had rebuilt the porch steps, and, while he was at it, he had replaced the torn "attack" screen in the door. He'd also stopped the annoying drip in the bathroom faucet, fixed the pulleys on all the windows so they stayed up without props and worked some magic that made the old gas stove light on the first try. And all that working only half days.

Lisa had learned that while he wasn't actively involved in what he considered a major project, he was doing some consulting work for the state university, which occupied most of his mornings. He usually showed up close to lunchtime, roaring into the yard on the motorcycle he used only when it wasn't practical to travel by foot. Gradually Lisa found herself spending less time at the park and more time working on the porch or in her one-room retreat. If Sam noticed the change in her habits, he didn't comment, and over the course of several days they fell into a comfortable routine that, instead of interfering with her concentration as Lisa had feared, seemed to increase her productivity.

Sometimes she fixed lunch for the two of them, and sometimes Sam stopped at the deli on his way, arriving with an assortment of goodies Lisa never would have tried on her own. Instead of ordinary ham and bologna, he brought spicy Italian cold cuts with names like capicollo and mortadella, along with roasted peppers and marinated mushrooms and thick, crusty rolls to pile it all on.

They talked while they ate, and Lisa was fascinated to discover that Sam not only built models of ships but lived on his own boat, as well. It was docked at a marina across the bay, and in response to her undisguised interest, he extended a vague invitation for her to visit sometime. Lisa resisted the impulse to demand when, just as she resisted asking if his job as a university consultant paid so little that he had to moonlight as a handyman. Easygoing as he was, Lisa had the impression that Sam revealed only as much about himself as he chose to, and that he didn't choose to reveal it all.

Still, it was inevitable that they would spend some time talking about themselves. And since Lisa had impulsively confided all the highlights of her life the very first time they met, they invariably ended up talking about what she considered Sam's much more interesting past. He spoke with authority about locating and salvaging sunken ships, regaling her with stories about the times he'd spent diving for treasure in the Gulf of Mexico and off the coast of remote islands south of the Florida Keys. Again Lisa wondered why a man who had supposedly been instrumental in the highly profitable salvaging of several historical ships would be reduced to spending his days this way. However, even her gentlest hints in that direction hit a stone wall.

One thing Sam did speak about freely and often was his childhood, conveying the impression that it had been a very happy one. He told Lisa about the big old house on Cape Cod, and later the one in Boston, where he'd lived with his parents, four brothers and sisters, his maternal grandfather, and an ever-changing succession of pets. It was the sort of family Lisa had always longed to be part of, and she could happily have listened to his stories of errant baseballs smashing windows and sibling pillow fights all afternoon.

Fortunately for the condition of the big old house that was hers to live in, Sam took his responsibilities too seriously to squander that much time. Almost as soon as they'd finished eating, he would clean up, then disappear to get started on whatever job he had planned for that day. The sounds of hammer and saw quickly became peaceful background music for Lisa, and though she was usually left with more questions than answers about Sam, she found an unfamiliar contentment in going about her work while he was close by doing his own.

Ironically, the part of his life that interested Lisa most intensely was another subject Sam seemed reluctant to open up about—namely, any romantic liaisons he might have. He never alluded to any woman in his present and only once revealed that there had been anyone special in his past. That was the time they had meandered their way into yet another fiery debate about Alexander and Elizabeth's relationship and had somehow found themselves on opposite sides of a shouting match about women's rights, then and now.

"You know, sometimes I wish we were back in the eighteenth century so I wouldn't even be tempted to discuss something like this with you," Sam had finally exploded in frustration.

"It's a shame I can't zap you back there," Lisa had retorted. "You'd fit right in."

"That's absurd."

"All right," she'd conceded in her most docile tone, "maybe you would need a powdered wig and a costume change, but your attitude is perfect."

"What attitude? Name one attitude, one quality of mine, one thing I've ever said to you that suggests I don't consider women my equal."

"You said I needed remedial lessons in common sense."

"That's you, not all women. You have to allow for individual differences. And I only said it because you'd rather break your back lugging groceries home than wait and ask me to do it for you."

"See? There you go again. Maybe I didn't want you to do it for me. But never mind me. You also said it was lucky for Elizabeth that she found a man who knew what she wanted even though she was afraid to ask for it. Try telling me that isn't straight from the male supremacist's handbook."

Sam had gazed skyward with a look of strained patience. "I was talking about something that happened almost three hundred years ago. That was a whole different world."

Lisa had arched her eyebrows. "Really? Is that your official scientific opinion?"

He'd replied through clenched teeth. "You know what I meant. That was then, and this is now."

"Which only proves what a slow learner you are. You know, it doesn't surprise me that you've never married."

"As a matter of fact, I came damn close once," Sam had retorted, exasperation clearly ruling his tongue. "And the only reason it didn't work out wasn't because I didn't think she had every right to her own opinion, but because she didn't have one. It gets pretty tedious having someone consult you before she can so much as pick out the color of the sheets she wants. I suppose I should have guessed what she was like the first time she handed me back a restaurant menu, smiled blankly and said, 'You order for me.' But as they say, love is blind. And I sure thought I was in love.''

"And it turned out you weren't?'' Lisa had ventured when he stopped shouting and fell into a preoccupied silence. The dark look on his face told her the memories she'd stirred weren't pleasant ones.

By the time he'd turned to her, however, his familiar smirk was back in place, signaling that he was once more in control of his emotions. "It turned out I was in lust. Once it simmered to a cool, I realized that not only did I not want to spend the rest of my life holding Darlene's hand through every imagined crisis, I didn't want to spend the rest of my life with her at all.''

"So you broke off the engagement,'' Lisa had concluded with a certain satisfaction. She'd been unable to work up even a shred of sympathy for the woman who'd managed to inspire such a blinding case of lust in a man who found Lisa about as tempting as he found bologna.

Sam had nodded. "Actually, it was a mutual breakup. Darlene finally managed to reach a decision all on her own, and she decided I was too unsupportive and insensitive to marry. I decided that before I let myself get more than hormonally involved with a woman again, I'd make damn sure she could stand on her own two feet and that she liked doing it. It's the only way she could survive being married to me. When I'm committed to a salvage effort, I can be out of touch for weeks at a time. Any wife of mine would have to have a life of her own so that there wouldn't be a big chunk missing whenever I wasn't around. Not,'' he'd concluded with a sudden glitter in his green eyes, "that I'd mind if she missed me a whole lot and let me know it when I got home.''

With that he had crumpled his napkin and stood, leaving questions about any current "hormonal involvements'' buzzing like hornets in Lisa's head. Cowardly hornets. Instead of charging forward to be asked, they all stayed inside and plagued her whenever she wasn't engrossed in her drawing or asleep.

At least it was satisfying to know that, for all he'd scoffed at her prerequisites for involvement, Sam had a few of his own. Their relationship had too much of an adversarial edge for Lisa to admit it to him, of course, but if he was telling the truth about wanting a woman with a mind of her own, Lisa admired him for it.

Did it even occur to him that she was just such a woman? If so, he did a good job of hiding it. Certainly the fact that what he was looking for in a relationship dovetailed nicely with some of her own desires—for an equal, independent partnership, at least—wasn't lost on Lisa. Sometimes when she looked at Sam, he was so damn sexy she longed to be persuaded to overlook the fact that he wasn't financially secure enough to make him the perfect man for her. The only hitch was that Sam apparently wasn't the least bit inclined toward such persuading.

Throughout the week she spent putting the finishing touches on her proposal, Lisa wavered between indulging in fantasies of what it would be like to be more than friends with Sam and dousing herself with the cold, hard reality that the man was neither suitable nor interested. Although there was, Lisa finally, sheepishly admitted to herself, room for movement on the suitable part of it. Enough time had elapsed since Ron's devastating ego-bruising for her to start being practical. The chances were good that in an imperfect world she was never going to meet the paragon of virtue, character and financial security she had in mind.

She probably ought to consider herself lucky to have stumbled across a man who not only appealed to her wildly but who also didn't see her as only a tempting piece of meat, a man who claimed he could easily tolerate, even encourage, the sort of independence she was determined to maintain. Yes, a few pragmatic brush strokes and, presto, Sam was suitable. Now how in the world did she go about getting his interest? For Lisa, who was more accustomed to discouraging unwanted male attention, going out of her way to attract a man was totally uncharted territory.

By Friday morning she was doing the final lettering on her finished samples with a black calligraphy pen. First thing Monday she planned to take the bus to Boston and hand-deliver the proposal to PaperThoughts. After that she was free to return to Chicago. Surprisingly, the prospect no longer filled her with the relief and excitement it should have, and Lisa knew the reason was Sam.

Somehow, with him around, the old wreck of a house had started to seem less like a bad joke on her and more like a real home. Part of it, Lisa knew, was the subtle way he had of reminding her that, like it or not, her tie to the Bennett house was real and deep. His consulting work required him to do some research at the Aquidneck Historical Society, and several times he'd brought Lisa copies of old articles he'd come across that mentioned the Bennett house or family. Once he had even badgered her into accompanying him there to see a handwritten account of the Bennett family tree dating back to the eighteen hundreds. Lisa had been fascinated by it, exactly as Sam had insisted she would be and as she had fervently denied. But aside from the way Sam was lulling her into facing her feelings about the house, the simple fact was that she liked him. A lot. And more every day.

She applied a flourish to a letter *M* and wished for the thousandth time that something reciprocal would spark between them before their time together ran out. What would happen, she wondered, if she simply summoned the courage to tell Sam that she was attracted to him in more than a platonic way? She dabbed an exclamation point into place and decided the outcome was too hard to predict; the whole idea too risky to explore. Of course, she could try to get the message across in a less direct manner. Like, say, greeting him at the door in a negligee.

Chuckling at the picture that conjured up, Lisa lifted her pen from the linen paper before it left a blot. She even owned the perfect negligee for such a mission—a lacy, crimson, plunging little thing that would either light a fire under him or prove he was unignitable. Fortunately for her dignity, she hadn't packed it.

After blowing gently on the fresh lettering to ensure that it was dry, she put the card she'd been working on aside and lifted the top one from the stack that remained. She wanted to avoid being either too direct or too devious in dealing with Sam. On the other hand, she didn't want to leave Jamestown and live with months' worth of second thoughts. If only there was some way to force him to take a good hard look at her as a woman instead of a pal. Then, no matter what happened, she would at least have the satisfaction of knowing it had been his choice whether or not to pursue matters.

Lisa paused with the pen over the paper, her expression thoughtful. Actually, she had to assume some of the blame for the fact that their relationship had gotten stalled on this palsy-walsy track. When they first met, she hadn't been very receptive to his offer of friendship, much less anything more intimate. If only they could start over. Suddenly Lisa straightened in her chair and stopped absently nibbling the end of her pen. Maybe they could. Maybe if she simply pretended to herself that they had just met, she would naturally say and do the right things to encourage him. It would almost be like starting over, sort of like a first date.

Her eyes sparkled, seeing possibilities instead of the paper before her. A first date would be perfect. Perhaps seeing her in a different setting would be the spark needed to change the way Sam thought of her. It was worth a try, at least. Unfortunately, since he was unlikely to suggest a date, she would have to do the asking. That is, if she had the guts.

Calculatedly Lisa eyed the pile of cards she had yet to complete, deciding they made a perfect carrot on a stick to help her keep her mind on what she was doing. She would leave it up to fate, deal with it as she had her Muses. If she could harness her straying concentration and finish the proposal by the time Sam arrived, she would invite him out to dinner. If not ... If not, she'd have plenty of *what if*'s to mull over on the plane ride home.

As she worked, a question streaked repeatedly through her mind. Was it wise to let serendipity guide her this way?

She might have reneged on her superstitious bargain with herself if the fates didn't make their wishes so abundantly clear. For the first time since he'd begun working around the house, Sam didn't show up until long after noon, giving Lisa ample time not only to complete the proposal and arrange it in her portfolio, but also to change into a deep aqua sweater that made her eyes seem the color of a tropical sea.

Not that it mattered. The aqua sweater and ivory linen slacks, the carefully coordinated jewelry, the painstakingly tousled waves of her blond hair—all was wasted on Sam. She might as well have wrapped herself in yesterday's newspaper. In fact, it might have been better if she'd wrapped herself in newspaper. Then he might have at least broken stride as he passed by, to check the sports page for the score of last night's Red Sox game.

Instead he breezed into the kitchen, where Lisa waited with damp palms and a prepared speech, announced that he had been tied up on campus and had already grabbed a quick lunch, then proceeded upstairs. Through a haze of disappointment and annoyance Lisa heard him add something about finding an electrical short, and he disappeared. Alone in the kitchen once more, she glumly eyed the neatly arranged ingredients for the ham and cheese omelet with which she'd planned to impress him. Annoyance was rapidly gaining on disappointment.

Who did Sam Ravenal think he was? Or, of greater concern, who did he think she was? Forget looks and sex appeal and all that nonsense, he had no right to barge past her as if she were a doorman around here.

Halfway up the stairs, hell-bent on telling him so, she reconsidered. The last thing she wanted to do was give Sam the impression that his inattention bothered her, especially when she was about to risk suggesting they get together for something fancier than pizza in front of the TV. It would make her appear exactly what she refused to be: vulnerable. No, she would bite her lip and hold back the lecture on manners for the time being. But she had no intention of waiting one more nerve-racking minute to ask what was on her mind.

Sam was busy in Miriam's room, and as Lisa stepped inside the doorway, she decided maybe it was a good thing it had worked out this way. He was standing on the narrow brass bed, fiddling with a light mounted on the wall, so all she had to do was talk to his back. That was infinitely easier than confronting the wry amusement that so often glinted in his roguish green eyes.

"So," she began, sticking her hands into the deep side pockets of her slacks to keep from fidgeting, "this is where the short is."

Sam glanced over his shoulder at her. He was wearing an ordinary green-and-black cotton shirt that somehow looked extraordinary stretched across his broad shoulders. Countless washings had faded his jeans to the color of a hazy sky and to a near-satin softness. He looked wonderful, and just the flash of his lopsided smile was enough to cause an oddly exhilarating tightness in Lisa's chest.

"It looks that way," he said in response to her remark about the short. He was once more squinting at the multicolored wires he had exposed. The tarnished brass fixture was lying on the bed by his sock-clad feet. The sight of his tan work boots on the floor made Lisa smile. At least his lack of manners wasn't total.

"I think I've traced the problem with that flickering bathroom light into here," continued Sam, still facing the wall. "But it's tough to be sure. Like everything else about this house, the wiring was done in stages. Some of it's concealed behind the original ceilings.''

"You mean these aren't the original ceilings?" inquired Lisa.

"Not all of them." He rapped his knuckles on the ceiling over his head. "This one definitely was added sometime after the house was built. There's a space above it. Some of these walls are probably new, as well."

Lisa thought about that. If the rooms had been laid out differently back then, would she ever figure out which room had been Elizabeth's?

"Why would anyone have fooled around with a house this old?"

Sam flicked her a dry look. "It wasn't always this old, pal, or this historically significant. Life-styles change, families need more bedrooms, or bigger ones, walls come down and go up." His fingers carefully uncoiled a knot of copper-tipped wires. "Personally, I think it adds character to the old place. I like trying to figure out what changes were made at a particular point in history and why."

"Like a big puzzle."

"Sort of." His fingers stilled, and he met her gaze. "Do you like puzzles, Lisa?"

The intense interest in his gaze stopped her from answering quickly or thoughtlessly. She shrugged, a little uneasy.

"Sometimes, I suppose... but only if I can solve them in the end. Once my curiosity has been piqued, I hate not knowing the answer, like when someone tells a long, involved joke and then forgets the punch line. Or a movie that leaves you still wondering what happened when the credits start to roll.

"Once when I was in high school," she continued, absently moving closer to the bed, "a friend of mine showed me this puzzle—it was a brainteaser, connecting lines and boxes in a certain way—and I would rush through my homework every day in study hall to work on it. She insisted there was a solution, and she had me going for months. Then, when I finally gave up and decided I was never going to figure it out on my own, it turned out she had forgotten the solution and lost the book she'd found it in. Of course, she still insisted a solution existed, and, you know, to this day when I start doodling, I end up working on the darn thing." Lisa suddenly realized she'd been rattling on in response to what had probably been a casual question, and she laughed. "Crazy, huh?"

Sam shook his head, his expression so solemn it was almost a grimace. For once she was absolutely certain it wasn't amusement that had narrowed his eyes, but she couldn't read the expression there.

"No, it's not crazy," he told her softly. "I'm the same way. The truth is..." He hesitated. His mouth tightened, making the grimace more pronounced. "Did you come up here for something?" he asked brusquely.

The question sounded like a reprimand, and she quickly decided the elusive look in his eyes must have been annoyance. She'd already discovered that he didn't like interruptions while he worked.

"Actually, yes, I did," she replied, taking a deep breath as he turned back to his project.

"Go ahead, shoot."

She searched for the words she'd rehearsed earlier, but they seemed to have deserted her, like rats fleeing a sinking ship.

As the silence lengthened, Sam glanced back at her. "Well?"

"I finished my proposal," she blurted.

He turned back to the wall and yanked on the wires with none of his earlier delicacy. "Swell."

Lisa didn't think he sounded too impressed. "And I thought, maybe if you were free sometime, we might celebrate." The invitation had started slow but finished like a tape on fast forward. Lisa gripped the bedpost, steeled for his refusal.

"Sure thing," he said. She didn't have time to savor that mediocre response before he added, "You want to give me a hand here?"

"That's not exactly what I had in mind for a celebration."

"Cute, Lisa. You want to help or not?"

You want to go jump off a cliff? she bit back.

"Help with what?" she asked instead.

"Just climb up here next to me," he ordered. "I'll show you what to do."

"I'm not touching any live wires," she declared when she was standing barefoot beside him. She knew the remark sounded as waspish as his lukewarm reaction had left her feeling.

Sam's barely lifted brows topped off a sardonic gaze. "Would you even know a live wire from a dead one?" he inquired.

"I suppose I would if I touched one," she shot back. "But I really don't want to find out. So if your electrical skills are as rusty as your social skills, I don't want any part of this."

"What the hell are you talking about?"

"Nothing." Now Lisa was staring at the wires while he looked at her.

"What was that crack about my social skills?"

"Meaningless," snapped Lisa. "It was meaningless. You can't very well comment on what doesn't exist."

"For God's sake." He went to jab his fingers through his hair in exasperation and instead beaned himself with the screwdriver he was holding. "Ouch!"

Lisa tried not to gloat as he rubbed his head.

"All right, Lisa," he drawled. "What's eating you? Is this all because I didn't go wild over the fact that you finished your proposal?"

"You hardly acknowledged it," she bit out, her eyes flashing as they finally met his.

"I'm sorry, okay? I think it's great that you finished. Now you can do what you've been dying to do and blow this joint. I'm ecstatic for you. You want me to jump up and down to prove it? I'll jump up and down. There!"

He jumped, making the old bed groan and creak almost as loudly as he was shouting. Before Lisa could climb down or grab the wall or even draw breath to tell him what an idiot he was, the whole thing collapsed beneath them with a riotous clanging of metal and an uprising of dust. At the last instant Lisa saw Sam's arms shoot out toward her, and then for a split second it felt as if she'd stepped off the edge of the world.

Not until she landed did she realize that Sam had reached out to cushion her fall. He had ended up on his back, half on the mattress and half off, and Lisa, to her acute embarrassment, had ended up on his front. Intimately so. She was straddling him in a position that reminded her of nothing so much as the predicament the heroine of *Romancing the Stone* had found herself in at the bottom of that mud slide. If Lisa had her way, she would never have to lift her face from where it was pressed to Sam's neck and face the laughter in his eyes.

Far too soon for her to have even started gathering her wits, she felt his hand wind through her hair to tip her face up.

"Lisa?" His voice was husky with concern. "Are you okay?"

"Yes. I'm okay." She moved her head only enough to nod, but in the process her eyes met his, and abruptly the answer became a lie.

She wasn't okay. Not even close. There was a fever spreading through her, and she knew it was rooted in the hard, lean body beneath her. Some instinct more powerful than that of self-preservation lifted her head higher, until her chin rested on the steel of his chest and she yielded to the luminous power of his gaze. His eyes were a sea of dark emeralds, and Lisa was drowning. His mouth was closer than it had ever been, close enough so she could smell the mint on his breath and feel the moist heat of it coming in rapid pants. As rapid as her own.

The realization that he was gripped by the same sizzling awareness as she was heightened her excitement. He was going to kiss her. She knew it as surely as she knew the sun would rise again tomorrow, and she welcomed it in the same elemental way.

"Lisa." It was barely a sound, soft and gritty.

"Yes," she whispered.

His head rose, bringing those erotically parted lips closer still. Lisa felt herself melting, her surrender complete.

"Yes, yes," she murmured again, her tone urgent and inviting.

Without warning, Sam's head dropped back to the hardwood floor. The movement was as jarring to Lisa as if a film had snapped at the most crucial point of the movie. She felt like screaming in protest.

Something had changed Sam's mind about kissing her. There was no way she had simply imagined his passion a few seconds ago. She was as certain of that as she was that he was now struggling to rein in his emotions. She was vividly aware of the wild pumping of his heart beneath her. By the time he spoke a minute later, however, his breathing was normal, his tone the lazy, casual one she recognized well.

"My back," he announced, "is killing me."

"Your back?" Lisa echoed as if he were talking about something totally foreign.

"Yeah. I think I must have landed on something, maybe one of the broken slats, and it's digging into me. If you could sort of...get off me...."

"Yes...yes...of course."

Lisa half rolled, half scrambled off his body, her face redder than a cardinal's robes. She was more than embarrassed; she was mortified. The glazed look on his face that she'd mistaken for desire had been pain.

She watched in humiliated silence as he eased himself to a sitting position and, wincing, rubbed the small of his back. On the floor where he'd been lying was what looked like a fabric bundle on a rod jutting from beneath the mattress.

"This must have been what was sticking into you," she suggested, reaching for it.

She would have reached for hot coals if it would distract him from what had just happened. The object stuck beneath the collapsed bed, and she had to lean forward on her knees and use both hands to work it free. It turned out to be a handmade contraption, devised so that it could be tightly anchored between the mattress and box spring with a loose pocket hanging by the side of the bed.

It looked like the sort of thing used to keep glasses or a magazine handy for reading in bed, but inside this pocket was a worn leather case with brass filigree corners. One of the corners arrowing upward had probably jabbed Sam. She held it up for him to see, but he was still too busy administering first aid to himself.

"Figures old maid Miriam would have her bed booby-trapped," he muttered. "I feel like I've been lanced."

Lisa was feeling a little lanced herself. She forced a quick, sympathetic smile for Sam, then, as if fascinated, lowered her gaze to examine the case in her hands. Had he been aware of her feelings a moment ago? she wondered. Or could she be so lucky as to have him really be as insensitive as his former fiancée had accused him of being?

"What did she get me with anyway?" he finally inquired, shifting on the mattress so he was facing her. "It felt like brass knuckles."

"Close. Brass corners." She held it up again. "Does it still hurt?"

"Like hell," Sam murmured, although he'd stopped rubbing his back and looked fully recovered to Lisa. His gaze lingered on her face for a moment—long enough to make her breath catch—before trailing down to the leather case she was holding. "What was a thing like that doing in her bed?"

"It wasn't actually in her bed," Lisa explained, holding up the fabric pocket to demonstrate. "I think it must have been hanging by the side in this thing, probably the side next to the wall."

"*Hidden* next to the wall," Sam amended in a tone of high drama. "What do you suppose was so important old Miriam had it hidden away?"

Shrugging, Lisa turned the case over in her hands. "I don't know."

"And you never will until you open it."

Lisa's fingers clenched on the smooth leather. "No."

"What do you mean, no?"

The curt refusal had slipped out unbidden, and Lisa wasn't sure exactly what she did mean by it. But the thought of prying into something Miss Miriam Bennett had obviously intended to keep to herself disturbed her. As Sam watched her, still waiting for an explanation, Lisa noticed for the first time the small lock securing the case and made a perfunctory attempt to open it.

"It's locked," she announced happily.

"That lock isn't anything a paper clip can't open," Sam replied. "Hand it over."

Lisa met his narrow-eyed gaze and thought it seemed almost a challenge, as if he were daring her to examine her feelings of reluctance and try to put them into words. Hastily she slapped the case into his open palm, trying to ignore the sensation of disloyalty that shot through her. To add to her discomfort she could have sworn she caught a hint of cynicism in the twist of Sam's mouth before he unfolded himself from the collapsed bed with fluid grace and crossed the room to rummage through the things on Miriam's dresser.

"Ah, success," he called over his shoulder, waving a hairpin in the air for her to see. A few seconds later he had the case unlocked and had rejoined Lisa on the floor. "Do you want to do the honors," he inquired lightly, "or shall I?"

Lisa snatched the case from him. "I will." She peeled open the front flap, then halted. "Actually, I'm not sure we should even be doing this. It's really none of our business what's in here. This is her personal property, after all."

"I'm sure Miriam, wherever she is, won't mind," Sam intoned dryly.

"Well, I'm not. She did go to a lot of trouble to hide it."

"Probably so it wouldn't be stolen if anyone ever broke in," he suggested. "Certainly she wasn't hiding it from her own flesh and blood."

Lisa's head shook vehemently. "I'm hardly that."

"Lisa, you're exactly that. And maybe if Miriam had known you existed, she would have wanted you to have whatever is in there. Maybe if she'd known there was another Bennett to live in her precious house, she wouldn't have ordered it to be demolished." He tapped the case with his forefinger. "And maybe something in here will help us understand why she did."

Still, Lisa hesitated.

"I thought you liked solving puzzles," Sam drawled.

Lisa wasn't sure if it was his mocking challenge or her own burning curiosity that finally got to her, but she slowly opened the case wider. Inside were several yellowed envelopes tied with a ribbon of faded violet satin. Tucked in one corner was an equally yellowed piece of tissue.

Carefully Lisa lifted the tissue out and with trembling fingers unfolded it to reveal an oval locket suspended from a delicate bow-shaped pin. It was about the size of a quarter and made of gold except for its clear glass face. Pressed behind the glass was a lock of very fine, very pale blond hair. The sight of it cradled in her palm filled Lisa with the by-now-familiar sensation of being connected to things that had occurred in this house long before she arrived.

"A hair brooch. Is that all?"

Sam's question intruded on her mood, shattering the warm feelings that had engulfed her.

"Yes, except for a few letters. A hair brooch," Lisa repeated, savoring the words. She looked up to see Sam shrug.

"That's what I've heard them called. They were quite the rage way back then, a unique way for a lady to wear a lock of her loved one's hair."

"I hadn't thought of Miss Bennett as having a loved one," Lisa murmured. "She never married, and everything I've heard about her suggests she liked it that way." Idly she ran her thumb over the glass. "I wonder who he was."

"I'll wager there's one sure way to find out. Read the letters, Lisa."

"No." This time the refusal was accompanied by a firm shake of her head. Hastily she slipped the hair brooch back into the case and scrambled to her feet. "Absolutely not. It's bad enough that Miss Bennett's will might be voided and her last wishes ignored. She shouldn't have to suffer the added indignity of having her privacy violated by strangers."

Sam was leaning back on his elbows, one dark eyebrow flexed in amusement. "Do you really think she cares?"

"*I* care," Lisa declared. "We're not reading these letters."

She expected him to argue or mock her, but he looked strangely pleased as he grinned and asked, "What's this rearing its ugly head, Lisa? Family loyalty?"

She tossed her hair over her shoulder, barely pausing as she strode toward the door. "Maybe. And maybe I've learned the hard way that everyone has a right to decide for herself what happens to the things that belong to her."

"Like Maxine's Musings?"

Lisa halted and whirled to face him. Her eyes flashed. "You're damn right, like Maxine's Musings."

"And like this house?"

"No. Yes. Oh, I don't know. That's so complicated." She held up the case containing the letters, her face set with determination. "But these aren't complicated. They're private. And they shouldn't be read just to satisfy some morbid curiosity.''

"How about to satisfy some healthy curiosity?" Sam persisted as she turned to go. "There is such a thing, Lisa. Think about it."

She made a noncommittal sound and took another step toward the door, only to have him detain her once more.

"Now, about that celebration...."

Chapter Six

Forget I ever mentioned a celebration," Lisa told him. "I have."

"Well, I haven't, and I won't. You earned it, and you're going to get it."

"Yes, I can imagine. Coffee and donuts on the porch while I hold the ladder for you."

"If that's what you've got your heart set on," Sam replied, grinning. "Personally, I was going to suggest something a little less...local. Are you still planning to go to Boston to drop off your proposal?"

"Yes," returned Lisa with a nod. "I wasn't kidding when I said I'm not trusting it out of my sight until it's safely in the publisher's hands."

"Good. It so happens I have some business of my own to take care of in Boston. I'll drive you up on Monday, and we can handle everything in one shot, including our celebration. I know the perfect place to have lunch. You'll love it, I promise. What do you say?"

No matter how perfect the place he had in mind, lunch on Monday simply didn't match the romantic setting she'd envisioned. It was also three whole days away. Still, this invitation was a step in the right direction.

She smiled at him. "It sounds wonderful."

"Good. I'll pick you up around eleven."

"You don't mean on that motorcycle?"

Amusement glittered in his dark green eyes. "You'd rather walk to Boston?"

"Couldn't we take the bus instead?"

"Uh-uh. I get bus sick."

"A rental car?"

"Lisa," he countered, impatience in his voice, "there's nothing wrong with taking my bike."

Lisa was valiantly trying to maintain her smile. "Except that I'll be totally windblown by the time we get there."

"So I happen to think you'd look great windblown. Sort of touchable for a change."

Was that a compliment? Although he was looking at the broken bed, not at her, as he said it, Lisa decided the remark still counted as a significant breakthrough. If windblown and touchable were linked in Sam's mind, then she would swallow her pride and look windblown. Besides, it occurred to her that Sam might not have the money for a bus ticket or a rental car *and* lunch. She would gladly pay her share, especially since the celebration had been her idea, but something warned that bringing up the subject of finances might drain what little romance the occasion possessed.

"I suppose I could always wear a scarf," she allowed.

Sam shot her a stern look. "You'll wear a helmet."

A helmet? With the beautiful ivory silk blouse she had already picked out to wear? Over her dead body, thought Lisa. As it was she'd have to wear slacks instead of a skirt. With her lips starting to ache from the effort of staying tipped up in defiance of her gut-level impulse to grimace, she didn't press the issue. There would be time enough to argue about the helmet on Monday.

"Monday at eleven it is, then," she said.

"Right. I'm going to have to knock off early today, and I'll be tied up all day tomorrow and Sunday, but don't worry, I'll get everything cleaned up here before I leave."

That was the very last thing worrying Lisa. Tied up all day tomorrow and Sunday with whom? she wanted to demand. With the question perched high enough in her throat to choke her, she nodded and nonsensically repeated, "Monday."

"Right." Sam glanced from the mess on the floor to the wires hanging overhead to Lisa, his expression a pointed dismissal.

After extending an offer to help, which he soundly refused, she murmured something about staying out of his way and left. All the way down the stairs she berated herself for not having thought of a subtle way to inquire about what or who was pressing enough to occupy his time for the entire weekend. Surely if he was seeing another woman that often, he would have mentioned something about her by now.

Wouldn't he?

Pouring herself a glass of ice tea, Lisa decided she might be better off not knowing.

With her proposal finished, she soon discovered she didn't have a lot to do to pass the time. Unfortunately, neither the fat mystery she'd been eager to dig into nor the afternoon showing of one of her favorite old movies on television was able to hold her attention.

Monday seemed to loom as a first date in more ways than one. It was as if she were sixteen again, consumed by mixed emotions and uncertainties as if they were all she had to think about, when actually she had dozens of more important things to do than sit there daydreaming about Sam Ravenal.

For instance she could.... Lisa stirred her ice tea with her straw and took a sip. Then she reached for the television remote control panel and irritably hit the off button. She could pack her clothes for the trip home, that's what she could do, she thought finally, with an absurdly hollow feeling of triumph and absolutely no inclination to go upstairs and get started.

Instead she decided to walk next door and give Helen the book she had bought for her while shopping yesterday. Several times since their first visit, Helen had knocked on the back door with a plate of homemade muffins or cookies, and once even a small seafood casserole. She always brushed off Lisa's protests with the claim that the recipe made far more than one person could eat. Lacking the culinary skills to reciprocate, Lisa had been searching for a way to show her appreciation and had finally spotted a new horticulture annual in the bookstore that she knew Helen, an avid gardener, would enjoy.

Helen blushed with pleasure when Lisa gave her the book, and, as Lisa had hoped, insisted she stay for a cup of tea. They talked a little about the work "that nice-looking young man," as Helen referred to Sam, was doing on the house. Then Lisa casually steered the conversation to Miriam Bennett.

"I know you said she wasn't fond of children," Lisa ventured at one point, "but surely Miss Bennett had friends her own age."

"None I ever noticed," Helen replied, placing a plate of homemade sugar cookies in front of Lisa. "No, Miss Bennett kept to herself, except for her mother, of course. And after that poor old soul died, I guess Miss Bennett was just so set in her ways it was too much bother to change."

"But what about gentlemen friends?" Lisa persisted, curious about whom the letters might have been from even though she refused to read them. "Maybe when she was younger...before you moved here?"

Helen chuckled at the suggestion. "Oh, pardon me, honey, I know she was your great-aunt and all, but I can't for the life of me picture Miss Bennett entertaining a man. No, she wasn't a bit friendly or sweet—not at all like you." The older woman's brow puckered as if she'd been struck by a sudden thought, and Lisa leaned forward in her chair. "But then, there was a rumor of some sort...."

"What sort of rumor?" Lisa urged.

"I remember hearing it right after we moved in, when I remarked to old Mr. Fournier—he's dead now, too, God rest his soul—how welcome all the neighbors had made us feel, except for the Bennetts. He snorted and asked what else could you expect from a senile old lady and a jilted old maid. Naturally, I was all ears to hear the story of how Miss Bennett had been jilted, but all he knew was that it was a traveling salesman of one kind or another, and that he'd courted Miss Bennett quite steadily all summer and then just up and left town before the first frost. That was years and years before we moved here, back when Miss Bennett was in her late twenties, I believe he said."

Helen shook her head as she lifted her teacup to take a sip. "Heavens, I'd forgotten all about that. You're good for me, Lisa. You help me clear out the cobwebs in this old head. I'll miss you when you're gone."

"I'll miss you, too, Helen," Lisa replied, a little surprised by how true that was.

She usually exchanged only neighborly greetings with the older woman, but she liked knowing she was there next door if she needed anything or simply wanted to talk. Despite their age difference, Lisa felt comfortable with Helen. Aside from Sam, the older woman was the closest thing to a real friend she had found in a long time. Their unexpected friendship was one more emotional bond Lisa hadn't anticipated when she'd come to Jamestown, and one more thread in her tangled, conflicting feelings about leaving.

By the time Lisa returned to her own house, order had been restored to the upstairs bedroom, and Sam was gone.

She quickly moved through the rooms, turning on lights and closing the windows to the ocean breeze, but still the house felt cold and lifeless. Suddenly with all her heart Lisa wished she hadn't intentionally lingered over tea to avoid Sam. Maybe if she'd returned earlier he would have stayed and talked for a while and eventually decided to skip whatever he had planned for this evening.

But no, she was far too clever to let fate alone handle this thing. She had plotted so craftily, deciding that as long as she wasn't going to see Sam again until Monday, they should start that day with as clean a slate as possible between them, without either of them having a chance to say or do anything to diminish its shimmering possibilities.

Now she longed for five more minutes with him no matter what he had to say. The long hours until eleven o'clock Monday morning stretched before her like an endless row of hurdles, and she wondered how an idea that had seemed so brilliant just a short while ago could suddenly feel like the most masochistic move she'd ever made.

It had reached the point where Sam dreaded answering the phone. It wasn't enough that he was waging a war with his own conscience, he also had to keep rationalizing his behavior to someone who clearly thought he had lost his mind.

"Let me see if I understand what you've been telling me," his friend said when he called Sunday night. "You created this farce about being hired to do repairs around her place so you could find something that you tell me probably isn't there, and you admit you're not really sure what it might be anyway. And now, on top of that, you feel too guilty to even look for it. Which I understood was the purpose of this whole thing. Do I have all that right?"

"I don't feel guilty, really. I just hate the thought of sneaking around there behind Lisa's back. I feel as if I'm betraying her."

"Betraying," came the pointed response. *"Two nights ago when we got together for a drink, you used the word* involved *four times in reference to Lisa Bennett. You know, if I didn't know you so well, I'd almost think you were falling for this broad. Tell me you're not falling for her, Sam."*

"I'm not falling for her. Exactly." Resting his head against the cabin wall, Sam hoped he wouldn't be asked to name the fine points that distinguished what he was feeling for Lisa from falling for her, because he'd be damned if he knew. He supposed that must mean he was falling for her.

"All right, that's it!" The exclamation came in such a loud burst of finality that Sam had to lift the receiver away from his ear for a second. *"It's over. Finito. I want out of this, Sam old buddy. I never should have let you talk me into getting involved in the first place. This, in case you haven't noticed, has become an uncomfortably prolonged lie. Either you tell her, or I'll have to."*

"I'll tell her," Sam assured him. It was no more than he had already decided on his own. He no longer had any worry that Lisa was mercenary enough to threaten or delay the entire project. The risk now was purely personal, and sooner or later he was going to have to face it.

"When?" came the curt demand.

"Maybe tomorrow."

"Definitely tomorrow. Or the matter will be out of your hands."

Sam nodded, his expression bleak. *"Tomorrow."*

When Lisa awoke on Monday morning she didn't bother to glance at the clock. She could tell from the raw pink of the sky outside her bedroom window that it was far too early to get up. She would have preferred to sleep until nine-thirty or so, leaving herself a luxurious amount of time to get ready for her date with Sam but not enough time to get frazzled over it.

Rolling onto her stomach, she buried her face in her pillow and wondered what the chances were that Sam would wake this morning thinking about her. She wondered if he thought of their lunch this afternoon as a date, and if the prospect even slightly frazzled him. Probably not, she concluded wistfully. Next she wondered if Sam would even remember that they had made plans to go to Boston together today, and her heart started to pound anxiously. Great, just what she needed: one more thing to keep her on edge.

With a disgusted sigh she threw back the covers. She knew from her experience yesterday morning that once her mind became charged with thoughts of Sam, she couldn't go back to sleep no matter how hard she tried. As she waited for warm water and ran a bath, she was struck by the ironic realization that at least she had plenty of things to worry about to fill the empty morning ahead. Inside her the layers of anxiety were as plentiful as those in a gourmet pastry.

She was concerned about how PaperThoughts would receive her proposal, and she was more than concerned about what had come to loom in her mind as today's do-or-die situation with Sam. Her feelings for him were so confused that from moment to moment she wasn't sure how she even wanted this afternoon to turn out. And then, hovering beneath all her other concerns was a growing uncertainty about how she was going to manage to close the door on the Jonathan Bennett House when the time came to get on with her life back in Chicago.

After bathing and drying her hair, she dressed in an old pair of jeans, a comfortable red sweater and sneakers. Her stomach was in no mood to receive breakfast, and a long walk on the beach would at least provide a change of scenery for her jitters. It was almost eight-thirty by the time she returned and was picking her way back up the bluff. At the sound of voices in the yard above, Lisa quickened her pace as much as she safely could and set foot on the lawn just in time to see a trio of boys scampering toward the sidewalk.

"Wait! Hold it, you guys!" she shouted, slightly amazed when they did exactly that.

They had frozen in their tracks beside the porch and now turned to face Lisa with comically sheepish expressions. They looked to be about eight years old, all of them dressed alike in jeans with the cuffs rolled up and windbreakers. Everything about them, from the scuffs on their sneakers to the patches on their knees and dirt smudges on their faces, was a testament to the glories of active boyhood. As Lisa slowly approached, they sidled closer to one another, standing shoulder to shoulder for courage in a way that left her fighting a smile.

"All right, you guys," she said, sweeping her gaze from one anxious face to another, "what were you doing in my yard again?" She wasn't absolutely certain these were the same boys Helen had reprimanded the other night, until they responded to her question with guilty shrugs rather than a denial.

"Nothing," the blond boy on her left finally blurted. "We weren't doing nothing. Honest, lady."

Lisa squinted at the back of the house as if checking for fresh chokecherry stains.

"We weren't bombing your house again, if that's what you think," he added in a rush. "Mrs. Van Egan said she'd tell if we did, and my mother said next time it'll be no bike for me for a week."

The small boy's tone was so horrified, it might have been the guillotine his mother had threatened him with. In that instant Lisa knew that, no matter what they had been up to, she wouldn't do anything to get them into trouble at home.

"Well, if you weren't throwing cherries, what were you doing?" she asked.

Again there was a general shuffling of sneakers before the apparent spokesman for the group looked up at her, his blue eyes wide. "We were ... sort of ... climbing your tree," he confessed. "But we weren't hurting it, honest."

"I see." Lisa looked around at the towering cherry tree with its maze of giant limbs, then back at the boys. "Aren't there any trees in your yards?"

"Not like that one!" he exclaimed. "That's a lookout tree. You can see pirates coming all the way from England from the top of that tree."

Lisa whistled in solemn appreciation of that tidbit. "My goodness, all the way from England? I had no idea. Do you boys come around often to climb the tree?"

"No, just sometimes," piped up the smallest of the trio, a dark-haired boy with a blue baseball cap pulled low over his forehead. "Maybe only once a year."

Lisa bit her lip to keep from chuckling at the innocent lie. "Once a year, huh? That's too bad."

"Why, lady?" the first boy asked. "Are you going to tell?"

"Tell?" Lisa shook her head, frowning as if the very prospect was ludicrous. "No, I only said it was too bad because now that I've taken a good, hard look at it, I can see that is a tree that needs a lot of climbing. And most days I'm just too busy to get out here and do it. I only wish I knew someone who would have the time to get around to climbing it more than once a year."

"You mean like us?" the light-haired boy asked in astonishment.

"That would be wonderful!" Lisa exclaimed. "That is, if you three aren't too busy."

She finally stopped fighting the smile and bestowed it on each of them in turn. Slowly, answering grins appeared on all three small faces as they realized that not only was she not going to snitch on them, she was actually going to let them climb the tree that had been forbidden territory for so long.

"We're not too busy, are we, Pete? Are we, Danny?"

Pete and Danny hastily assured Lisa that they weren't.

"We could climb it anytime you want," offered Danny, who had been silent until now. "Except after the streetlights come on."

"Well, I'll leave the time up to you," Lisa returned. "But there are a few conditions you have to agree to." They all nodded eagerly. "I want each of you to promise never to come alone. That way, in case anything happens there will always be someone to go for help. And I don't want any pushing or fighting or horsing around while you're up there. Agreed?"

"Agreed," they chorused.

"And," she continued, "I want all of you to check it out with your folks first."

"You mean before we get to climb it even once?" Pete asked, looking longingly at the tree behind her.

"That's what I mean," confirmed Lisa.

"But, lady, we climb trees all the time. They know we do."

"Well, I want them to know you're going to be climbing this particular tree. Mrs. Van Egan told me you were good kids, so I'm going to trust you to ask them. In fact, if you go right now," she added on an impulse intended to soften the blow of not being able to scale the tree that instant, "it will give me time to scout around the basement for some rope and a few boards. I was thinking that old tree could use a lookout platform."

"A lookout platform," Danny echoed in awe. "I'm going to ask my mother right now. C'mon, Josh, I'll race you."

Blond Josh was hard on Danny's heels leaving the yard, with Pete bellowing "Wait for me!" as he brought up the rear. Grinning at the sight of them, Lisa headed for the basement. She had no idea if she'd find either rope or wood down there, or, if she did, how to turn them into a lookout platform. But she was confident she could rig up something that would please the boys and at the same time keep herself busy for the next hour or so.

When the boys returned, she had them come downstairs to help her carry up the heavy plywood and coils of rope she'd found. Through trial and error they finally succeeded in wedging the board horizontally between two limbs and used the rope to fashion a pulley system complete with a pail tied to one end for hauling things up.

The boys were thrilled. The term *platform* was quickly cast aside. This was nothing so lowly; it was a fort, a club-house, a military base, and Lisa was a genius. Too nice to be a grown-up, as Josh put it. When the last knot had been tied, the four of them gathered around the old tree to survey their accomplishment.

"Awesome," pronounced Josh.

"Wicked awesome," added Pete.

"Rad."

"Wicked rad."

Danny nodded in full agreement. "Awesome rad."

"Rad?" queried Lisa.

"Radical," Josh explained. "The best."

Lisa mimicked Danny's solemn nod. "You're right. It is awesome rad."

"Who's going to be the first to try it out?" Josh asked after a proper period of silent admiration.

"Me!" the other two yelled simultaneously.

"Hey, why not me?" demanded Josh.

Then they all looked at Lisa.

"Lisa ought to go first," Josh announced generously. "It was her idea." The other two boys nodded.

"No, really, I—" Lisa stopped short in the middle of saying she really didn't want to go first, last or in between when she saw disappointment flicker on all three small faces. So she's just a stodgy old grown-up after all, they seemed to be thinking, reminding Lisa of all the times as a child she'd begged her mother to share in her fun, and all the times she'd been brushed aside.

"I think," she went on, "that I should go last. That way I can watch and see how you guys get up there. Remember, you've had a lot more practice at climbing this tree than I have."

"She's right," Danny agreed. "But don't worry, Lisa, we'll show you how."

"Yeah."

"It's easy."

"A cinch."

After a short discussion they decided a coin toss was the fairest way to determine the climbing order, and in no time Josh, Danny and then Pete had clamored up to the make-shift platform. Kneeling in a row, they hung over the edge, offering words of encouragement and boasts about who would save her if necessary, as Lisa struggled to join them.

About halfway up she broke a nail, and a few seconds later she caught her hair in a branch, but eventually she made it. She gave the boys plenty of time to show her around their fifteen square feet of paradise, admiring the details of the view they pointed out and agreeing there was potential for a second tier at some future date. She was just about to brave the climb down when she heard Sam's familiar deep-pitched voice calling her name.

"Oh, my God!" exclaimed Lisa, clamping her hands to her face in horror. "It can't be eleven o'clock already."

Danny proudly peeled back his jacket sleeve to reveal a shiny new Transformer watch. "Ten forty-one," he informed her.

Lisa glanced down at the grass stains on the knees of her jeans and the bits of leaves and bark stuck to her sweater, and she could have cried. Talk about putting her best foot forward.

"Lisa?" Sam called again.

She could tell from the volume of his voice that he had checked the house and was now headed this way to look for her.

"Ten forty-two," intoned Danny.

Looking around frantically, as if there could possibly be some escape route that would take her safely to the house without having to confront Sam, Lisa decided that if she could have fit in the nearby squirrel hole, she gladly would have climbed in.

"Lisa?" Sam shouted. "Are you out here?"

Except for Danny, who was keeping an eye on his watch, the boys had been regarding her in puzzled silence. Now

Lisa felt a tug on her sleeve and looked down into Pete's earnest brown eyes.

"Lisa, I think somebody's looking for you," he said.

"I know, honey," she told him. Sighing, she called out, "I'm over here, Sam."

Sam had drawn close enough so that she could see him through the leafy branches as he slowly turned in a circle, surveying the deserted backyard. Lisa wasn't surprised to note that he hadn't gone all out in dressing for their celebration. But then, why should he? she mused with grudging admiration. He looked as impressive and commanding in a plain white shirt, gray slacks and leather boots as most men did in a three-piece suit.

"Lisa?" he said again, his tone clearly puzzled.

"Over here," she repeated. Then, feeling her dignity crumble, she added, "*Up* here."

Following the direction of her voice, Sam moved a few steps closer, peering up at the tree quizzically. A massive, low-hanging branch hid the platform from view until he was almost directly underneath. When he finally caught sight of the makeshift tree house, his bewildered expression gave way to a wide grin that crinkled the corners of his eyes. He stared up at Lisa, who was flanked by her tiny cohorts.

After a few seconds his gaze left her face to wander over her woodsy-look sweater and rumpled jeans, all the way down to her scruffy sneakers. His smile slowly faded, and for the very first time Lisa detected a spark of decidedly male interest in his appraisal. More than a spark actually, she decided, her spirits rising dramatically. His dark green eyes were definitely smoldering. It didn't even dim her delight that he quickly masked the response before she had a chance to ponder why he would find her more appealing disheveled than he ever had when she had painstakingly dressed to impress.

"Damn," he drawled finally, once more presenting her with that amused grin, which, until a few seconds ago, Lisa had always found so maddening. "If I didn't see this with my own eyes . . ." He let the comment trail off, his meaning quite clear. "Are we having fun?"

He glanced at the boys as if to include them in the question, and predictably they were quick to respond.

"Sure."

"I'll say."

"Wicked fun."

Knowing how the description could escalate, Lisa hurriedly spoke up. "The boys were climbing the tree, and I thought it would be better—easier for them—this way."

Sam nodded, his grin intensifying. "Uh-huh."

"And safer, too," Lisa went on, endeavoring to cast a practical light on her involvement. "I thought it would be less dangerous if, once they were up here, they had a place to stand."

"A fort," Sam added, making it clear that he had once been an eight-year-old boy.

"I guess you could call it that," Lisa returned.

"Uh-huh. And then what would I call you?" Sam inquired, the innocence in his tone not at all in accordance with the teasing glint in his eyes. "Are you the captive princess? Or their leader?"

The peals of laughter all around her told Lisa that both suggestions pleased the boys just fine. She shot Sam a look intended to quell his grin of utter enjoyment, but it had exactly the opposite effect.

"Neither," she insisted. "I was simply helping. After all, what's the sense in you doing all those repairs to the house to avoid a lawsuit, only to have one of the boys fall out of the tree and break his arm?"

"You could have just ordered them not to climb the tree," Sam pointed out.

That was exactly what Lisa knew she should have done, but the anxious sounds of disappointment his remark drew from the boys made her glad she hadn't.

"Well, I didn't," she declared.

"No, you sure didn't," agreed Sam, but it was satisfaction, not condemnation that permeated his soft tone. "Are you finished up there now? Or did you want to change our lunch date to dinner? Or maybe a midnight snack?"

Date. He'd said it, and suddenly Lisa found it easy to return his smile. "No, I'm quite finished."

Her smile dwindled as she stepped to the edge of the platform and paused, trying to figure out how to reverse her upward climb.

"Need a hand?"

The laughter in Sam's question brought a quick refusal to Lisa's lips. Luckily, she had the sense to keep from blurting it. Far more embarrassing than admitting she needed help would be having to lumber her way down while Sam stood by, watching every clumsy move, his mouth curved in that mocking twist.

"How gracious of you to offer," she purred.

Sam laughed. "My pleasure. No, don't try to climb down," he ordered as she turned and prepared to start down. "Just sit on the edge and slide off. I'll catch you."

"You mean jump?" Lisa exclaimed, shaking her head fervently. "No way. I'm too heavy for you to catch. You're not even that much bigger than I am."

There was definitely male pride at work behind the sardonic look Sam gave her. "I'm big enough to catch you, pal. Now, sit."

Resisting the urge to tell him she didn't respond well to canine commands, Lisa sat with her legs hanging over the side of the platform.

"Now slide out to the very edge," directed Sam.

She wiggled forward as far as she dared.

"Now just slide down into my arms."

"But..."

"Slide," he growled.

In the split second before she closed her eyes and pushed off, Lisa saw the muscles in Sam's shoulders and thighs tense as he planted his feet firmly on the grass and lifted his arms to her. She fully expected him to topple beneath her falling weight, leaving her in the same humiliating position as when the bed had collapsed beneath the two of them. Instead, landing against his chest felt as Lisa imagined hitting a granite wall might. His hands caught her beneath her arms, steadying her for an instant before allowing her to slowly slide the length of his body.

Lisa's eyes widened as her breasts glided across the hard, muscled terrain of his chest. The sensations jolting through her were so vivid the barriers of her sweater and his shirt might not have existed. She was slightly breathless by the time her feet gently touched ground.

Even then Sam didn't release her. Moving one hand so it was pressed flat on her back, anchoring her to his chest, he taunted, "Now who's big enough, hmm?"

All she could manage was a soft laugh, but it was obviously enough of a concession to satisfy Sam's masculine pride. Dropping his hands to his sides without moving away from her, he asked, "Are you ready to go?"

With her mind still reeling from the warmth and the soap-scented closeness of him, Lisa started to nod absently, then broke off abruptly as his question registered. "No, I'm not ready," she told him. "Just look at me."

"I have. You look fine."

The husky way he drawled the word *fine* rendered it a synonym for *beautiful*, and Lisa was startled at how beautiful she felt at that moment. How that was possible when she was grass-stained and dirty, she was too misty-minded to fathom. She very nearly let him sweep her away to Boston, twigs and all, when common sense intervened.

"I can't go like this," she insisted. "I'm going to the card company."

"You said yourself you'll probably only talk to the receptionist."

"Probably," Lisa stressed. "But you never know. Besides, I don't even want the receptionist to see me with leaves stuck in my hair."

Chuckling softly, Sam plucked a leaf from her hair as tenderly as if it—or she—were made of spun glass. "I suppose you're right. But make it fast, okay?"

"Okay," she promised softly.

After a quick goodbye to the boys, who were already engrossed in their play, she hurried inside to clean up. As she washed her face and applied her makeup, Lisa wondered if she had imagined the warm caress in Sam's voice that seemed to say he wanted her to hurry so he could be with her and not simply because he was eager to be on their way. Imagined or not, it spurred her to record speed as she stepped into a pair of pleated black slacks that she predicted would survive a motorcycle ride with a minimum of wrinkles. She topped the slacks with a rose-colored sweater that went well with her taupe leather flats, the only low-heeled shoes, besides sneakers, she'd brought. Adding a braided gold chain and matching earrings as she scurried down the stairs and detouring to pick up her portfolio from her den, she still made it to the front sidewalk, where Sam was waiting, in less than ten minutes.

"Was that quick enough?" she teased.

"No," he murmured. "But it was well worth the wait."

Lisa wanted to bask in the warm look he ran over her, but it was quickly replaced by an expression of no-nonsense determination as he lifted a black-and-silver helmet from the back of the motorcycle. He held it out to her and extended his other hand for the portfolio.

"Trade," he ordered. "I'll strap that and your purse onto the back while you put this on. No, don't argue," he admonished as she attempted to protest. "If you want to ride with me, you wear a helmet." He stared at her implacably, the helmet swinging by its strap from one finger.

With her lip curled in distaste, Lisa shoved the heavy portfolio and her handbag at him and grabbed the helmet. "Oh, give me the damn thing if that's the way you want it."

"That's the way I want it," he affirmed.

He neatly wrapped her possessions in a greenish-gray tarp, then strapped the bundle into place beneath the seat.

"Perfect," he said, giving it a final pat. He ambled back over to Lisa, who was now wearing the unflattering helmet and what she hoped was a very unfriendly expression, and gave her chin an identical pat, murmuring another "Perfect."

Lisa would have whacked him if he hadn't quickly moved out of range, easily swinging one leg over the bike, then glancing over his shoulder at her expectantly. "I didn't think to ask," he said, "but you have ridden a bike before, haven't you?"

"Of course." Not, she added silently. Better to let him think her reluctance was motivated by good taste and not fear.

"Then what are you waiting for?" he queried. "Climb on."

"I am, I am." She sidled a little closer. "You know, I can't believe I didn't hear you pull up on this thing."

"I coasted from the corner," he explained. "The gas gauge is broken, so I never know exactly how much is in the tank. Since we'll be covering a lot of miles today, I figured I'd conserve to be on the safe side."

Lisa was about to ask if it wouldn't be simpler, not to mention safer, to stop at a gas station and fill up, when she remembered his precarious finances and paused to rephrase the suggestion more tactfully.

"Sam, if you think we need gas, I have a credit card for the station on the other side of the park."

"No, we'll be fine," he returned, looking neither pleased nor insulted by her offer to pay. "Besides, that's not on our way to the highway. That is, if we ever get on our way."

"All right, I'm getting on now," Lisa assured him, lifting one hand to brace herself, only to have it hang in midair as she looked for a place to plant it.

"Try using my shoulder, Lisa," Sam directed placidly.

She did, thankful for the solid feel of him as she swung her leg over the motorcycle seat, which turned out to be even wider and higher off the ground than it had appeared. She was equally thankful for the thick padding on the seat, remembering that it was a good sixty miles to Boston.

"All set?" he asked over his shoulder.

"Whenever you are."

"Better hold on tight," he urged. Then he lifted himself off the seat to come down hard on the starter, and the motorcycle roared to life.

Lisa had been so conscious of wanting to touch Sam, to feel her arms around him, that she had self-consciously kept her grasp loose. As soon as they started to move, however, she found she had no choice but to wrap her arms tightly around his waist. After the first few minutes of panic before she got used to the way the bike leaned as they took corners, Lisa started to relax, and by the time they reached the highway she was filled with excitement. She felt as if she were flying and more gloriously free than she had ever been before. The probability of arriving in Boston wrinkled and tousled was forgotten as she tipped her face into the wind, closed her eyes and let Sam fly away with her.

After a while she brought her mouth closer to his ear and shouted so he could hear her. "Thank you."

He turned his head just enough for her to catch a glimpse of his mouth, and she saw more than heard him shout, "For what?"

"For not letting me take the bus," she shouted in reply.

This time his only response was a nod and a smile, but the smile told Lisa he understood what she meant.

Riding behind a man on his bike was, Lisa discovered, a strangely intimate experience. In the absence of conversation she felt closer to Sam than ever. Close enough and comfortable enough with him to let her head rest on his back whenever the bite of the wind became too fierce. She loved the feel of her arms around him, the pressure of his lean hips on the insides of her thighs, and the soft brush of his long hair against her cheek. The only bittersweet moment of the whole ride occurred when she was struck by the thought that if today didn't work out as she hoped, this might be the only chance she'd ever have to hold Sam this way.

Since both their destinations were in the same general area, they left the motorcycle in a high-rise garage and walked. Lisa agreed with Sam's assessment that their first stop should be PaperThoughts. They arrived around lunchtime, and as she had predicted, the receptionist was the only one there to accept the portfolio. The woman promised it would be delivered to the proper office that afternoon.

"It's amazing," Lisa declared, stepping back outside onto the crowded sidewalk with Sam. "I thought I felt relieved when I finished working on the proposal Friday, but that was nothing compared to this. I feel..." She searched for the right word.

"Like celebrating?" suggested Sam as he gracefully steered her around a street vendor hawking T-shirts. The hustle and bustle of a big city at midday was familiar to Lisa, and it fed her exhilarated mood.

"No. More like...dancing on rooftops," she countered with a laugh.

"Fine. It so happens that my lawyer's office is on the top floor. While I dash in and sign a few papers, you can go on up and pirouette on the roof."

"Thanks, but I'm sure I'll be able to contain myself." As they were swept along by the crowd, she glanced through the parade of passersby at the windows of the shops along Commonwealth Avenue. "Maybe I'll satisfy my urge to do something outrageous by buying something in one of these stores. They all look suitably outrageous. That will also give you time to see your lawyer without me tagging along."

Sam turned to look at her, and she briefly felt the pressure of his hand on the small of her back. The touch struck Lisa as almost possessive, and it started the familiar coil of hope and confusion twisting inside her once again.

"But I want you to tag along," he insisted. His eyes lit with a mischievous glint. "And I know my lawyer will be very interested in meeting you."

Despite Lisa's pleas for an explanation of that mysterious remark, Sam was stubbornly unresponsive for the block and a half that remained until he drew her to a halt in front of a tall brownstone and held the door open for her. The elevator inside was the old-fashioned kind that required an operator, and Lisa was forced to politely match Sam's silence as they rode to the eighth floor. The elevator doors opened directly into the reception area of the law office, suggesting to Lisa that the firm was successful enough to occupy an entire floor in one of Boston's high-rent business districts. And there on a quietly tasteful sign was the answer to her question. COSTIGAN, RAVENAL AND TREMAIN, ATTORNEYS-AT-LAW it read.

Lisa felt panic bubble up. She was hardly properly dressed, much less emotionally prepared, to meet Sam's father. And the man was bound to be curious about her role in his son's life. Which might be a blessing in disguise. After all, wasn't she curious about the same thing herself? If only she'd worn the ivory silk blouse and linen suit as she had first intended. Damn his old motorcycle, no matter how much she'd enjoyed the ride.

Self-consciously Lisa smoothed her slacks as she gazed around the outer office. Everything about the place was as tasteful as the nameplate. From the hunter-green carpeting to the mahogany paneling and impressive brass accents, it was the epitome of expensive understatement. Just the right setting to inspire confidence in a client. Unfortunately, it was having quite the opposite effect on Lisa.

Before she had a chance to voice her concerns about meeting his father, Sam was busy greeting the pretty brunette seated at the receptionist's desk. The woman obviously recognized Sam immediately, and, smiling, she motioned for him to proceed down the short hallway behind her. He pulled Lisa along with him.

"Sam, slow down," she urged in a hushed whisper. "I ought to comb my hair or something."

"Your hair is fine."

"Fine for a rat's nest," she hissed, doing her best to tame it with the hand he wasn't yanking on. "Why didn't you warn me?"

At last he paused, but his fingers were already gripping the brass knob of the solid mahogany door at the very end of the hall. "Warn you about what?"

"That your lawyer also happens to be your father," she returned with exasperation.

"Maybe because my father's not my lawyer," Sam responded casually as he swung the door open to reveal an office that looked as wide and intimidating as a lion's den. "My mother is."

Chapter Seven

Why was it, Lisa anguished silently, as the woman behind the massive desk stood and glided toward them, that meeting a man's mother was always so much more traumatic than meeting his father?

However, this was hardly the time to stand there pondering the problem. Sam stepped forward to gather his mother in a quick bear hug. While they exchanged greetings, Lisa quickly took stock of Mrs. Ravenal. She was nearly as tall as her son, Lisa noted, and slender, with silver-blond hair neatly coiled in a soft twist at the back of her head. And she was dressed in a dark pleated skirt and pale gray silk blouse that made Lisa feel even more out of place in her casual slacks and sweater.

"Mom," Sam said as he released her from the hug and turned to face Lisa, "this is Lisa Bennett, a good friend of mine."

"Ah," Mrs. Ravenal murmured, smiling and reaching out to clasp Lisa's hand with both of hers. There was a wealth of curiosity underlying her soft "Ah," but Lisa suspected that, in spite of her lawyer's instincts, she would never come right out and voice it the way a father might.

"Hello, Lisa," she said instead. "I'm happy to meet you. It's so seldom the family gets to see Sam these days, much less meet any of his friends."

"I'm happy to meet you, too, Mrs. Ravenal. Although if Sam had told me who his lawyer was," she continued with a glance at Sam, "and that I would be coming with him to your office, I would have dressed up a little more."

"You look fine to me," Mrs. Ravenal assured her. "And my son looks neater than I've seen him in years. What on earth do you suppose that means?"

The sparkle in Mrs. Ravenal's blue eyes told Lisa exactly what the older woman thought it meant, and she responded with a noncommittal shrug. For his part Sam stood by with his hands in his pockets, looking supremely unaffected by all that was being said about him.

"Besides," his mother continued, "a thirty-year-old man has a right to feel a little awkward telling a woman he's bringing her to meet his mother." Turning and stepping back toward her desk, she added, "Although why that same supposedly sensitive man doesn't feel the least bit awkward about dumping legal problems on his poor overworked mother at the last minute is beyond me."

"I want to keep you sharp," Sam retorted in a teasing way that told Lisa much about the good-natured affection that marked his relationship with his mother.

Mrs. Ravenal arrowed him a sardonic look. "Such a thoughtful son. Whatever would I do without you?"

"Have more time for paying clients?" he suggested.

Laughing, his mother reached across the desk for a manila folder and flipped it open so that Sam could see the contents. She placed a pen beside it. "Paying clients? I'll have to give that a try someday. In the meantime, here are those sales contracts, Sam, all ready for your signature."

"Real estate transfers," he explained with a quick glance over his shoulder at Lisa, causing her a bit of surprise. Somehow the notion of anything as financially solid as buying and selling real estate didn't mesh with her image of Sam. Picking up the pen, he leaned over the desk and quickly scrawled his name on the papers without bothering to read them.

Watching him, Lisa marveled at the display of such utter trust. But then, she supposed mothers should be utterly trustworthy. As should husbands. It had simply been her misfortune to be cursed with the exception in both cases. She gazed at Mrs. Ravenal, who had leaned closer to Sam to draw his attention to something in the papers spread before them. What would it be like to have a woman like her for a mother? A woman who was affectionate and caring and fun. And successful. It suddenly occurred to Lisa that Sam had been telling the absolute truth when he insisted he wanted a woman with an independent spirit. Growing up with this sort of role model, how else could he feel?

Lisa's train of thought was interrupted when Mrs. Ravenal straightened and flipped the folder shut.

"As soon as the checks arrive, I'll forward them to you," she told Sam.

He replied with careless shrug. "There's no hurry."

"Says who?" his mother joked with a glance at her watch. "I have to be in court in an hour. I do, however, have enough time to take Lisa and you to lunch if you're willing to settle for the little joint on the corner. The food is unremarkable," she apologetically explained to Lisa, "but the waitresses are quick."

"Another time, Mom," Sam said before Lisa could respond. "Lisa and I have already made plans for lunch."

"All right, then, some other time when you don't have plans. That way Lisa and I will be able to have a nice long chat." She smiled at Lisa. "And I hope it's soon."

"I do, too, Mrs. Ravenal," Lisa replied.

With a wink at his mother that struck Lisa as conspiratorial, Sam opened the door for them to leave. Lisa walked decorously by his side back down the hallway, past the smiling receptionist and silent elevator operator, waiting until they were safely out of the building before whacking his arm with her fist.

"I can't believe you let me walk in there that way!" she declared.

"Ouch! What way?"

"Unprepared. I had no idea when you said you had to see your lawyer that it was your mother, and you knew it."

"Of course I knew it," he agreed without apology. "If you had known beforehand that she was my mother, would you have come along?"

"Probably not."

"See?"

"No. Why was it so important to you that I come along to meet your mother?" Lisa held her breath in anxious anticipation.

"Because I thought meeting her might prove I'm not the total Neanderthal you seem to think I am."

"Why should it? Even total Neanderthals sometimes have perfectly nice mothers. Everyone knows that Neanderthal tendencies are a male sex-linked genetic defect."

She'd thought it obvious that she was joking, but a look of stony frustration settled on Sam's face as he stalked along by her side. This conversation wasn't going as she'd hoped.

"Sam," she began, tugging lightly on his sleeve, "I don't really think you're a Neanderthal."

"Maybe not, but you call me unbearably macho when I say that Alexander Brandon had a right to carry Elizabeth off the way he did ... and that just maybe she wanted him to do exactly that but was afraid to admit it."

"Well, yes ... and no," Lisa hurriedly added when he reacted with a sound of irritation. "Let's forget about Alexander and Elizabeth, shall we? For better or worse, they settled their differences a long time ago. I understand why you wanted me to meet your mother, and if it makes you feel any better, you were right.''

"I was, huh? Suppose you tell me what you think I was so right about?''

"The other day when you told me about your broken engagement and insisted that any woman you got involved with would have to be strong and independent, I had my doubts that you really believed what you were saying. Not that I thought you were lying," she quickly explained. "I just thought that you didn't know what you were asking for in a woman who truly had a mind and a will and a life of her own. But after meeting your mother, seeing how successful she is and how you feel about her, I can see that you did.''

"I guess what I really found hard to believe—when I first became interested enough in the opposite sex to notice it—was that a woman could be any other way *but* strong and independent.''

Sam's pace slowed as understanding replaced his brief burst of frustration with her, and Lisa no longer had to strain to keep up. It was past two o'clock, and the general activity on the sidewalk was a little less frenetic than it had been an hour ago. The medley of the city sounds formed a kind of barrier, isolating the two of them from the rest of the world as they talked and walked, their shoulders bumping, their hands brushing. Each touch was fleeting, but even that was enough to send sparks sizzling through Lisa in a burning burst of sensation.

Struggling to keep her tone or manner from revealing that she was melting inside, she asked, "Did your mother work as a lawyer even when you and your brothers and sisters were younger?''

Sam nodded. "Always. She never had any intention of doing anything other than practice law. She'd been weaned on it—the Costigan part of the firm was my grandfather— and she merely incorporated marriage and a family into her plans as they came along. She worked at being a mother just as seriously as she did her law practice.

"I'm not going to try to tell you she was Betty Crocker," he admitted with a wry smile, "but none of us ever felt shortchanged. Of course, when I was a kid I never fully appreciated what a phenomenal thing she was doing—handling a high-pressure career and meanwhile managing to raise well-adjusted children and sustain a happy marriage."

"That is quite a feat," agreed Lisa, wistfulness and bitterness mixed in her tone. "I mean, look at what a mess I've managed to make out of two of those three."

The sudden weight of Sam's arm across her shoulders felt right, as if it was a fundamental extension of herself that had been missing all these years. Yet at the same time, his action was so thrillingly unexpected it took her breath away.

"Don't be so hard on yourself," he urged. "Neither the failure of your marriage nor the sabotaging of your career was your fault."

Sam's arm was holding her so close that his hip rubbed against hers as they walked. It suddenly felt to Lisa as if there were air instead of concrete beneath her feet. Tingles shimmered up her spine, ending in tiny explosions of excitement that cascaded all the way to her toes.

"And at the risk of being branded an insensitive male all over again," he continued, "I have to say that I think being married to the right man made it possible for my mother to achieve what she did. Now, don't get prickly until you hear me out," he ordered.

Lisa could have laughed out loud. She was beyond getting prickly or resentful or indignant. She was far too mesmerized by the sheer closeness of his warm, rangy body to concentrate on anything but him. She wanted to keep walking forever, all the way to the end of the earth, staying safely tucked beneath Sam's strong arm, listening to the gritty music of his voice.

"Not that I don't think my mother couldn't have been a damn successful lawyer on her own," he continued, "maybe even more successful than she is, if that had been her only goal. But it's the balance she achieved that's so remarkable. Marriage and children add another dimension to pursuing a career. It's one hell of a giant step beyond living solo. And if you try to take that step with someone who's headed in the opposite direction, you're not going anywhere.''

"I agree," Lisa assured him. "Your father must be a special person, too.''

"He is. He's the head of the history department at a small college and pretty successful in his own right.'' A smile lifted the corners of Sam's wide mouth. "But he's also something of a character. He doesn't dress for success, doesn't play the role of corporate husband very well, doesn't make nearly as much as my mother does and doesn't give half a damn.''

Lisa shook her head with a small laugh. "It doesn't sound like a perfect match.''

"But it sure as hell worked," Sam pointed out happily. "It used to drive my grandfather crazy that a daughter of his could be happy with a man who'd rather read Thoreau than *The Wall Street Journal*. But none of that ever mattered to the two of them. They always agreed on the important stuff and never competed on the rest.''

They had come to a busy intersection, where the traffic light was blinking DON'T WALK. Without removing the arm that rested across her shoulders, Sam angled his body so he was facing her. His eyes were dark green and very serious as they probed hers.

"Love shouldn't be a battle of wits," he said so softly and solemnly that Lisa had no idea how to respond.

The light changed to WALK, and when Sam and she didn't move quickly enough, the crowd behind them parted and surged around them, leaving the two of them standing there, their gazes locked, suspended in a moment that seemed to hum with something important Lisa didn't fully understand.

What was he trying to say? Why on earth was he speaking about love to her when he still persisted in that irksome habit of addressing her as *pal*, and when up until now he'd never so much as touched her in a way that could be considered anything but platonic? Even now she had to wonder if he hadn't put his arm around her more out of pity than any desire to hold her. She wished he would say something else, give her some clue as to what was going on inside his head, before she said something about her own feelings that she might regret.

But before he spoke, he cleared his throat, and a less volatile look shattered the vulnerability she had seen clouding his eyes. And then all he said was, "How hungry are you, anyway?"

Starving, something deep inside her cried. But realizing that he was probably referring to food rather than her growing hunger for him, she responded with a careless shrug. "Hungry enough for lunch, I guess."

The truth was that, even though she hadn't eaten all day, she wasn't remotely hungry, and when Sam asked if she was too hungry to make one more stop before they had lunch, she assured him she wasn't.

When he led her to the ivy-draped brick building that housed The New England Historical Society, Lisa assumed their visit was related to whatever his consulting project was. Not until they were settled in one of the small private alcoves and he opened the heavy, unwieldy book he'd obviously reserved ahead of time did she realize it had something to do with her.

"I know you're probably close to overdosing on Bennett history," Sam began almost apologetically. "But you do seem fascinated by the legend of Alex and Elizabeth, and when I got talking to the librarian at the college and she mentioned that they had records here of trials dating back that far, I thought you might like to take a look."

"Oh, I would!" exclaimed Lisa. "Do you mean this is actually the transcript from Alexander Brandon's piracy trial?"

"Not exactly the transcript," Sam explained, carefully turning the yellowed pages. "The woman I spoke with when

I phoned to check it out told me that it's more of a written record of what occurred rather than a word-for-word transcript as we know it today. But she did mention that for some of the trials, including this particular one, they have on file . . . yes, here it is.''

He stopped turning pages and shifted the book to make it easier for Lisa to see. On the page before them was a copy of a handwritten letter, the script far too ornate to be recent.

"Is it from Elizabeth?" Lisa asked eagerly as she ran her gaze down to check the letter's signature.

"No, it was written by Alex," Sam said just as she came to the strong scrawl of his name beneath the words, *Your friend.* "He wrote it to a man by the name of Patrick Halloran, a supposed friend of his. Instead of doing as the letter requests, however, and delivering a message from Alex to Elizabeth, Halloran sold the letter to the prosecuting attorney, which is how it ended up here, kept on file as evidence. Rather, the original is. These copies are all that are available without special permission."

Lisa was more interested in the contents of the letter and how it fit into the puzzle of Alexander and Elizabeth. "What message was this friend supposed to deliver?" she asked.

Sam nodded toward the book. "Read it for yourself. I already know basically what it says from my phone conversation."

It took Lisa longer to read than a typed letter would have, but as her eyes grew accustomed to the archaic penmanship and use of language, she discovered that Alexander had written from prison to ask his friend to assure the men of his crew that their captain had every confidence he would be joining them before long. He had then requested that Halloran personally visit Miss Elizabeth Bennett and carry to her the message of his devotion and impress upon her the fact that Alexander's greatest treasure and the best hope for their future together rested within the *Black Star.*

"Why would he want to tell her a thing like that?" she wondered aloud, frowning as she lifted her gaze from the letter to meet Sam's. "After all, the *Black Star* was resting at the bottom of the sea by the time this was written."

"I'm not really sure what he meant. For one thing it bothers me that he referred to the treasure as being *within* the *Black Star*. I'm certain that even back then a seaman would have said *aboard*. But if you overlook that piece of the puzzle, I suppose you could conclude that he was trying to get across the message that he intended to recover the sunken treasure, trying to convince Elizabeth that it would be worth her while to stick by him."

Sam cast a disapproving glance at the book as he continued. "Certainly that's the way it was made to appear at his trial. They used this letter as evidence that Alex had illegally plundered foreign ships for the sole reason of personal gain. And then sentenced him to die for it."

"Thank goodness he managed to thwart them in the end," Lisa murmured, running her fingers across the copy of the letter as if to get a better feel for the man who had penned the original from his prison cell all those years ago.

"Even though in doing so he gained the freedom to compromise one of your ancestors?"

She glanced up to confront a mocking challenge in Sam's eyes. Her fingers itched to abandon the letters on that lifeless piece of paper to trace instead the lines that fanned at the corners of his beautiful eyes.

"Even so," she murmured.

By the time they finished poring over the record of the trial and every other pertinent document on file, it was after five o'clock, and Lisa's neck was stiffer than if she'd spent the day bent over her sketchbook. As much as she'd enjoyed the afternoon, it was a relief to step outdoors and draw a deep breath of fresh air. It was an even bigger relief to learn that the restaurant they were going to was located overlooking the Charles River only a few blocks away. Lisa suddenly realized she was starving.

"It looks like I wasn't all that far off this morning when I suggested this might turn out to be a celebration dinner," Sam remarked on the way.

"Lunch, dinner." Lisa shrugged. "As long as it's edible I'll be happy."

"I'm sorry. I should have fed you much earlier. Just because I get so lost in that stuff that I forget everything else doesn't mean you should have to."

"You didn't hear me complaining," she reminded him.

The expression in Sam's eyes softened as they moved over her face. "That's right, you didn't complain, did you?"

"No. But I will," she warned, "if this restaurant has a dress code and we don't get in."

Sam chuckled. "Trust me, this restaurant does not have a dress code. As a matter of fact, it doesn't even have menus."

He wasn't kidding, Lisa soon discovered. The Fish Bucket was unadulteratedly informal, a wood plank floor, red-checked tablecloth kind of place, with the daily offerings scribbled on a blackboard just inside the entry. It hardly mattered, Sam told her as he hurried her past the blackboard without bothering to read it. Almost everyone who came to the Fish Bucket came to eat lobster. He clearly assumed that she would be happy doing likewise but had the decency to look a little stricken when it finally occurred to him to ask if she liked it. As much as he deserved to be teased for all the times he'd teased her, Lisa didn't have the heart to do anything but quickly assure him that she loved lobster.

What she didn't particularly relish was the prospect of having to pluck her dinner out of the Plexiglas tank at one end of the informal restaurant. As ugly as the grayish-green crustaceans were in their uncooked state, Lisa didn't like to think she held their fate in her hands.

"You're not really controlling their fate," Sam reasoned, amused by her reluctance as he selected a huge lobster. "You're simply taking advantage of it. One way or the other, all these fellas are going to make that final trip to the kitchen before long."

Although not completely persuaded, Lisa finally forced herself to choose a lobster, softheartedly avoiding what she considered to be the babies in favor of a medium-sized specimen. She then tried not to think about what was happening in the kitchen while she and Sam returned to their corner table by the window to sample the crackers and house cheese dip until their dinners arrived.

Somehow the lobster she had chosen looked a lot bigger on her plate than it had in the tank, and a lot more complicated than the lobster thermidor, she often ordered out. Lisa was still eyeing it judiciously, pondering the neatest way to go about removing the meat from the bright red shell, when Sam reached across the table with a chunk of butter-drenched lobster already speared on the tip of his fork.

"Here you go," he said. "Open up."

After only a slight hesitation Lisa obligingly opened her mouth and accepted the offering. It was warm, slightly salty and slightly sweet—delicious—but so was the look in Sam's eyes. She was so spellbound by it that she could do little more than murmur appreciatively.

"Worth the wait?" he inquired, his tone low and grainy, barely audible in the noisy restaurant. He must be referring to the lobster, she told herself, yet the roguish green eyes lighting a fire inside her seemed to say, that was not at all what he was talking about.

"Yes." She cleared her throat but still ended up sounding throaty. "Yes. It was worth the wait."

"And all the trouble?"

"Yes."

"Good."

His gaze held hers for another scorching moment, then slowly lowered to her plate. A smile stretched his mouth. "Would you like me to crack that open for you?"

"No, I can manage—" Lisa broke off and shrugged sheepishly as his smile deepened into a grin. "Yes, I guess I could use some help."

The table was narrow enough that Sam could easily reach her plate, and after only a few deft maneuvers with the nutcracker, he had rendered the lobster meat easily accessible.

"Thanks," Lisa said as he turned his attention back to his own plate.

"Anytime."

Anytime. Lisa caught herself short in the rush of sweetness that word sent coursing through her. What was wrong with her? She was reading implications into everything he said, analyzing each inflection, hearing primal undercurrents in his every tone. She had to be crazy. But if she was, she had the distinct impression she wasn't alone.

Surely it wasn't only her imagination or her longing to have something happen that made Sam seem different today. He *was* different. Not in any earth-shattering way—he was always charming in his own offbeat style. The difference was subtle and hard to pinpoint, but it was real. Lisa could feel it even if she couldn't define it, and anticipation began to throb within her.

The Fish Bucket's single stab at elegance was the lighted candle propped in an empty wine bottle on each table. The shadows it sent playing over Sam's face softened its sharp angles but did nothing to soften its impact on Lisa. In the flickering glow his eyes glittered more darkly than ever, and the rough smudge of incipient whiskers along his jaw gave him a reckless air she found far more enticing than the food in front of her.

It was difficult to eat and stare at him at the same time, and after the first few bites had satisfied her hunger, she had to fight to keep from dropping her fork in favor of watching Sam. His lean, strong hands fascinated her, as did the faint dusting of black hair visible at the open neck of his shirt. She visualized the way that hair would fan across his chest and then narrow to a pencil-thin line as it dove beneath his belt buckle. But it didn't even require anything that masculinely alluring to fascinate her where Sam was concerned. She was beguiled simply by the way he chewed and wiped his mouth with a paper napkin.

"Full?" he inquired, glancing up to find her watching him.

Startled, she shook her head rapidly, then looked down to the fork abandoned on the edge of her plate. Her hands were in her lap, their tense twisting hidden.

"Not yet, but I'm getting there," she told him.

Retrieving her fork, she discovered that all the easy bites of lobster had been taken and she was going to have to work for the rest. She stalled by munching on a french fry, then, following the lead of everyone around her, resorted to using her fingers to hold the tail shell open while she pried the meat loose. She chewed each small bite slowly, savoring the taste along with the realization that Sam suddenly seemed far more interested in her than in his dinner. His gaze was pure heat, and when she finally met it with her own, the air between them fairly crackled.

"I think," he observed, "that this was a mistake. I'd hoped you'd like it here, that you might be able to relax and let down your guard for a change, but I guess you would have been more comfortable at another sort of restaurant, after all. Someplace less earthy, eating a meal that's less...messy."

"No, I love this," Lisa countered fervently, still holding the cracked tail in her hand. How could she tell him that, if anything, it was her own feelings, not the setting, making her uncomfortable? "Really."

"Come off it, Lisa. You hate being mussed up...even though that's when I like you best," he added with unexpected wistfulness. "What you like is being in order and in control."

"Maybe that's true most of the time, but I'm enjoying this, too." Lisa heard the desperation in her effort to assure him, and she strained to rein it in. With a smile intended to be carefree, she held up the sticky fingers that had been gripping the lobster tail and added, "Can I help it if I haven't had much experience eating lobster in the rough?"

His answering smile was wry. "So that's it. I should have guessed. You're the only one I've ever seen go through fifty napkins on the first claw." She grimaced as he smirked at the small mountain of paper napkins beside her plate. "Everyone knows you're supposed to lick your fingers when you eat lobster at the Fish Bucket."

"I never lick my fingers in public," she retorted.

Her haughty look faded fast as, without warning, Sam's hand shot across the table to lock around her slender wrist so securely that she couldn't have pulled away from him even if she'd wanted to.

"You don't, huh?" he drawled. "Then I guess I'll just have to do it for you."

Lisa's heart stopped. He wouldn't, she thought, even as he drew her fingers relentlessly closer to his mouth, telling her with the familiar reckless glint in his eyes that he damn well would. His lips parted, and he moved her hand so that her fingers made contact with their smooth warmth.

Then his tongue flicked across the sensitive tips of her fingers, and Lisa trembled. She forgot where they were, forgot the people talking and laughing all around them, forgot everything but the wet heat of Sam's mouth and the yearning that built inside her as slowly, one by one, he licked her fingers clean.

Even after he'd released her hand with obvious reluctance, his gaze held hers captive. Lisa struggled for words as everything inside her turned liquid with longing.

"I . . ." she faltered.

Still staring at her with a look of raw hunger, Sam shoved his plate aside and muttered, "Let's get out of here."

Chapter Eight

Lisa stood by while Sam tossed enough money onto the table for dinner and a tip, then followed him to the door of the Fish Bucket. Once outside, she expected him to say something about what was so obviously happening between them, but he didn't. With her hand held tightly in his, they walked in silence to the garage where they'd left his motorcycle.

When he helped her fasten the strap on the helmet, she expected him to kiss her at long last, but he didn't. And then they were streaking through the cool black night with nothing and everything settled between them.

Lisa rode with her arms locked around Sam's waist, her head resting on his strong back. A smile formed on her lips as she realized how strangely content she felt, considering the volatility of the situation. Inside her a sense of peace and confidence was entwined with nervous anticipation. She had seen the desire on Sam's face earlier, and the war of emotions plaguing him during their short, silent trek from the restaurant to the garage, and she knew exactly what he was going through.

Hadn't she fought her own attraction to him? Hadn't she struggled to keep their friendship from growing into something more? It had taken her time to come to terms with her feelings and accept that maybe she and Sam weren't as ill suited for each other as they'd both insisted. He would need time, as well. After all, she wasn't "his type."

Lisa's smile burgeoned into a grin against his back. That's what he had told her in no uncertain terms right from the start. But no matter what he'd said back then, there was no doubt that he now shared her intense desire. Though he would have to work it out in his own mind, Lisa knew that, for better or worse, however briefly, they were going to come together. Tonight, tomorrow, it was going to happen.

Her mellow philosophical mood lasted as long as the ride home, then shattered in an explosion of eagerness as they approached her back door. All the way up the walk and the steps, his hand rode the small of her back, the possessiveness in his light touch electrifying to her senses. Lord, how she wanted to know what he was thinking.

She wanted him to tell her—no, she wanted him to *show* her—that he found her as exciting as she did him. She wanted to feel his arms around her, and his mouth on hers, kissing her with the crushing, demanding finesse she knew intuitively was his. Shockingly, for a woman who had always found her physical impulses easy to control, Lisa realized that with Sam she wanted everything. And she didn't want to wait.

"Thank you," she said as she unlocked the door. Her voice was soft, her breathing as erratic as the pounding of her pulse.

"For what?"

The tight, harsh edge to Sam's words brought her gaze to his eyes. Even in the dim porch light she could read a glittering reflection of her own impatience, and her heart swelled. "For my celebration, of course. I—"

"Don't," Sam broke in. The roughness in the command thrilled Lisa rather than making her uneasy, because she knew the inner turmoil that was causing it. "Don't thank me yet. It's not over."

"It's not?"

He shook his head slowly. "No. And you damn well know it."

Lisa knew, and she didn't even consider pretending otherwise. The time for pretending was past, and as Sam's head lowered, she closed her eyes and tipped her face up to meet him. Maybe because she'd imagined this so often during the past few days, her arms wound around his neck as if from long habit, and finally, after all her waiting and fantasizing, he was kissing her.

So often, she knew, the anticipation of something was much better than the reality. It amazed her that, with Sam, that wasn't so. The damp warmth of his mouth and the hard, lean reality of his body were more exciting than even her wildest imaginings. He was, as she'd suspected, as she'd hoped, as she'd fantasized, an ardent, demanding lover. His tongue gently traced her lips, then parted them with a rough thrust that made her shiver.

Nothing in her limited sexual experience came close to this white-hot desire ignited by his kiss alone. With Ron, sex had always been like climbing, climbing and never quite getting there. Her only other lover had been a college professor who'd had little patience or concern for her inexperience. As Sam's tongue rocked against hers, she marveled at how swiftly and easily he had swept away her naïveté. She had been so sure she could live happily without intimacy, and now she discovered she hadn't even known what real intimacy was. Tonight she was going to learn.

She sensed that Sam wasn't going to hurry himself or rush her, and a sweet sense of languor claimed her body. She felt at once numb to all normal sensation and unbearably sensitized to the sight and smell and feel of Sam. His hand had found its way beneath her hair to caress the back of her neck and hold her still. His deep, searching kiss went on and on until she was gasping for breath. He lifted his mouth from hers to kiss her eyelids and the pulse point that thundered at the edge of her jaw.

Then, with his tongue in her ear, shooting currents of excitement straight to the pit of her stomach, he whispered, "Take me inside, Lisa."

The plea left her weak. She knew he was talking not only about the house but also about her body and her life. With trembling fingers she turned and opened the door for him. Once inside the house, they moved through the kitchen and up the narrow stairs without turning on lights that might alter the mood. Lisa held Sam's hand tightly as she led the way to her bedroom at the end of the hall.

Just inside the bedroom door, she hesitated. The pale moonlight filtering through the lace curtains made the single bed stand out boldly, and she was suddenly struck by the enormity and irreversibility of what she was about to do.

Before she had time to let second thoughts intrude, however, Sam reached out and gently spun her to face him, pulling her against him. Cradling her close to his chest, his arms encased her like the bars of a steel cage. Only these bars moved, seductively stroking her back, pressing her closer, urging her to feel his passion in the pumping of his heart and in the hardness he was rubbing slowly against her belly. Her need rose up to match his. Fledgling doubts and second thoughts were blown away in an explosion of desire as he bent his head and took her mouth again.

"I want to see you," he murmured when he finally stopped kissing her. His hands didn't still, however. They roamed over her, from her shoulders to the backs of her thighs, causing her to move sinuously against him in a way that delighted them both. "I want to see your body while I'm making love to you. May I turn on a light?"

"I'll do it," she whispered.

Reluctantly she peeled herself away from him and moved to turn on the small lamp on the dresser. Its dim bulb and yellowed shade bathed the room in a seductive glow. When she turned back, she discovered that Sam had followed her the few steps to the dresser, as if he couldn't bear even the slightest delay until he was touching her again.

She moved into his arms easily, their bodies a perfect blend in size and texture. Their chests and bellies nuzzled each other, but where he was as hard as stone she was soft and yielding. His strong fingers kneaded her shoulders, and her muscles fluttered in response. Slowly he moved his hands lower, coasting around to the front so that they grazed her breasts in passing. A soft, fractured sound of need escaped her. She wanted to grab his hands and drag them back to cover her breasts, but they were already at her waist, sliding up and under her sweater, and the touch of his warm hands on her bare flesh left her helpless.

With his trademark deceptively lazy ease, Sam pulled the rose sweater over her head and tossed it aside. His arms remained around her, but he levered back just enough to glance down at her, and the sight of her naked from the waist up except for her nearly transparent ivory lace bra seemed to please him wildly. His eyes flashed with desire, and he released a ragged groan as he quickly lowered his head to kiss her through the delicate lace.

It was as much a bite as a kiss, and Lisa couldn't help flinging her head back and tossing it from side to side as his teeth raked over the tightly pebbled crest. He nipped and then soothed the sweetly tortured flesh with his tongue, again and again, making her hotter and wetter until finally his lips closed firmly on her nipple, sucking from her a near scream of pleasure.

Murmuring rough, blunt words of encouragement, he moved his mouth to her other breast, making her pant and tremble all over again. In disbelief Lisa felt a swelling pressure building between her legs, where he hadn't even touched her yet. She unconsciously clamped her thighs together, then heard the rumble of Sam's deep, satisfied laughter and felt her cheeks burning even hotter than the rest of her.

Dear God, what must he be thinking? Ron had let her know that a man expected a woman to be responsive but demure, and she had been, right up until he'd stopped seeking any sort of response at all from her. Certainly she had never been this frantic or uncontrolled with any man in her life. Should she tell Sam that? Explain that this wasn't like her at all? But how could she, when she didn't understand it herself? And when, in spite of the voices of reason and embarrassment trying to intrude, she wanted him to go on making her feel this way.

She must have tightened up with self-recriminations, because against the curve of her breast Sam was murmuring for her to relax, and his hands stroking her back suddenly sought to soothe as much as arouse.

"Please, baby, don't pull away from me now," he implored, his breath a warm caress in itself. "This is right. It's meant to be. You'll see... you'll see. Trust me."

The calming timbre of his voice worked magic. Lisa's uneasiness disappeared. She didn't flinch as he unfastened the button of her slacks and lowered the zipper. His hand flattened against her belly, the tips of his fingers nudging beneath the elastic waistband on her bikini panties. Her stomach muscles clenched violently. That spiral of delicious pressure wound tighter, making her hips yearn toward him in slow, rhythmic thrusts.

He urged her on by cupping her buttocks with his other hand and guiding the pace of her thrusts. At the same time he brought his mouth back to hers and kissed her roughly as his fingers slid deeper inside her panties. Lisa tightened her arms around him so she wouldn't collapse. His fingers tangled in the soft gold curls between her legs and slid lower still, separating her, opening her.

Driven by sheer need, Lisa lurched against him, lowering her head to his shoulder as one soft moan after another escaped her. The lower half of her body was moving instinctively, bracketed by his knowing hands, one pushing her onward, the other seeking, learning, giving. Using the heel of his hand to impart a steady pressure, he slid one finger deep inside her, and that was all it took to push Lisa off the very top of the mountain he'd built for her.

For several seconds she felt as if she were hurtling through space on giant waves of pleasure. They gusted around and through her, leaving her shaking and breathless. When she touched down, though, reality was there waiting, and the waves of pleasure turned into an avalanche of embarrassment.

Lord, Sam had barely touched her, and she'd climaxed. And so... loudly. Even now she could hear the echo of her cries, and the memory made her face burn with humiliation. And worse, she was so...wet. She could hear that, too, as Sam's fingers continued to play lightly between her legs.

"Sam, I'm sorry," she burst out without looking at him. She could feel his surprise even before he used his free hand to tip her face up to his, and she saw it mixed with the passion in his eyes.

"Sorry? For what?"

"For being so..." She hesitated, stumped. How in the world did she say it? "For being so... quick. That's never happened before."

He searched her anguished eyes. "Do you mean that it never happened that quickly or that it never happened before, period?"

Lisa swallowed hard and still couldn't dislodge the uncomfortable lump in her throat. "Both, I guess. And I'm not usually so...noisy," she continued, in a rush to get it all out and over with. "Ron hated when I made noise."

"Wait, wait." Sam shook his head as if to clear it. "You're telling me your ex-husband hated for you to make noise when he made love to you?"

Lisa nodded, puzzled by his incredulous expression. Of course, she realized all men probably weren't as exacting in their demands as Ron had been, but she'd bet no man liked having a woman race on ahead without him the way she just had.

"Lisa, oh, Lisa." He kissed the top of her head and shifted to wrap both arms around her, pulling her close. "Your ex-husband was an ass. I *want* you to make noise when I love you. I want you to moan, scream if you want. And I want you to talk to me, tell me what feels good and what you don't like." He grinned. "Talk dirty to me if you know how. And as for being quick..." His eyes glittered. "Don't you know what a kick that is for me and my fragile male ego? I loved it, Lisa. You were like fire in my hands. And finding out that it was the first time you've ever climaxed only makes it better. I never want you to worry about anything like that when we're together, do you understand?"

He shook her lightly even as she nodded. Relief seeped through her, warming her, making her feel as light as air.

"Fast, slow," he went on, "it doesn't matter. There are no rules, no time limits. This isn't an endurance contest."

As he spoke he had drawn her closer to the bed. Now he fell back onto it, pulling her on top of him. "This is just me loving you."

"And me loving you," she whispered, meaning it with all her heart, even though she suspected Sam had been using the term *loving* in a purely physical sense.

"Then show me," he crooned, stretching beneath her like a big lazy cat. He folded his arms behind his neck, smiling. "Make love to me, Lisa."

For only a second did she regard his words as a challenge. Then she saw there was no mocking glint in his eyes, only smoldering heat, and she realized it was not a challenge but an invitation. Her smile was wise and womanly as she lifted her fingers to his shirt and slowly worked the buttons open. When she reached the last one, she peeled the shirt aside and ran her hands over his bare chest.

Just the feel of him excited her, the crisp tickle of curling black hairs against her palm and the warm resilience of his flesh beneath her wandering fingertips. She closed her eyes, relishing the varying textures of him, and then opened them again to watch his expression as she lowered her head to explore him with her lips and tongue.

Sam's hands left their relaxed position behind his head to grasp her shoulders. He was definitely not relaxed. The quickening of the pulse in his throat when she touched her tongue there and the restless, random twitch of his hips told Lisa that his hunger for her was testing his powers of control. It was a heady feeling knowing that he was as needful as she had been a moment ago. It gave her the courage to let her fingers trace the narrow line of dark hair that bisected his belly, to find and flick open the flat metal fastening on his slacks. She lowered the zipper slowly, and as she did, the backs of her fingers rubbed the hard ridge beneath it, causing Sam's fingers to bite into her shoulders. His breath was coming in harsh, labored gasps.

Lisa had straightened in order to unbutton his shirt, and now she sat straddling his thighs, gazing down at the slash of underwear exposed in the open V of his zipper. She remembered Ron's passion for colored designer briefs and experienced a burst of sheer appreciative adoration that Sam's underwear was old-fashioned white cotton. The choice struck her as solid somehow, like the feel of his arms around her, like everything about him. Solid and dependable.

"God, Lisa, don't stop now." His urgent rasp snapped her full attention back to him. "Are you going to finish this," he demanded hoarsely, "or shall I?"

Smiling wickedly, Lisa curled the fingers of one hand beneath the elastic on his briefs and with the other petted a path down the center of his chest. "Impatient, hmm?" she purred.

"No." He grinned, but his obvious agitation undercut its usual careless effect. "Not impatient. Frantic is what I am. And close to committing a felony if you don't hurry up and touch me. Please, Lisa."

She did, quickly lowering his shorts to discover that the thick patch of dark hair beneath was surprisingly soft, the skin there shockingly hot. Sam shuddered as her fingers closed around him and almost immediately rolled her onto her back beneath him with a powerful surge. With rough urgency he stripped both of them of what remained of their clothing, then covered her with his body, insistently nudging her legs apart to make a place for himself.

It seemed Lisa wasn't the only one with a short fuse tonight. She lifted her chin as he hailed kisses along her throat, the sleek, hot tip of his arousal probing her eagerly. Then she arched against him with instinctive fervor as with one mighty lunge he entered her. She kissed his ear and the side of his neck, weaving her fingers through his long silky hair and lifting to meet each furious thrust of his hips as he carried them both higher and higher.

Again that all-new sensation built inside her. She heard Sam's breath catch and felt all his muscles tense only a fraction of a second before her entire body seemed to explode with pleasure. As if from a distance she heard his exultant cry of completion echo her own, and she knew that at that moment he had been rendered every bit as shattered and as richly whole as she was.

Sam collapsed on her with a shudder that shook his whole body, and Lisa loved the sense of cushioning his spent weight, no matter how difficult it made it for her to catch her breath. She was a little sorry when he eventually rolled to his side, still holding her close.

His lips moved over her face, brushing her eyelids, her cheekbones. He drew back a little, and when she opened her eyes to look at him, he smiled.

"We're very quick, you and I," he said without a hint of dissatisfaction.

Lisa leaned forward to touch her tongue to his roughly whiskered chin, the way she'd wanted to do the very first day they met. "And very loud," she added.

"Not to mention wet." They were both damp and sweaty. He pressed his hips closer to hers, grinning shamelessly and growling, "I love it."

Now say you love *me*, urged Lisa's heart. Say it so I can.

It was the truth. Right or wrong, she loved him. Physically, emotionally, in all the ways she knew how to love and in some she didn't yet understand. She realized now that she had been falling for days and was finally all the way there, completely in love with Sam Ravenal. Sam, a man who had claimed he only wanted to be her friend and who had just made violent, heartbreakingly tender love to her without saying a single word to suggest he might now want something more.

What if he didn't want anything more? What if he was offbeat enough to consider sex merely an inevitable, casual reality between a man and woman who were together as much as they had been lately? Lisa gave in to the sleepy urge to close her eyes and tried to push worrisome thoughts away. She would simply have to give him time, no matter how much she wanted to demand answers and explanations— even a declaration if she could wring it from him. Which she knew with absolute certainty she couldn't. If she couldn't talk Sam into accepting her version of history, she would never be able to talk him into love.

She lay silently beside him as sleep gradually took control of her senses, still willing him to say something. But he was just as silent, giving her only a few husky words of praise on which to build her hopes before he drifted off to sleep in her arms.

"It was good, Lisa," he murmured against the damp curve of her neck. "Real good."

Sometime during the night or early in the morning, Sam must have gotten up to turn off the lamp, because when Lisa awoke, the pink-gold light in the room flowed only from the sun, and he was gone.

Gone gone, Lisa knew without even getting out of bed. Not simply downstairs making coffee or taking an early-morning jog along the beach. All the dreaded doubts and possibilities she'd managed to shrink away from the night before came back full force.

Obviously he hadn't been in the mood this morning to hang around cuddling, willing to let whatever happened happen. Lisa had been banking that he would be, hopeful that the sex Sam himself had said was "real good" would chip away at whatever preconceptions he had about her not being right for him.

She was exactly right for him. Why couldn't he see that? As exactly right as he was for her. True, they had differences of opinion—very colorful ones on occasion—but on important matters they were totally in sync. Besides, Sam would rather she argue with him than meekly submit to his views. And even when they were sparring the hardest, she knew he enjoyed being around her.

The only thing about her that Lisa knew had earned Sam's outright disapproval was what he considered her excessive concern with her glamorous image. And maybe, she reluctantly acknowledged, her determination to marry only for security and equality the second time around.

So there were two things about her he might find upsetting. Two pretty major things, granted, but given the spectrum of possible failings, two still didn't seem such a big deal. Particularly when you considered the irony that, when push came to shove, both qualities had about as much substance as cotton candy. Lisa was not and had never been "glamorous" at heart, only by design. If Sam preferred her windblown and in jeans, she could happily spend the rest of her life that way. As for all her pragmatic prerequisites for a relationship, they had collapsed like the defensive blustering they were when Sam came into her life.

Ignoring the part of her that wanted to pull the covers up over her head and cry, Lisa got out of bed, took a bath and dressed. Her choice of faded jeans, sneakers and a comfortable old sweater was very deliberate, and she even felt recovered enough to smile as she looked in the mirror to comb her hair. Clean face, straight hair and a pair of tiny gold ball earrings her only jewelry—surely that was a sight to melt Sam Ravenal's heart.

That is, if he showed up to see how *un*glamorous she could look when she put her mind to it. The sudden panic that tightened her chest at the thought that he might not return disappeared as quickly as it had come. Sam would come back. For one thing, he was too conscientious to abandon the commitment he'd made to repair the house. But he would also return to put things right between them after last night.

In spite of her injured feelings and disappointment, Lisa felt she understood why Sam had left without talking to her this morning. He hadn't wanted to say anything until he'd decided exactly what he wanted to say. She'd seen him struggling with his feelings last night, and no doubt he hadn't sorted them all out yet. Whatever he felt for her, even if it was still strictly friendship, Lisa knew that Sam cared for her too much to lie there this morning and mouth pretty promises unless he meant them. Whatever he finally said about last night, whether she liked hearing it or not, she could count on the fact that, coming from Sam, it would be the truth.

And maybe it would even be something she wanted to hear. It was possible that as he thought things through he might come to the same realization she had: that he'd fallen in love with her. Then she could safely reveal what was in her heart. Of course, there was also the chance that he might want to write off last night as a momentary impulse, which, for the sake of their friendship, they shouldn't repeat. Or worse, he might declare that they shouldn't go on seeing each other even as friends. He might even suggest it was time for her to go home to Chicago.

Panic again clutched at Lisa as she realized that the words *home* and *Chicago* no longer sounded synonymous to her.

What on earth was she going to do back there without Sam? What was she going to do if he showed up at her door this afternoon or tomorrow or the next day, spouting some nonsense based on the fallacy that they were ill suited for each other?

It took Lisa next-to-no time to accept the fact there was only one possible thing she could do. She would hear him out, try her best to understand, and then do whatever it took, including moving heaven and earth, to change his mind.

Chapter Nine

Sam had quietly felt his way down the narrow staircase of the Jonathan Bennett House in the predawn darkness, but he'd been forced to turn on the light to navigate the downstairs hallway. The second he flipped it on, he stopped in his tracks at the sight of Lisa's latest bit of decorating.

Gradually her presence in the house had radiated out from the tiny den she'd all but closeted herself in when she first arrived, and that had pleased Sam more than he deemed safe to tell her. However, it wasn't pleasure or satisfaction he felt now, looking at the framed sketch she'd hung in a prominent place in the front hall, but rather a bitter self-loathing.

It was the very first of Lisa's sketches he had ever seen, the one on which she'd scrawled *You charm-bag, you* beneath a character that was undeniably based on him. Charm-bag. Sam slammed his hand hard against the light switch, condemning the house to blackness once more. He'd rather trip over every damn stick of furniture in the place than face that right now.

Charm-bag. A humorous caption. Too bad it was so far off base. It should have read *Sleaze-bag* instead.

He listlessly made his way through his morning's work on the university campus, feeling as if the word should be emblazoned across his chest. He definitely deserved his own modern-day, male version of a scarlet letter more than poor Hester Prynne ever had. He was a sleaze of the worst kind. One who was sinking to a new all-time low with each passing day.

It had started back at the beginning, even before he'd cleverly set Lisa up by contriving that supposedly chance first meeting. And the lies had gotten more intricate ever since. One lie was used to support another, and then another was necessary to protect that one. In a way, the omissions were even more damning—all the little things he didn't tell Lisa, *couldn't* tell her, because to do so would bring this nightmare crashing down around him.

Not that he didn't deserve it. Sometimes he even longed for the richly deserved justice of Lisa's anger. But he knew that her reaction to the truth would be more than anger. It would be a heartbreaking blend of fury and pain, and it would destroy what had come to be the most important thing in his life: the chance to spend it with Lisa.

Hurling a metal-ringed folder across his office with such force it broke open and rained important papers everywhere, Sam raked his fingers through his uncombed hair and asked himself for at least the thousandth time since he'd skulked out of Lisa's bed what the hell he was going to do now. It wasn't bad enough that from the start he'd been lying and misleading and outright manipulating her. Now he'd gone and done exactly what he had appeased his conscience by swearing he would never do: he had made love to her with all the lies and deceit still between them. And sleaze that he was, he'd enjoyed every minute of it.

Well, maybe not every minute. He sure as hell hadn't enjoyed that moment in the early morning when he'd woken with Lisa asleep in his arms and faced what he had done. She'd looked so fragile and vulnerable lying there. Inside him had surged a fierce protectiveness, and along with it the bitter realization that what she most needed protection from was him. She'd survived the duplicity of her ex-husband, but for all her supposed self-sufficiency, Sam knew the divorce had left her shaken. And now, like some savage cleanup squad, he had come along to finish the job of destroying her.

The real hell of it was that he couldn't think of any way to avoid it. The situation had taken on a twisted momentum of its own, almost as if the two of them were speeding toward the edge of a cliff with no brakes and no steering mechanism. Yep, a real melodrama, and if he weren't starring in it, he would probably snort with amusement. It was almost absurdly comical when you considered that the truth wasn't anything so bad. He wasn't an ax murderer or bigamist or anything. Unfortunately, given Lisa's background, it was bad enough. How could he have let something that began so benignly get so out of control?

Sam's mouth creased with rabid self-disgust. It had happened because he had made the ultimate mistake for a scientist, that's how: he had plunged into this project without factoring in all the possible contingencies. Never once had he so much as considered the possibility that he might fall crazy, out-of-his-mind in love with Lisa Bennett.

A stuck-up broad, too pretty for her own good—that's what he'd decided Lisa was the first time he laid eyes on her. Sexy, though. He had enjoyed seeing her strut her designer black wardrobe, had enjoyed watching her walk in those too-high heels. Hell, he had enjoyed watching her, period, as he sat there day after day, watching and waiting and doing nothing that might reveal she was his one and only reason for frequenting the park. But then, in his life he'd enjoyed watching a lot of women with whom he wouldn't want to hold more than a two-minute conversation. He hadn't been kidding that first day when he told Lisa she wasn't his type.

Then little by little, and against her will, he knew, she had started to open up to him, and before that first afternoon was half-over, he couldn't remember what his type was or had been before Lisa. Those big blue eyes and the sweet, light smell of her had severely scrambled his thought processes. There was only one reason he had refused her invitation to stay for dinner that night. It was the same reason he had pulled back and stayed away several times since, and it wasn't because he had anything better to do. There wasn't anything else, including breathing, that he wanted to do more than be with Lisa. The reason he'd bolted and spent the night alone on the boat, with only a six-pack and a bag of Doritos for company, was fear. He was constantly afraid that the hurricane of his feelings for her was going to blow out of control, ruining everything. And so, he'd persisted in the ludicrous, farcical role of her friend.

Lurching back in his chair, Sam propped his boots on his desk and stared past them with a bitter twist of a smile. Her friend. Her pal. When all he could think of every blessed waking moment—and quite a few sleeping ones, as well—was how she would feel and taste and move under him when he finally got around to making love to her. The fantasy had driven him for days now. And last night it had driven him too far, past reason and caution, past decency. He felt sorry that he'd let it happen, and guilty, and most of all he felt scared.

When he'd first approached Lisa, his reasons for being less than truthful had been selfish. He'd been strictly interested in expediency and hadn't wanted to risk the possibility that if she knew the whole story, she would get in his way. Then the situation changed. Sure, his reasons for playing things close to his chest were still selfish in a manner of speaking, but they gradually ceased to have anything to do with the quest that had brought him from Boston to Rhode

Island in the first place. He'd become much more concerned with losing Lisa than he was with finding what he'd come here for.

And losing her was exactly what was going to happen if he didn't think of a way out of this trap he himself had built. He should have followed his instincts—not to mention Roger Tillinghast's persistent nagging—and told her everything the second day, instead of fabricating yet another story about being hired to make repairs around her place. He'd hoped that maybe after they got to know each other better as friends, she'd be less likely to condemn him outright when she inevitably learned the truth. Instead, as he got to know her, he began to understand that vulnerability and mistrust ran through her like the veins of color in marble. He realized, too, that, like marble, the wrong kind of pressure would break her in two. Like the pressure of finding out that once again she'd been used by a man for his own gain.

He knew she would bolt as soon as she caught on, that she wouldn't stick around and give him a chance to explain how he'd never intended for things to get this convoluted. So he had hidden his real feelings behind that nauseating best-buddies routine and prayed for a way out of what was becoming a tighter no-win situation all the time. He couldn't tell her he loved her and hope to do anything about it until he'd told her the truth. And he couldn't tell her the truth because it would mean losing her trust and any chance that she might learn to love him back. He'd been living on borrowed time, swaying between heaven and hell. Then, last night, when she had looked at him with those eyes that scorched and beguiled, he hadn't been able to keep from reaching out and taking what he wanted so badly.

At the time he'd been beyond caring that it might be simply loneliness motivating Lisa to want a man she clearly considered beneath her standards. Maybe, subconsciously, he'd hoped that great sex might be the miracle that would bind her to him in spite of her inevitable disappointment in him. And the sex *had* been great, like nothing before in his life. But it had also been revealing, exposing other, deeper insecurities and needs in Lisa's prismlike nature.

Instead of making the telling easier, it had made it one step closer to impossible. It was as if by drawing nearer to her, he was also closing more doors on their future, until now there seemed to be only one possible way out of this. That is, if he'd sunk low enough to take it.

The door to Sam's office swung open, interrupting his thoughts. He swung around to see Marcia Serennson, a student assistant in the Oceanography department. As usual, her tortoiseshell glasses had slipped down on her nose, and she wrinkled it as she spoke in an unsuccessful attempt to push them back up.

"Sam," she began as soon as she stepped inside his office. "Lewis is on the phone, and he says they need you at the dock right away."

"Tell him I'm not here," Sam directed, reaching a decision about what to do about Lisa.

Marcia greeted that unprecedented request with a confused squint. "I can't. I already told him you're here, and he wants to talk with you before you leave to meet him because—"

"I'm not going to meet him," Sam broke in. "Not now, anyway. And I'm not talking to him on the phone."

"But Lewis will—"

Sam silenced the young woman with a look as he stood and grabbed his denim jacket. He already knew what she was going to say, that Lewis would be furious when he heard Sam had refused his request to join him and the student crew working on locating and raising the *Black Star*. And Marcia was right. Lewis Costa, chairman of the Oceanography department and, technically speaking, Sam's boss at the moment, had a notorious temper.

"All right," he conceded impatiently, pushing past Marcia to reach the telephone on the desk in the outer office. If anyone was going to bear the brunt of Lewis's anger, it ought to be he. "I'll tell him myself."

He did, explaining as concisely as possible that something important had come up, that he would be there when he could, and that, no, he hadn't turned up any new information on the possible coordinates of the ship's location. He hesitated only a heartbeat when Lewis demanded to know if the important matter that had just come up had to do with the *Black Star*. Yes, Sam told him, it definitely did.

For years locating the *Black Star* had been his most enduring dream. It had, at least in part, dictated his choice of a college major and a career, and he had made many professional decisions since with that ultimate goal in mind. It wasn't uncommon for someone in his field to have a fixation on a particular sunken ship, but even among the most addicted divers Sam had never revealed that for him, raising the *Black Star* was more than a dream. It was his destiny. He'd never thought anything else could ignite in him such fierce, reckless passion or such determination just to see and touch and, yes, to possess. Now something, or rather, someone, had. Lisa. And while it might not be in the sense Lewis Costa had in mind when he asked, Lisa and the *Black Star* were very much intertwined in Sam's life.

Sam's first thought when he knocked on Lisa's back door and got no answer was that she had packed up and gone home, back to Chicago. He was immediately assailed by threatening possibilities, each one like the flick of a whip on his soul. Maybe she had been so angry at his taking off without any explanation that she decided to do the same, permanently. Worse, she might have been so horrified by the fact that she'd gone to bed with him that she hadn't had the stomach to face him again.

Even before he heard the sound of her laughter down by the old cherry tree near the bluffs, however, he'd calmed down enough to know that Lisa wouldn't leave without saying goodbye to him. She had too much sensitivity and too much backbone under her softness to run away. That only slightly eased his trepidation over what sort of reception to expect from her. He circled the house, forcing him-

self to maintain a slow, almost aimless pace as he
approached.

He knew his steps had been silent as he crossed the thick
grass carpet, yet almost as if she were equipped with some
sixth sense, Lisa turned and watched him draw closer. Her
expression was unreadable, neither smiling nor, as Sam was
willing to admit he deserved, openly contemptuous.

He recognized the kid by her side as one of the boys
who'd been there yesterday, and if Lisa was hiding her feelings at seeing him, the boy wasn't. He looked distinctly
perturbed that Sam had intruded on their intense discussion. Sam knew exactly how the kid felt. He was a little
perturbed to find the kid hanging around again. He would
have outright told him to take a hike if it wasn't for the definite impression that he, not the boy, was the interloper today.

He wanted to be alone with Lisa so he could take her in
his arms and taste her mouth. It was already driving him
crazy, all shiny and wet from the way her tongue had
dragged nervously across it as he drew to a halt as close to
her as he dared. Her hair hung loose to her shoulders. Tousled by the wind, it looked as enticingly untamed as Sam
imagined it might have looked if he'd had the courage to
stay and wake up with her this morning. He'd love to have
seen her sleepy-eyed, her hair tousled from his fingers instead of the wind. His gaze drifted lower, memorizing the
way her worn jeans and soft, clingy sweater fit her curves
like designer silk. Sam burned to tell her how beautiful she
looked, backlit by the late-morning sun.

Instead he jammed his hands into his jean pockets to keep
from touching her and said, "Hi."

"Hi," she returned, brushing a wispy lock of pale gold
hair away from her cheek.

Their gazes locked, and Sam thanked God their eyes were
more eloquently equipped to share their feelings than their
tongues seemed to be. While Lisa's face remained tightly
unexpressive, Sam could read in her eyes a maelstrom of

emotion that made him want to soothe and explain and re-assure. *Slow*, he cautioned himself, his hands clenched into tight fists in his pockets. Take it slow. You don't want to risk scaring her off before you've even made her yours.

"So, Lisa, can we, do you think? Can we, huh?"

They both blinked rapidly, disorientedly, as the boy's voice pierced the spell holding them immobile. Slowly they turned to glance down at him, Lisa with a small indulgent smile, Sam with barely masked annoyance.

"I don't know yet, Danny," she replied in answer to his eager questioning. "I suppose I'll have to climb up there first and check it out. We're discussing the possibility of a second level for the fort," she explained to Sam.

"I see." He nodded and stepped closer to the tree, peer-ing up through the branches. "Oh, yes, that's definitely a possibility. Maybe with an extended balcony for better scouting. I can see it now."

"Yeah?" Danny's tone was awestruck, his eyes as round as silver dollars as he obviously envisioned what Sam was suggesting. "Really, mister? A balcony? You think we could build a balcony?"

Sam ran his gaze over Lisa before looking at Danny, not-ing as he did the wry expression that suggested she was at-tuned to his motives. "Sure it's possible. In fact, I'll give you a hand with it myself. Only not right now."

"Yeah? Then when, mister?" inquired Danny with squinty-eyed skepticism.

"Tomorrow," Sam countered on an impulse born of desperation. He would have promised to call in the Army Corps of Engineers to get rid of the kid. "Of course, that's provided you round up your buddies for extra manpower. And," he added pointedly, "provided you beat it now so I can talk with Lisa about something very important."

It took Danny all of five seconds to eye Sam up and down and apparently conclude that he could be trusted. Sam hoped Lisa was taking note and that she put stock in the old saying about kids and animals being excellent judges of character.

"You got yourself a deal, mister!" Danny exclaimed, grabbing his bike from where he'd dropped it nearby. "Me and Pete and Josh will be here first thing tomorrow. See ya, Lisa."

"See you, Danny," she called after him as he cut a bumpy path across the lawn and headed off down the street, no doubt to find his friends and brag about the deal he'd made on their behalf.

Once the boy was out of sight, she turned to look at Sam. He saw her shoulders rise with a preparatory sigh as she turned, as if she were steeling herself for something unpleasant. He saw the glint of determination in her eyes, as if she refused to be swayed from some foregone conclusion made in the early hours of the morning when she'd awakened to a cold, empty bed. And a feeling of dread ran like ice water through his veins.

"We have to talk," he told her quietly.

"About what?"

"I think that's obvious. About last night."

"I think last night speaks for itself. I'd rather talk about this morning."

Sam nodded grudgingly. He'd guessed right. She wasn't going to give an inch. "All right. First let me say I'm sorry about leaving before you woke up. It was . . . a sleazy thing to do."

Lisa appeared to be considering his self-appraisal. "Yes," she finally concurred, "I think *sleazy* covers it nicely." Then, with an impatient toss of her head, she demanded, "Were you really that afraid to face me, Ravenal? Afraid I was going to say something sloppy about commitment? Or worse, expect you to?"

"I don't know what I was afraid of," he admitted, wincing inwardly at what amounted to yet more not-quite-truthful hedging. "Or what I expected. One thing I didn't expect was for last night to end the way it did. Not that I'm sorry it happened," he quickly added when Lisa jerked her head away as if to hide her reaction from him. He put his hand on the back of her neck, loving the warm softness of her, fighting the urge to pull her into his arms and show her what he was having such a hard time putting into words.

"Lisa, I'm glad we made love last night," he said quietly.

Lisa glanced sideways at him through the shimmering gold veil of her hair, then swept it aside to meet his gaze fully, solemnly. "So am I, Sam."

Closing his eyes, he drew her against his chest, rubbing relieved kisses into her soft, fragrant hair. At least, thank God, she didn't regret what had happened. Granted, that didn't necessarily mean she was ready to confess how totally wrong she'd been about him or that she'd changed her mind about what she wanted in a man. But it might mean there was something here to build on if he was willing to work at it. That was the best he could hope for and more than he deserved.

"C'mon," he said, gently nudging her toward a sunny spot close to the bluffs. "Sit over here with me. I meant it when I said we needed to talk."

"We seem to communicate better when we *don't* talk," Lisa pointed out with a slightly wry sensuality as she settled beside him on the warm grass. "Maybe we shouldn't spoil things by talking."

"I happen to be of the opinion that what I'm going to say won't spoil anything. Lisa…" He hesitated, daring to lightly trail his fingertips along the outside of her thigh as he groped for words. He couldn't seem to keep his hands off her, and he was immensely relieved that she didn't seem to mind.

"Lisa, I know what we both said when we first met, about not being each other's type, and we were right, I suppose. I mean, you weren't slow or shy about ticking off your shopping list as far as men were concerned, and I don't think anybody would make the mistake of saying I qualify."

As he watched, she shrugged awkwardly, and her cheeks warmed to the color of overripe peaches. "Oh, I don't know. You're not exactly—"

"Cut it, Lisa," he broke in roughly, not wanting to hear all the things he wasn't in her eyes. "We both know what I'm not." Forcing a grin, he added, "If it makes you feel any better, it works both ways. I sure as hell never figured myself with anyone like you."

"What's wrong with me?" she demanded, eyes flashing as darkly as blue-black ice.

"Nothing, nothing...when you leave yourself alone, like yesterday. It's only when you go getting all gussied up and prissy that you give me a royal pain."

"Ask me if I care," she drawled in spite of her heated flush, which seemed to suggest that she just might. "By 'gussied up' I assume you mean a little tastefully applied makeup and clothes that don't look as if I wore them to my high-school class outing and every day since?"

The haughty look she dragged over Sam's old jeans and work shirt turned him on. But then, in the state he was in, any look from Lisa would probably turn him on.

"A little tastefully applied makeup? I saw your bathroom, Lise," he reminded her, affectionately shortening her name. "You have more paint and brushes than Benjamin Moore. And more clothes than Bloomingdale's."

"Hardly."

"Oh, no? I'd love to get a look at the trunk you must have needed to haul them here from Chicago. Ten to one the airport porter is still in traction."

She shook her head piteously. "You can be such a jerk sometimes. It's not a crime to want to look nice, you know."

"That's the point. You always look nice to me, like right now, like yesterday."

"Well..."

She shrugged, looking away from him to stare down at her casually crossed ankles. Her mouth twitched at the corners as if she might break into a pleased smile if she weren't struggling to subdue it by biting her bottom lip.

"Thank you," she said finally. "I guess it's just that I don't feel I look good unless I'm dressed nicely and wearing makeup. No, that's not true," she suddenly admitted with a long sigh. "The truth is that it has nothing to do with caring about the way I look. It's just that the only time I feel really confident or in control is when I'm..." She rolled her eyes in self-disgust as she concluded, "When I'm dressed to impress. Believe it or not, it helps to keep strangers at a distance, and lately I just haven't felt up to dealing with strangers."

"*Strangers*, translated *men*?" When she nodded, Sam reached out to caress her cheek. He wasn't sure if the light touch soothed her as he intended, but it made *his* nerve endings sizzle.

"Lisa, control and self-confidence aren't something you can buy in a bottle from Elizabeth Arden. They come from in here." He tapped her head lightly before dropping his hand back to his side. "I know how helpless you must have felt when you found out how your husband had appropriated your ideas, but you're *not* helpless. Not by a long shot. Instead of getting caught up in resentment, you rebounded. You're smart and you're resourceful, and I for one think you can handle anything you decide to tackle. Look at how quickly you put your new proposal together. And how well you've handled your stay here, even though you hated this place at first."

"Maybe," Lisa allowed. "But, much as I hate to admit it, I think all that had a lot to do with you, and the fact that you've been such a good friend. At first I was miserable. I felt so alone. Then you happened along, and everything seemed to come together for me. My work, even my feelings about this house." Her sigh was tinged with irony. "I guess you can't call it *self*-confidence if you get it from someone else, huh?"

"Oh, I don't know. A really smart person probably wouldn't make such picky semantic distinctions and would definitely, at all costs, hang on to whatever worked for her. Which is sort of what I wanted to talk with you about," he continued with all the grace and precision and ruthlessness of a hockey player spotting an open shot at the net. "You said I've helped you, but the fact is, we're good for each other, Lise. Maybe not in the sense that we were each halfheartedly searching for, but in ways that are just as important. Maybe even more important."

"Such as?"

"Friendship. How many couples do you know who are actually best friends? Or who stay that way after they've become lovers? That's the other important thing we've got going for us. Great sex."

Again her eyes skittered away from his. "Yes, well..."

"It was, you know," he insisted, gripping her chin to force her gaze back to his. "Or maybe you really don't know, at that. So let me tell you. It was great. Rare. Special."

"I sort of... felt that way, too."

He smiled, his insides a tight coil of nervous anticipation, waiting for her to smile back. When she finally did, he reached for her hand and brought it to his mouth to taste the smooth, soft skin of her palm. "With your penchant for independence and my crazy work habits, the last thing either of us needs in our life is someone overly demanding emotionally. And it makes good sense not to turn your back on a safe, satisfying sexual outlet simply because you don't hear violins playing every time the person walks by."

He almost bit his tongue on *that* lie. Violins, hell. Lisa's impact was that of a symphony orchestra. "We don't need violins, Lisa," he continued nobly. "What we need is each other." He stroked the inside of her wrist with his thumb, encouraged by the sight of goose bumps rising along her arm. "So, what do you say?"

With his thumb still on her wrist, he felt her pulse trip wildly. Her eyes widened, then narrowed as they searched his almost disbelievingly. "I...I'm not sure. I'm not even sure what it is you're saying, Sam."

"I thought it was obvious, but I guess not. It's pretty simple really," he said, while inside he was reeling from feelings that were about as simple as the blueprint for a nuclear power plant. "What I've been trying to say is...marry me, Lisa."

Chapter Ten

Lisa stared at him in shocked silence, then gave a nervous spurt of laughter. "You're teasing me. You have to be. Either that or you're crazy. Sam, you don't marry a person when there are so many things about them you don't even like."

"I wouldn't exactly say there are *so* many." He quickly held his hands up in surrender as her expression moved from disbelief to dismay. "Kidding, only kidding. C'mon, Lisa, you know I like you just fine."

"I like you just fine," she mimicked sarcastically. "That's great, Ravenal. Exactly what a woman wants to hear from a man when he proposes to her."

Sam reached for her hand and held it between both of his, slowly stroking until she abandoned her huff and deigned to look at him.

"I like you fine," he said once more with quiet insistence, all the while curbing the nearly violent urge to tell her he loved her and then to roll her beneath him right there on the lawn and show her exactly how much.

Some twisted shred of decency even he didn't fully understand held him back. Somehow he felt that if he revealed now how much he loved her, she would ultimately see that as just one more trick he'd used to manipulate her into doing what he wanted. He'd prefer to bind her to him legally without making any declarations, in the hope that her commitment to him would serve as a safety net later, when he told her everything.

She would be mad as hell, sure, but he would be her husband then, and somehow he would find a way to make her understand and forgive him. And when he finally did tell her that he loved her, she would have to believe him, because the words would be fresh and pure, untainted by his own stupid, shortsighted finagling.

"I like you very much, Lisa," he told her honestly. "I admire your creativity and your intelligence. I can't think of anyone I'd rather argue with, and you excite me more than any woman I've ever known. Maybe all that doesn't add up to the traditional grounds for marriage, but I'd say it's a hell of a lot better foundation for one than most couples have. Now, what do you say?" he asked again.

What *could* she say? Lisa considered all he'd laid before her and found she couldn't argue with any of it. She respected his intelligence, too, as well as his talent for working with his hands and his unmistakable passion for his job as a marine archaeologist. And he excited her. In fact, if last night was any indication, a smart woman would marry Sam Ravenal for the sex alone. And then there was the clear, simple fact that she loved him, a fact she wouldn't dare admit to him. Yet.

"Yes," she breathed as a smile seized control of her mouth. "I say yes, yes, yes."

"You mean it?"

The look of sheer wonder in Sam's luminous green eyes told Lisa that his lazy, self-confident approach had been at least partly an act, and that reassured her. Sam might not know it yet, but she was going to see to it that their marriage was a very traditional, *loving* one, or die trying.

"God, you do mean it," he growled, reaching for her and bringing her down on the grass under him in one fluid lunge. "You won't be sorry," he said against her laughing mouth, "I promise you that."

Lisa parted her lips at his gentle prodding, and his mouth slowly made love to hers, his tongue licking lightly at the corners, then surging inside with a pounding rhythm that left her weak and hungry at the same time. When he pulled away enough to look into her eyes, Lisa was flooded with love for him. Slowly, though, an ugly uncertainty reared its head.

"Sam," she began tentatively. She was unsure of the bounds of this unusual marriage he was proposing but dead certain that at least some of the ground rules had to be clear up front.

He dipped his head to nuzzle her neck. "Mmm?"

"I know you said this won't be a strictly traditional marriage in all ways, but there are some, well, one really..."

"Lisa, just say it." His tone was laden with amusement.

"Other women," she blurted. "I couldn't stand—"

"You'll never have to," he assured her before she could finish. "Maybe you misunderstood me. I'm not proposing to you as a lark. In terms of faithfulness I expect our marriage to be very traditional. On both our parts. I want my ring on your finger and my last name after yours, at least in our private life. Professionally you'll probably choose to continue using your own name. But make no mistake, you'll be my woman in every sense, respected and cherished."

And loved, Lisa added to herself. He might not be ready to accept or admit it right now, but without even knowing it Sam was giving her every reason to believe that love would come.

A lazy smile tilted his mouth. "Do you think your independent nature could stand all that if I promise that I'll never interfere with your work? And never question your decisions about what's right for you professionally?''

"I think I'll manage."

"Good." He brushed his mouth against hers but circumvented her attempt to deepen the kiss. "As long as we're talking terms, we might as well tackle that other killer problem: finances."

Lisa could have bit her tongue off for all the things she'd said about wanting a man who was fabulously wealthy and sickeningly secure. "Sam, I really didn't mean any—''

"Of course you did," he contradicted. "And not without reason. The truth is that I can afford to support the two of us in reasonable style, and I will."

Lisa was confused. "But if my proposal sells, then—'

"You can do whatever you want with the money."

"And what," she shot back with an exasperated sigh, "if I choose to squander it by buying you outrageously expensive presents—say, mink earmuffs and eighteen-carat gold toothpicks?"

He laughed as he bent his head to kiss her again. "Whatever makes you happy, pal—as long as you don't expect me to use any of that crap."

"Sam?"

Groaning with impatience, he muttered, "Be quiet, Lisa. We don't have to settle every little problem right this minute, while I'm doing my damnedest to kiss you. We have until Saturday, after all."

This time Lisa planted her hands against his shoulders and shoved as he closed in. "Saturday?"

"Sure. This is already Tuesday. There's the waiting period for the blood tests and license to consider. Not to mention the fact that I'm committed to a major balcony construction project bright and early tomorrow," he added with no small amount of regret. "We can't possibly be married any sooner than Saturday."

"Wrong, Sam, we can't possibly be married as *soon* as Saturday," she corrected. "I don't have anything ready. I need a dress and—"

Sam's fingers covered her lips, gently silencing her. "Lisa, you're beginning to sound prissy again."

"Tough. I'm not getting married in blue jeans just to please you."

"And I'm not getting married in a monkey suit to please you."

They glared at each for all of three seconds before dissolving in laughter.

"Sounds like we're off to a great start," he observed dryly. "What do you say we stop arguing about it and surprise each other?"

"Fine."

"Because I was just thinking there would be one very definite advantage to having you get all decked out in stockings and lace and stuff." His eyes glittered mischievously as he slowly ran his hands along her sides. "I'd get to take it off you after the ceremony."

"True," she agreed, her voice thick and throaty as he dipped to caress her collarbone with his lips.

"*Immediately* after the ceremony," he breathed against her skin.

"Oh, yes . . . yes . . ."

The sound of a twig snapping close by brought Lisa's gaze around in a hurry. She gulped as she recognized the feet approaching at a spry pace and pushed frantically at Sam's shoulders without success. He remained stubbornly amorous until Helen, who by then had ground to a sudden, embarrassed halt only a few feet away, spoke up.

"Oh, heavens, now I've gone and done it. I thought you were alone here, Lisa. Leave it to an old lady to rush out without her glasses and intrude. I can see you young folks aren't interested in blueberry muffins just now." She gestured with the foil-wrapped plate she was carrying as she turned to go.

"No, Helen, wait!" Lisa called after her.

This time when she shoved, Sam moved, although she could tell from the sardonic look he gave her that in his condition he felt as awkward sitting up as she had with him sprawled on top of her. She prayed Helen wasn't kidding about needing her glasses to see clearly, because the soft fabric of Sam's jeans did little to camouflage his enthusiasm. She tossed him a grateful smile when he diplomatically drew his legs up, crossing his arms casually atop his bent knees.

"Helen, I know you've said hello to Sam a few times, but I don't think you two have been formally introduced." Lisa quickly handled the introductions, earning another wounded look from Sam as he was forced to get to his feet to shake Helen's hand. Lisa stood to join them, brushing grass from her jeans and her hair.

"Helen, I want you to be the first to know that I think I'm getting married."

Sam eyed her yet again, this time with a blend of amusement and challenge.

"I mean," she hastily amended, "I *know* I'm getting married. To Sam." As if her starry-eyed look at him wasn't a dead giveaway that he was the man.

"Lisa, how wonderful!" Helen exclaimed, beaming from her to Sam. "And, Sam, congratulations to you. You're getting a very special young lady."

"I know that, Mrs. Van Egan," Sam returned, his gaze steady on Lisa. "I'm a lucky man."

"I certainly hope the wedding will be close by so that I can attend," Helen went on. "Lisa will be such a beautiful bride."

"Yes, it will be," Lisa told her, a little amazed that she hadn't even considered that the wedding might take place anywhere else. "There really isn't anyone back in Chicago I would want to be there." Lisa hurried on as both Sam and Helen reacted to that declaration with mild surprise. She didn't want to risk spoiling her mood with lengthy explanations about her mother. "As a matter of fact, Helen, it's going to be quite soon. Maybe even Saturday."

"Definitely Saturday," Sam interjected in a tone of steel.

"An impatient groom," chuckled Helen with obvious delight. "But then, I could see that for myself."

"I guess Saturday it is," Lisa conceded, laughing in spite of a trace of embarrassment. "Helen, Sam and I haven't really had a chance to make any arrangements yet, but I'd like it if you would stand up for me."

"Oh, gracious!" she exclaimed, clearly thrilled by the request. "An old lady like me? Surely there must be someone else, someone younger, you'd rather have."

"There isn't," Lisa insisted firmly. "I really don't know anyone else here, but even if I did, I'd want it to be you, Helen. Just having you to talk things over with has meant more to me than you'll ever know."

"In that case, I'd be pleased to be your matron of honor," Helen declared. Stepping forward, she gathered Lisa in a quick hug with the arm not wielding the plate of muffins. As she moved away, her smile dwindled into a perplexed frown. "But what on earth will I wear? I'll have to coordinate with whatever you choose, and—"

She broke off as Sam let loose a groan of dismay. "Clothes again! Is that always the first thing a woman thinks about when she decides to do something? I swear, it's a conspiracy." He glared at Lisa and Helen as they both broke into amused grins.

"You'll have to excuse him," Lisa told Helen in an openly affectionate tone. "He has this strange hostility toward anything not made of denim."

Helen's grin stiffened into a staunch look of reproach. "Tch, tch. You can just forget about that, young man. As I always told my sons, a man can't go wrong in a dark blue suit with a white shirt. And a tie, of course. Nothing too flashy—a nice maroon stripe is always appropriate."

"Yes, ma'am," Sam replied. His look could almost be described as humble if you didn't know him well enough to discern the glint in his eyes. "Dark blue suit, white shirt, not-too-flashy maroon tie. That's exactly what I had in mind."

"Good," the older woman pronounced with a that-settles-that air. Her eyes held a sparkle of their own as she added, "Now I'll just be getting out of here so you can talk over your plans in private. The last thing two people in love need is a third wheel hanging around."

At the mention of love Lisa's gaze shifted to Sam's face. It was natural for Helen to assume that two people planning to be married were in love. What wasn't natural, and what sent the icy tremor snaking along Lisa's spine, was the implacable warning look in Sam's eyes as they met hers. Remember, it seemed to caution, love was not a part of our bargain. Lisa forced her thoughts away from the germ of sadness his expression planted in her heart as she said goodbye to Helen, thanking her for the blueberry muffins as she turned to leave.

When she and Sam were alone, she slanted him a scoffing smile. "A blue suit is exactly what you had in mind, huh?"

Sam didn't look the least bit contrite. "You wouldn't have wanted me to tell her what I really had in mind, would you?"

He reached for her as he spoke, and Lisa knew instantly what he really had in mind.

"That all depends," she countered, laughing and struggling to keep the muffin plate steady as he swung her up into his arms. "Were you thinking about what you were going to wear to the wedding?"

"Definitely not. I was thinking more about what you're wearing right this minute." His mouth found her neck beneath the soft, satin length of her hair and trailed kisses all the way to her ear. "I was wondering how long it would take me to get these clothes off you if I really put my mind to it."

Shivering with excitement from his moist, heated mouth on her skin, Lisa arched her neck. "And how long would it?" she asked huskily.

He lifted his head, his gaze dark and hungry and reckless enough to unleash all her civilized restraints. "Do I have to stop for buttons?" he asked. "Or can I rip?"

"Don't stop," she whispered, her gaze locked on his, her words coming hard and breathless around the sudden, overwhelming need in her. Her fingers wove through the long, thickly curling hair at the back of his neck to pull his head down even as she strained in his arms to reach his mouth. "Don't stop, Sam."

With some distant portion of her mind, Lisa marveled that he was able to walk and kiss that way at the same time. In her whole life she'd never met a man who could kiss half so spectacularly even without distractions. He barely broke stride to relieve her of the plate in the kitchen, then somehow managed to conquer the narrow stairs without letting her go. A very talented man. She told him so as he tumbled her onto her bed.

"You think that was talent?" he teased with a provocative leer. "Just wait."

"I can't," she confessed softly. Her arms trembled as she opened them to him. "I can't wait, Sam."

With a quick look he assessed her mood, correctly judging that it wasn't a time for teasing, and Lisa was grateful when he lowered himself to the bed beside her and took her in his arms. He loved her slowly, fully, but without any playful holding back. He seemed to sense that she needed from his body the affirmation he wasn't able, or willing, to give with words.

Despite his earlier talk of ripping her clothes, he removed them so effortlessly that Lisa was barely aware of each piece leaving her body until she was naked and so was he, the slide of flesh against flesh unbearably erotic to her overheated senses. At least in this physical way he gave freely of himself, exploring her with his hands and his mouth, so intimately that Lisa feared she would have no secrets from him, body or soul, when he was done.

Amazingly, she didn't care. She might be taking the greatest risk of her life by marrying Sam, but this time she was taking the risk with her eyes open, and she would withhold nothing. As his hand moved between her legs, she parted them eagerly.

Last night she had been dazed by the unexpected impact of his loving, but in the clear light of day she realized that for the first time in her life she wanted to surrender everything. She wanted to give and give, not out of a sense of duty or because it was expected, or even to win his love in return, but simply for the joy of giving herself to the man she loved.

Sam rose above her, bracing himself on his arms. His face was damp with perspiration and tightly etched with desire.

"Stay with me," he demanded in a hoarse growl, pulling her from the beautiful web of her own thoughts.

She did, keeping her eyes open and focused on his as he lowered his hips, pressing against her with the burning strength of his arousal. Lisa slipped her hand between their damp bodies to encircle him with her fingers.

The muscles in Sam's arms twitched in response, and he sucked in a deep breath, but he didn't so much as blink as she guided him to her, stroking that softest part of herself with his warmth for as long as either of them could stand it before he had to thrust inside her and she had to have him there.

The fact that he was watching her watch him made the moment even more erotic. He held her gaze as he entered her and then as his body rocked against hers, slowly, back and forth. Neither of them said a word, but Lisa knew Sam was as enraptured as she by the sheer magic of their joining.

The link between them was primitive and physical, yes, but also mystical and eternal. And Sam could say all he wanted about sex and friendship and his string of oh, so practical considerations. Lisa knew it was not only their

bodies that came together on that sun-dappled bed, ex-
ploding in a blaze so hot it fused them together for all time,
but their hearts as well.

It was a severe test of her self-control not to tell him so in
the lazy aftermath of their lovemaking, while they lay side
by side, still wrapped in each other's arms. Again some instinct counseled her that it might be better to let Sam discover the truth about their relationship in his own way, in his
own time. So she bit her lip, knowing as she did that, no
matter how hard she tried, she couldn't wipe the happy smile
off her face or erase the glow of love from her eyes or strip
the tender adoration from her every touch.

And she couldn't stop looking at him and touching him.
She loved everything about him and couldn't seem to drink
in enough of the sight of his lean, muscled body or the feel
of all the smooth and rough textures that were his. Idly she
trailed her fingertips along the firm line of his throat, trac-
ing his collarbone and then straying lower. When she lightly
touched his nipple he sighed, and Lisa smiled with surprise
and a heady sort of pleasure.

"You like that," she murmured, touching him again,
feeling the slight change from flat to pebbled.

Sam watched her face as she touched him, and along with
a physical thrill he felt a rush of tenderness at the innocence and vulnerability he saw there. The woman had been
married, for God's sake, yet she approached his body with
the sort of awestruck wonder of a kid with a new toy. Not
for the first time he thought that, aside from being a bastard, Lisa's ex-husband was also an idiot.

"Yes, I like that," he confirmed. "And that," he added
as her hand stroked his chest and glided to his shoulder. Her
palm molded the curve of his biceps. "And that. Ah, Lisa,
you're so good."

Tilting his head, he kissed her mouth hard to keep from
telling her how much he loved her. The need to tell her, to
sweep aside every lie and shadow that hung between them,
filled him with impatience. Saturday seemed a dangerous

lifetime away. He lifted his head to look at her, brushing back the hair from her forehead.

"Lise, why don't you want your mother to come to the wedding?"

Instantly that familiar shuttered look appeared in her eyes, with him on one side of it and God only knew what doubts or fears on the other.

"I've already told you," she replied in a suddenly careful tone, "we're not close."

"Lots of mothers and daughters aren't close," Sam felt obligated to argue. "That doesn't mean they don't send each other Christmas cards and get together for weddings occasionally."

"It does for us."

"Lisa, she's your mother, and you're getting married—"

"And having her at the wedding would ruin it," Lisa broke in before he could finish. Her tone was strident, almost angry, and with gently kneading fingertips Sam could feel the muscles of her back tighten.

"I mean it, Sam," she continued. "I know this is something you probably can't understand, coming from such a close family with a wonderful mother like yours, so please, just accept it at face value. All I ever was to my mother was a name on child support checks, and when they stopped coming, she never missed a chance to let me know what an unwanted burden I really was."

Horrified, Sam tried to pull her close, but Lisa's body was too tense to melt into his the way he longed for. He wanted to pull her inside him so that no one ever again could put that shattered look on her face.

"She actually said that to you?" he asked softly, not knowing how to begin to soothe a pain that was rooted so deeply.

Lisa laughed, a harsh sound devoid of humor. "Oh, she said it all right, although it wasn't necessary. I knew it without being told, just from the way she looked at me. Then one day it all changed."

When no joy entered her tone, Sam was afraid to ask what had changed and how. He continued to rub her back in silence until she was ready to go on.

"It was when I was seventeen," she revealed finally. "She read an article in some magazine about the fabulous money models make, then took a good look at me and saw dollar signs. I was, she decided, model material."

"She was right. You're beautiful, and you're elegant."

Lisa shook her head defiantly. "No, she was wrong. Oh, I'm pretty enough in person," she conceded with an impatient toss of her head, "but put me in front of a camera, and I freeze. I didn't have the pizzazz it takes to be a successful model, and I sure as hell didn't have the desire, although I pretended to so that just once she would be pleased with me or proud or something besides... resentful. But I was hopeless, and every photographer and agent my mother dragged me to told her exactly that. It was humiliating."

Sam could see that remembered humiliation in her eyes before she squeezed them shut.

"As a last resort," she continued without looking at him, "she took me to some crummy little studio to see this washed-up photographer who was shooting underwear advertisements for the back pages of men's magazines." She slanted Sam a sardonic look from beneath lowered lashes. "I trust you're familiar with the sort of ad I'm referring to?"

"I've seen a few in my time," he admitted, taking pains to keep his tone easy. It wasn't sympathy that rose up in him now, but fury, great blinding waves of it that would have enabled him to calmly strangle Lisa's mother if he could have gotten his hands around her throat at that moment. "You were seventeen when she did this?"

"Eighteen by then," Lisa corrected. "And I'd had it. When that grubby little man put his hands on me, and my own mother stood by smiling as if he had every right to—because he was, after all, willing to fork over hard, cold cash for the privilege—something inside me snapped. I stood my ground right there and told her that I didn't want to be any kind of model, that I wanted to go to college and study art, and that thanks to the help of a teacher at school, I'd applied for a scholarship that just might make it possible.

"She was furious," Lisa continued softly, staring at his chest as if it were a window to her past. "She called me a loser, accused me of giving up on my dream. I don't think I ever did make her understand that it was *her* dream, not mine, and that I wasn't giving up, I was fighting for my life."

"Wasn't she happy when you won the scholarship?" Sam asked. "It saved her from helping with your tuition."

"As if she would have," Lisa returned dryly. "No, Sam, she wasn't happy. She was totally disgusted. She told me that if I wanted to chase some pipe dream to go ahead, but not to think I had a free ride with her whenever I felt like dropping in. The day I left for college was the last time I saw her until after I'd married Ron, and Maxine's Musings took off."

"Somehow I could have predicted that," Sam remarked harshly. Something told him Lisa wasn't nearly as well insulated against her mother's cruelty as her shrug seemed to indicate.

"We had lunch, once. And I sent her checks regularly while I could still afford to. I probably will again if my proposal sells," she revealed with a self-derisive smile.

Sam was outraged. "Why?"

"Because she's my mother, and because I know she could use the money. But I *don't* want her at my wedding. I don't want her in my life in any real, tangible way." She met Sam's gaze with a look of such raw pain, it tore a path straight to his heart. "My mother is a user. I know that, and, knowing it, I should be strong enough not to let her get to me. But I'm not sure I am. Maybe someday I'll be able to make peace with her, but for now I don't want any complications in my life. I just want you, Sam."

Instinctively her body pushed against his, and somehow he managed to return her smile until her face was safely buried against his chest. Then he grimaced with something close to panic. Damn. How could she know that he was the biggest complication of all? And how on earth was he going to stop himself from breaking her heart? He couldn't even form a coherent thought, yet at last he was able to see the whole picture spread before him in full, ugly color.

He saw Lisa's scheming mother, as well as the college professor she'd once told him about—the one who'd drooled over her paintings until he got her into bed, then forgot her name overnight. And he saw her ex-husband coming up right behind them with his arms open, ready to supply the love Lisa needed so desperately, for as long as it took him to work his own number on her. He saw all of them, offering her promises with one hand while they picked her clean of whatever she had that they wanted with the other. What disgusted him most of all, though, was that he saw himself right there with them.

Chapter Eleven

No! The word exploded in Sam's head, shattering the crystal-clear pictures from Lisa's past. He wasn't using her. He was doing the only thing he could to make sure they had a chance. And somehow when the time came, he would make her understand that.

"Sam?"

He rubbed the top of her head with his chin, mostly to keep her from looking up until he'd managed to chase the worried expression from his face. "Hmm?"

"Do you think it would be okay to have the wedding here...in the house, I mean?"

"I think it would be all right to have it hanging upside down from an airplane over the ocean if that would make you happy."

"The front parlor will be fine, thank you. I know it's small, but it sort of seems right that we should be married here. And, Sam?"

He finally met her gaze.

"Just because I don't have any family that I care to invite doesn't mean you can't invite yours."

"We're kind of spread out now, and it's a little late notice to get them all together, I'm afraid. I'll tell you what, why don't we keep Saturday just for us? Later, after everything is straightened out, we'll let my mother throw a big party so you can meet everybody. She'll love it."

"If you're sure they won't be hurt because they weren't... after what's straightened out?" she asked with a quizzical frown.

Sam's mind whirled frantically. "Details. You know, like where we're going to live, that sort of thing."

"I hadn't even thought of anything that practical," she confessed.

"That's understandable," he drawled, sliding his hand over her legs suggestively. "You've been otherwise occupied this morning."

"True, but now I'm ready to get down to business."

"I thought that's what I was doing," he grumbled as she absently transplanted his wandering hand from her belly to the less interesting region of her shoulder.

"Had you given any thought to living here in the Bennett house after we're married?" she asked.

Her smile seemed to tremble with hopeful excitement. There had been so little tradition or permanence in her life, Sam hated to crush this small seedling of it, but he knew if he encouraged it now, it would only hurt her more in the end.

"No," he said more brusquely then he intended. "Somehow I don't think that would work out." He hesitated, then added in a more gentle tone, "How about living on my boat with me?"

Slowly, under the steady warmth of his smile, the spark reignited in her eyes, and Sam felt his heartbeat slow to normal again.

"Well, I haven't actually seen your boat," she hedged, "but somehow I don't think that will work out, either."

"Landlubber," he gibed playfully.

"Not at all. It's more the close quarters I was thinking of. You and I can be . . . uh, volatile at times."

He laughed. "You have a point. We'll work something out."

"Sure," she agreed with a magnanimous shrug. "After all, we have four whole days, at least one of which you'll be busy playing general contractor for a group of eight-year-olds."

He groaned. "Don't remind me."

Laughing, Lisa grabbed the pillow he was attempting to burrow under. "Actually, that's what I was getting at a minute ago when I asked if you'd thought about living here. I was hoping you'd say no, because spending some time with Josh and the other boys has given me this great idea for the house."

Sam eyed her skeptically. "What sort of great idea?"

"A children's museum. I've given it a lot of thought, Sam, and it would be perfect."

She hurried on without giving him a chance to tell her he didn't have to be convinced. He already agreed it was a great idea. But very quickly he became captivated by Lisa's animated sales pitch and was glad he hadn't spoken too soon. He watched her with gentle, adoring eyes as she propped herself up on the pillows and argued her conviction that today's kids needed, and would be thrilled by, the opportunity for a hands-on exploration of the past. She described the house the way she envisioned it, as a kid-proof historical museum, complete with a restored kitchen to produce samples of bread and cookies made from scratch and a room dedicated to pirate lore.

"Somehow we'd have to work in the legend of Elizabeth and Alexander Brandon," she decreed. Then, with a snap of her fingers, she exclaimed, "I've got it! You could donate your model of the *Black Star*, and we could get copies of those letters we found in Boston. Do you think there might be a portrait of Elizabeth tucked away anywhere?"

"The attic?" Sam suggested indulgently.

"The attic! I almost forgot. That's the best part. There should be big trunks of old clothes up there so the kids can dress up. I'm sure lots of people would be willing to make donations. And maybe one or two of those old-fashioned pedestal mirrors for them to see themselves in. Dressing up in Grandma's attic has to be every kid's dream, and I'll bet there are a lot of kids today who come from broken homes or who don't live close enough to a real grandmother to visit her attic." She came to an abrupt halt and glanced at him, as if a little embarrassed by her rambling enthusiasm. "So, what do you think? Dumb? Impossible?"

Her look was so openly longing for approval that if she had suggested building the museum on the moon and having him haul all the materials there single-handedly he would have agreed wholeheartedly and worried about how later.

"I think it's a terrific idea," he told her honestly.

Her expression eased toward relief. "Really? I know it depends on the outcome of the will and all, but maybe this would be an acceptable compromise. I'm the closest thing to a legal heir, and if I agree to the museum and the town approves, it just might work. I can't imagine who would object." Her eyes clouded. "Except Miriam. I'm pretty sure she'd despise the whole idea, and I can't help feeling guilty. It is her house, after all."

"Was," Sam corrected. "And you can't know for sure how she would have reacted to your idea. Besides, she's dead, and the children who will benefit from the museum are very much alive. And I, for one, think you're brilliant." He kissed her mouth. "And gorgeous." Again his lips took hers, lingering. "And delicious. And the only thing I'd like to do half as much as keep you in bed all day is check out the attic."

"The attic?" Lisa sounded faintly disoriented, and when her eyes finally blinked open, Sam saw that they were already smoky with desire.

It thrilled him that he could arouse her so quickly, and he decided he was a fool to leave her bed to go poke around in a dusty old attic. There was, however, a method to his madness. The museum idea presented another possible bond between them, and he planned to forge it as deeply and solidly as he could. He wanted their lives so entwined that the very idea of living without him would be more painful to Lisa than his lies. Plus, his active participation would testify that he'd never had any designs on the house personally. Maybe it would be easier for Lisa to forgive him if it was clear that from the beginning he'd been driven not by profit, but by destiny.

"Yes, the attic." Grabbing her hand, he yanked her from the bed and, he hoped, from troublesome second thoughts about what Miriam Bennett would and would not approve of. "If we're going to present this museum idea to the executor of the estate and the town officials, we'd better know what we're talking about—size-wise, safety-wise, clothes-in-trunks-wise. Speaking of clothes, have you seen my... oh, there they are."

He quickly pulled on his jeans and shirt and then helped Lisa, ignoring her laughing protests that he was only slowing her down. It was, Sam discovered at the ripe old age of thirty, almost as much fun to dress a woman as to undress her. Eventually they made their way up to the attic, and once Sam had opened the tiny windows in the eaves, it wasn't half as musty as he'd anticipated.

It wasn't very dusty, either, and they agreed that Miriam had been even more meticulous about the house than they'd imagined. The space was, however, cluttered. Boxes lined the walls and were piled to the roofline in all four corners. Boxes of old books, old china, old bed linens and, to Lisa's boundless delight, old clothes. She eagerly opened one carton after the other, releasing the scent of camphor into the air.

Watching her, listening to her exclaim over each faded gown and timeworn military uniform she unearthed filled

Sam with a suffocating emotion he wasn't able to identify. For the first time in years he wanted to weep and wasn't sure whether it was from joy or sadness. Although she didn't say so, he knew these weren't merely old clothes to Lisa, but bits and pieces of a heritage she'd never even known she had.

She *was* the child she'd spoken of, the one from a broken home. Applied to Lisa, the overused phrase *broken home* became unbearable in Sam's mind. She was the child without a grandmother—without any family, really, only a father she'd never met and a mother she'd have been better off without. And now here she was, an adult, on her knees searching for fragments of a childhood that never was.

At that moment Sam would have given anything for the power to change history. But he couldn't. He couldn't give Lisa a past, only a future. He wanted to fill her life with all the things it was missing. He wanted to give her love and security and a family. He wanted to insulate her from everything that was ugly and mean in the world so that only beauty would ever touch her again.

She turned to him, laughing and posing behind a heavily ruffled dress of red satin. "Now, *this* is prissy," she declared, and with a wide smile Sam tried to hide the fact that his heart was pounding so hard it was difficult to breathe.

"Do you want to try something?" she offered. "There's a great striped suit here somewhere. Forties vintage, I believe. It's definitely you."

Sam shook his head. "No, you go ahead. I'd rather watch."

"No way, pal. Watching is not work."

"And that is?" he asked, arching his brows and pointing at the dress she still clutched to her body.

"Definitely. It's a tough job, but somebody has to sort through all this great stuff. As long as clothes aren't your field of expertise, why don't you check out those boxes over there?"

Sam knew an order when he heard one, and he ambled over to the stack of cartons she had indicated and settled for watching her surreptitiously while he pretended to work. Actually, exploring the attic had been high on his list of priorities when he'd maneuvered his way into doing odd jobs around here. Funny how quickly a man's priorities could change.

He suddenly thought of Lewis hard at work down at the dock, wondering when the hell his hotshot marine archaeologist was going to show up and no doubt cursing Sam with some very inventive language. As he had often in the past few weeks, Sam felt torn between wanting to be there and wanting to be here. Not that he had much to offer the university crew in his present state of mind. It wasn't that he no longer wanted to find some clue to the *Black Star*'s location if there was a clue somewhere in the house to be found. He just didn't want to have to sneak around behind Lisa's back to do it.

He rather carelessly worked his way through the pile of boxes Lisa had indicated, encountering nothing more interesting than some old *Farmer's Almanac*s, which, on another day, he would have contentedly spent hours poring over. As he was shifting cartons around for better access the toe of his boot caught on a raised floorboard in the corner. The handyman inside him couldn't simply ignore it, and he tried to hammer it back into place with his heel, reluctant to concede that the aged wood was stronger than he.

"Problems?" Lisa called.

"Nothing I can't—" he slammed his heel down hard, wincing as a shock wave of pain streaked up his leg "—handle."

"Doesn't sound that way," she observed from directly behind him. Glancing around, Sam saw that she'd moved closer and was a witness to his immature battle with an inanimate object.

"Doesn't feel that way, either," he admitted, rubbing his thigh. "Maybe I should try using my head."

"No, please," she pleaded, her expression one of exaggerated dismay. "I don't want a bruised groom."

"Cute. I didn't mean use my head to hit it, although that might not be a bad idea. I meant to figure out what's holding it." He crouched down, pulling out his pocketknife and using it to pry the end of the board up. "It's probably just swollen and needs to be shaved down a little, but—"

He broke off as the board gave way enough for them to see the space beneath, and Lisa's quick intake of breath echoed his own surprise. Even in the dim light it was easy to see a box wedged between the floor joists, its lid studded with what looked like diamonds. Black diamonds. Set in the shape of a star.

"Sam, look," Lisa breathed, crouching beside him as he quickly knelt and yanked on the floorboard, splintering the dry wood as he ripped it free. "A black star...do you think it has something to do with...oh, of course it does. It has to."

"Yeah, that would be my guess," he returned, knowing exactly what her excited, disjointed phrases meant. "It seems incredible that anything could have stayed here all these years without anyone knowing about it, though."

"Maybe it didn't."

Reaching for the box, Sam paused to glance at her. "What are you getting at?"

"I'm not really sure," she replied, shrugging. "But what little I've learned about the Bennett family tells me they were a pretty secretive bunch. Maybe they knew the box was here and preferred that no reminders of such a scandalous incident in family history be made public. Or maybe it was just such a well-kept secret for so long that recent generations didn't know of its existence."

"It sure would be nice to have old Miriam around to answer a few questions."

"Maybe." Lisa's tone was softly philosophical. "And maybe we wouldn't like what she had to say. I think I'd prefer to put the pieces together for myself. Now, are you going to open the box or not?"

"I didn't want to move too soon," he replied dryly. "I remember how you almost bit my head off for wanting to read those letters."

"That was different. We didn't find this box hidden beneath the bed of someone who had died very recently."

"Oh. Date of death matters, I take it." He grinned at her, amused, beguiled, so much in love that he ached. "You want to do me a favor? Keep me informed of the rules as we go along. This is getting complicated. Now, is it all right to open the box on Tuesday morning or should—"

He broke off as Lisa's fist connected playfully with his shoulder.

"Just open it," she ordered.

Carefully he removed the box and fiddled with its hammered metal clasp. It still worked, and he lifted the lid to find nothing but a faded, water-stained blue velvet lining.

"Empty," he announced.

Lisa's sigh reflected his own disappointment. "How anticlimactic. Who would go to so much trouble to hide an empty box?"

"Who would leave a will directing that their family home be bulldozed?"

"Do you think insanity is hereditary?"

Laughing, Sam leaned over to kiss her lightly. "I'll risk it."

"Mmm. A man who's not only sexy but brave. What more could I ask for?"

"Well dressed, but I wouldn't press my luck if I were you."

While they joked, he'd been idly examining the box more closely. It was about ten inches long by five wide and three deep, the lid slightly domed. As soon as he ran his fingers across the aged velvet lining the lid, he knew there was something there. It wasn't difficult to peel the fabric loose from the frame. He whistled softly between his teeth as he held up the folded papers that had been concealed beneath.

"Looks like I spoke too soon," he told her.

"What are they?"

Excitement quickened Lisa's tone, just as it had quickened the pulsing of his heart. There looked to be three documents altogether, all of them so brittle with age Sam was afraid they might fall apart in his hands. Laying the others aside, he very slowly and carefully unfolded the one that had been on top.

"A note," he announced, although Lisa had already sidled closer to look over his shoulder.

"'My love,'" she read softly, slowly deciphering the ancient lettering. "'I know you will understand the importance of these documents, and that I can safely entrust them to your care until that time when my life depends on your bringing them to me. A.'" She looked up at Sam. "*A*. For Alexander Brandon, do you suppose?"

He nodded, at once eager and strangely reluctant to examine the other papers, knowing they could well hold both the answer to a riddle from the past and a giant threat to his future. Above all he didn't want his direct involvement with the *Black Star* to be revealed too soon.

"Sam," Lisa prodded, nudging his shoulder. "Hurry up. I'm dying of curiosity."

Even more slowly than before, he unfolded the second paper, recognizing it instantly. "It's a letter of marque from the king of England," he explained, "formally authorizing Brandon to seize unfriendly craft at sea."

Distantly he heard Lisa's chattering response, but he was too caught up in a numbing flood of satisfaction to make sense of her words.

It existed. After all these years of believing and conjecturing, he held in his hands proof positive that the acts for which Alexander Brandon had been condemned were those of a legitimate privateer, not an outlaw. He reached for the final document, his historian's mind already knowing what he would find. This time there were two papers folded together. "French passes from two of the ships Brandon had plundered."

"What are passes?" Lisa asked after he had absently identified them. She tugged impatiently at his sleeve. "Sam, talk to me. What does it all mean?"

He looked up from the papers to find her eyes wide and flashing with excitement, and he smiled at her.

"I'm sorry, Lisa. I guess I got distracted. What it means is that Alex Brandon was telling the truth at his trial when he claimed that Bennett and the others had sponsored his voyage, and that the king himself had approved it with letters of marque. It also proves that, regardless of the fact that two of the ships he plundered turned out to be those of England's allies, when boarded they presented passes stating otherwise. Namely, that they were French ships, making them fair game at the time."

"Why would the ship captains do that? I mean, if he was working for England, and they were allies, why would—"

Sam cut her off, grinning. "Because the open seas weren't quite as civilized back then as they are today. Pirates reigned supreme, and while movies have led us to believe they all flew the skull and crossbones, the truth is they flew whatever flag suited their purposes at the moment. In turn, legitimate ships resorted to doing likewise, running up whatever colors they thought would save their hides. It was common for a ship to carry an assortment of flags and passes. It was all an elaborate, deadly game of bluff." He fingered the papers before him. "Obviously the captains of these two ships guessed wrong when Brandon confronted them."

"So he thought they were the enemy and seized them?"

"More or less. Most often a privateer was only interested in whatever cargo a ship was carrying. He might sink the ship afterward or, if he was in a benevolent mood, leave it to drift without sails. Only if a ship really caught his eye would he commandeer it—like the sloop Brandon claimed and renamed the *Black Star*."

"Because of the box?"

Sam considered her suggestion, then nodded. "That makes sense. He probably spotted the box during one of the raids—it looks like something that would grace a wealthy captain's quarters—and decided it would make a nice souvenir for Elizabeth. The box most likely was his inspiration for renaming the ship."

Lisa released a mild sigh of disappointment, her lips curving downward. "I was sort of hoping the name was inspired by something more romantic, like the color of Elizabeth's eyes."

"I don't know about Elizabeth Bennett's eyes," Sam said, reaching out to stroke her cheek, "but yours could definitely inspire me to name a ship after them. They're beautiful. Not black, but blue. And not cold or hard like diamonds... more like fire. Blue Fire." He shrugged awkwardly. "Not very poetic, I'm afraid."

"I think it's very poetic. Oh, Sam..."

Her eyes glowed as she swayed toward him, and Sam knew that, given another second, she would tell him that she loved him. Fear clutched at his gut, strangling his desire to hear the words. Not now, please, not yet. Let him maintain the safety of this pretense just a little longer, just until Saturday.

"But if I did have occasion to name a ship for you," he said, purposely turning away from her, "I could never bear to sink it the way old Brandon had to sink the *Black Star*."

"You sound so sure that's what happened."

"This proves it. Once and for all." Sam gestured toward the sheets of browned parchment spread before them. "The fact that Alex gave these to Elizabeth for safekeeping proves that he knew ahead of time that he was going to be double-crossed. To protect the ship, he would have sunk it offshore. He had the foresight to know that the proof of his innocence might mysteriously disappear if the authorities got their hands on it, so he delivered it to the safest place he knew—the hands of the woman he loved. That's what he must have been getting at in the letter we saw in Boston, when he wrote that his fate and their future rested *within* the *Black Star*."

As he spoke, the pieces began to slip into place in his head. "It wasn't the ship he was referring to," he explained to Lisa, "but this box. He was trying to tell Elizabeth that these documents were hidden in the box he'd given her, counting on her to bring them to him when the time came."

"Which she obviously didn't do," Lisa pointed out.

Sam thought he detected in Lisa's voice a little disapproval of her distant ancestor.

"Maybe because she wasn't able to," he suggested. He was rewarded by the spark of hope that flared to life in Lisa's eyes. Hell, he sure never figured he'd be defending Elizabeth Bennett. "We know she never received the message Alex sent; maybe she never saw the box, either. Maybe Alex brought it ashore with him the day he returned and her father intercepted it. That certainly would fit in with his scheme. It's a fact that Jonathan Bennett did his damnedest to convince Elizabeth and anyone else who'd listen that Brandon had planned to make himself a respectable place in society by marrying her."

"And you think she believed him?" It was as much accusation as question.

"I did," Sam admitted after a thoughtful pause. "But now that I've met a Bennett woman myself, I'm not so sure. If you're any indication, I'd say Bennett women are a pretty determined bunch, and pretty independent thinkers. If Elizabeth really loved Alex, her father would have had to do some heavy convincing to turn her against him. Personally, I still think that when Alex finally got himself free and got a message to her, Elizabeth was waiting outside there for him with bells on."

Lisa cocked an eyebrow at him. "Bells?"

"Well, maybe not bells exactly. But silk and lace definitely. Something rather like this, I imagine," he added, dropping his voice to a husky murmur as he slipped his fingers inside the neck of her blouse to toy with the strap of the ivory lace bra he'd "helped" her put on earlier. He smiled as he heard her breath catch.

"I see." Her voice was as husky as his. "And do you imagine this often?"

"All the time." Hooking his finger under the strap, he used it to pull her toward him, and placed his mouth against hers, rubbing lightly. "All the time."

With his hand cradling the back of her head, Sam held her still while he kissed her with slow, deep strokes of his tongue. He was debating with his conscience over whether the attic floor was too hard to lay her down on—and losing—when Lisa pulled away to look up at him with a concerned frown.

"Sam, I was just thinking...."

"While I was kissing you?" he demanded.

She shrugged with a matter-of-fact air. "I can't help it. This is important."

"So's my kissing," he felt obligated to grumble. "Go ahead. What's so blasted important?"

"The box. Do you suppose those are real diamonds?"

"They sure ain't cubic zirconium."

"Then do you think it's safe here?"

"It has been for over two hundred years. I definitely think it could have survived through one little kiss."

Lisa laughed. "I'll kiss more freely if I know it's safe. What do you think we should do with it?"

Sam knew exactly what he planned to do with it, but he wasn't ready to tell her, and the resulting guilt accomplished what he'd thought impossible: it distracted him from thoughts of kissing Lisa.

Feeling a sudden resurgence of his sleazy side, he said, "I suppose we could take it to the university and ask them to lock it in the library safe until we come up with a better idea."

"That sounds perfect," Lisa agreed. "But do you suppose you could take it there yourself?"

The fact that that was exactly how he'd prefer to handle it only made Sam feel guiltier. "Sure."

Lisa stood, brushing the dust from her jeans. "Good."

"Would it be overstepping my bounds to ask if this means that you have other plans for the afternoon?"

Grinning, she shook her head. "No, it wouldn't. And yes, I do. Big plans. I'm going shopping for a wedding dress."

"And I'm sorry I asked," he groaned because he knew she expected it.

Carrying the box easily under one arm, as if it didn't represent the physical culmination of an excruciatingly long effort, Sam followed Lisa downstairs, kissing her goodbye on the second-floor landing after duly expressing his confusion over why she had to change clothes just to go try on more clothes. Then he continued on his way to find Lewis Costa and show him this irrefutable proof that the *Black Star* had to lie in the general area they'd been searching, proof that if they kept at it with their computers and ultrasound equipment, the sea would soon have to yield what she had safeguarded for hundreds of years. The *Black Star*.

And that was what Sam wanted, what he had wanted ever since he was a kid and his grandfather had first told him the story of their family's most famous renegade, Captain Alexander Brandon.

So why the hell wasn't he happy about it?

That evening it was Sam who placed the phone call. Although it was late, he had no doubt there would be someone at Roger's office. He only hired workaholics.

"Tillinghast and Howell law offices," said the crisp generic female voice that answered. "May I help you?"

"Yes, this is Sam Ravenal. I'd like to speak with Mr. Tillinghast, please."

"I'm sorry, Mr. Ravenal, you just missed Mr. Tillinghast, and I'm afraid he'll be away for the rest of the week at an out-of-town trial."

Sam broke into a grin. This was too good to be true. No Roger around to lecture him about what a mistake he was making. Maybe it was even an omen that everything was going to work out all right for Lisa and him.

"That's too bad," he responded. "I'll just leave a message for him then. It's not urgent—in fact, don't bother trying to give it to him until he returns next week."

"Whatever you wish, Mr. Ravenal."

"Tell him that regarding that little matter we've been, uh...debating, it's all taken care of. And tell him I'm getting married on Saturday. He'll know the rest."

"All right, I'll leave it on his desk for him. Thank you for calling. And congratulations," the woman added.

"Thanks," he replied. "For everything." He was still grinning as he hung up.

Chapter Twelve

It was late in the week before Lisa paused long enough in the midst of the happily hectic avalanche of details and arrangements her life had suddenly become to acknowledge the totally consuming nature of her love for Sam. It hit her unexpectedly, in one crystalline lucid moment, when she realized how everything else that happened, no matter how important or longed for, paled in comparison.

If not for Sam, the phone call she received on Wednesday from PaperThoughts would have seemed the culmination of all her dreams instead of simply a wonderful bonus. The head of the company's development team phoned to tell Lisa that they loved her proposal and to offer her a generous advance on a contract for enough material to keep her busy for months. Somehow Lisa found words to accept, while her single overriding thought was to find Sam and share the news with him.

Sam's reaction, when he learned that she'd made such a spectacular sale, had been a perfect combination of pride and excitement, delivered with that uniquely cocky grin that

said he'd known all along she could do it. It was much the
same when Lisa reported to him the results of each small,
successful step toward making her idea for the Bennett
Children's Museum a reality.

Lisa had been adamant that, in addition to shopping and
planning for their wedding and honeymoon aboard Sam's
boat, she was going to make time to at least put the museum idea into motion. And she had been pleasantly surprised to discover that Sam agreed wholeheartedly. He'd
even gone so far as to take over the tasks of finding a minister and pianist for the ceremony on Saturday, as well as
arranging for flowers and refreshments, so that Lisa was free
to do a little research on existing children's museums.

Once she felt confident that she knew what she was talking about, she arranged a meeting with the executor of
Miriam's estate, William Fredericks, along with the chairman of the town committee and a representative of the local historical society. Their reaction to the idea was even
more enthusiastic than Lisa had dared to hope. Everyone
involved was overjoyed, not to mention relieved, that she
might have come up with a workable plan to save the Jonathan Bennett House from being destroyed.

Mr. Fredericks volunteered to research the legal feasibil-
ity of having the town formally refuse Miriam's bequest in
order that the historical society might step in and establish
the museum with private funds. The society's representative announced that she planned to start lining up potential
donors immediately, and the discussion ended with Mr.
Fredericks's promise to call a second meeting as soon as he
had something to report.

Their confidence was contagious, and Lisa left the meeting happy, although still plagued by a persistent twinge of
guilt over leading the drive to circumvent Miriam's last
wishes. Her guilt didn't even fully disappear when she
shared her idea with the final—and to Lisa, most important—group of interested parties. Danny, Josh and Pete
obligingly dragged themselves away from the impressive
second tier Sam had added to their fort long enough to lis-

ten to her description of the prospective museum, and they unanimously pronounced the idea to be "*awesome rad.*" Lisa answered their questions and discussed their suggestions about what ought to be included in the museum until her jaw ached, but it was worth it to see the anticipation shining in their eyes.

Everything seemed to be slipping into place with well-oiled precision. Lisa knew it was naive, recklessly so, but she couldn't help feeling as if fate had decided to transform her life into an absolute, unblemished model of utter bliss. Even her conscience pangs over Miriam and her concern that Sam still had not technically admitted to being in love with her didn't dim her happiness.

Lisa had decided not to fret over what Sam said or didn't say, but to let his actions speak for him. And his actions spoke in only the tenderest of terms, telling her more vividly than all the flowery words in all the love sonnets ever written how he felt about her in his heart. Whatever that feeling was, whatever Sam wanted to call it, it was enough for Lisa.

If there was a single slight shadow that danced through her thoughts at odd moments during the week before their wedding, it wasn't so much a worry or a doubt as a puzzle. It had first cropped up the afternoon she and Helen were making the rounds of Newport's most elegant shops in search of the perfect wedding dress. They had found it in a tiny Bellevue Avenue shop that specialized in French designs. Sewn entirely of the palest peach handmade lace overlaying a matching silk slip, it had long narrow sleeves and a high neck. The instant Lisa caught sight of herself in the dressing-room mirror, she knew that even if the price tag represented a big chunk of her advance check, she had to have it.

Helen encouraged the purchase, assuring Lisa that a wedding called for a certain amount of extravagance, and adding that, as luck would have it, she had a cerulean blue dress that would coordinate beautifully. Afterward they had toasted their successful venture with ice-cream sodas at the Newport Creamery.

"Thanks for coming with me, Helen," Lisa said. "I probably would have bought that dress anyway, but without you cheering me on I might have felt a whole lot guiltier about spending so much money on something I'll probably never have occasion to wear again."

"You never know," Helen chided, smiling. "That's exactly what I thought about the blue dress I bought for my son's wedding, and now you've given me a chance to show it off again."

"Before a very small audience," Lisa reminded her.

"I think it's the most romantic thing I've ever heard of." The older woman sighed. "A private wedding in that handsome old parlor, just the bridal couple and their witnesses, some soft piano music... What about pictures?" she suddenly asked, snapping out of her starry-eyed mood. "No matter how small the wedding, you have to take lots of pictures to remember it by when you're old and feeble like me."

Lisa laughed aloud at the notion of the attractive, jaunty woman seated across from her being described as either old or feeble. "Sam has asked one of his friends from campus—a real camera buff—to handle the pictures. And he, along with the minister and the caterer, will make up the entire crowd of seven. I only hope Sam's family and friends will understand that he didn't want to inconvenience them by inviting them on such short notice. We're planning to celebrate with them later, and since I don't know very many people around here to invite anyway..." She trailed off, leaning forward to sip from her straw, then pausing with a thoughtful smile. "On the other hand, I probably ought to invite the entire neighborhood out of sheer appreciation."

"Whatever for?" countered Helen with a trace of the good-natured crankiness Lisa had learned any mention of certain neighbors could provoke.

"Sam," she replied, grinning unabashedly. "After all, if your neighborhood group hadn't gotten together and hired

Roger Tillinghast to find me and bring me here to James-town, I never would have met Sam or—''

Lisa broke off as Helen's slightly confused expression deepened into a frown. She was shaking her head back and forth firmly.

"No, no, my dear," she contradicted Lisa. "You have that all wrong. We never hired any attorney. My goodness, however would we come up with the money for such a thing? Why, just getting some people to chip in a few dollars for a baby gift is like pulling teeth. I remember—"

"But, Helen," Lisa interrupted, for once too impatient to enjoy her friend's reminiscing, "the very first night we met, I mentioned this to you, and you agreed that it was lucky Mr. Tillinghast was able to locate me."

Helen's white head bobbed enthusiastically. "And it was. A blessing for all of us. But I never said we hired him to do it. We're not that organized a group, by any means. We just get together to complain, write letters to our committee-man if the streets aren't plowed to our liking. At Thanks-giving we do always manage to put together a big basket...."

Helen fell silent as she caught sight of Lisa's preoccupied frown. "Perhaps you misunderstood," she suggested in a gentle tone. "Maybe it was Miriam's estate that hired someone to find you."

Lisa shook her head. "No. Mr. Fredericks, the executor of her estate, took pains to tell me that he wasn't involved, that to use funds from Miriam's estate to circumvent her will would be a conflict of interest. Why, I wasn't even sure he'd be able to work with me on the museum idea. I never questioned that it was the neighborhood group who'd hired Mr. Tillinghast. It just made sense that they'd want to stop the destruction of the house at all costs."

"Not if you knew them," Helen remarked drolly. She leaned forward, her lips pursed almost angrily. "Did this Tillinghast fellow tell you he was working for us?"

Lisa peered down at the gold-speckled Formica tabletop, trying to remember exactly what Roger Tillinghast *had* said when he first came to see her in Chicago and during the few phone conversations they'd had since.

"I can't swear that he ever actually came out and said it directly," she admitted finally. "And any checks I've received have been drawn on his office account, so there's no clue there. But I know I didn't just make it all up. That is definitely the conclusion Mr. Tillinghast wanted me to draw."

"I wonder what on earth for?"

"Yes," Lisa agreed softly, looking past Helen to the sidewalk outside and seeing nothing but the questions whirling inside her head. "I wonder."

If there hadn't been so much else going on in her life at the time, Lisa would have been obsessed with putting an end to her wondering. No one else, however, seemed to rank the question of who had paid to find her, very high on the list of priorities.

She got the definite impression that Helen thought Lisa's memory had glitched due to pre-wedding jitters and was simply too kind to say so directly. Sam didn't even glance up from the Yellow Pages listings of musicians when she told him about it that evening. When prodded, he seemed equally content with any of several possibilities: that Lisa had misunderstood whatever Tillinghast had said, that a single concerned neighbor and not a group had hired Tillinghast, or that perhaps Helen wasn't totally reliable about the facts of the situation.

"Call Tillinghast and ask him outright," was Sam's best advice.

Unfortunately, when she tried calling that night, all she got was his answering machine. When she tried again the next morning, all she got was an explanation from his secretary that he would be out of town all week. No, the woman had sniffed in reply to Lisa's polite request, of course she couldn't provide any information about Mr. Tillinghast's client list in his absence. Reluctantly Lisa resigned herself to following Sam's next best advice—to put it out of her mind until after their honeymoon.

It wasn't all that difficult. What was difficult was trying to focus her thoughts for longer than a few seconds on anything that didn't have to do with Sam. He had grudgingly gone along with Lisa's sentimental suggestion that they each sleep alone, in their own beds, until Saturday. She wasn't sure if abstinence, like absence, was supposed to make the heart grow fonder, but she learned firsthand that it could make a person go almost crazy with anticipation. It was with an aching sort of relief that she kissed Sam good-night on Friday, knowing that the next time he took her in his arms it would be as her husband, and that there would never again be any need for restraint. Tomorrow she would be his.

Saturday dawned with such unblemished beauty that Lisa was sorely tempted to move the late-morning ceremony outdoors. However, the mere suggestion sent Helen into a tailspin. If there were any pre-wedding jitters in the house, Lisa decided, listening to her friend sputter about arranging for music outdoors and moving flower arrangements, those jitters were safely contained in her matron of honor.

Lisa felt enclosed in an almost sensual calm as she bathed and dressed, smiling as she donned the slightly scandalous lacy white corset that was her wedding present to Sam. She knew he shared her sizzling anticipation, and that he would appreciate this gift, with its satin garters and thigh-length stockings, far more than a watch or brass bookends.

Closing her eyes, Lisa savored the heavy, melting sensation that gripped her body as she imagined Sam's expression when he slipped off her dress and saw what she was wearing underneath. Her mind provided a series of vivid pictures of the long night ahead. She quickly opened her eyes to check the clock on her dresser. Nine-thirty. It was going to be a long day, too.

The sound of the florist's delivery truck turning into the driveway filled Lisa with relief, and she quickly dispatched Helen to sign for the flowers. At last there would be something for Helen to do besides flutter around the bedroom arranging and rearranging things until Lisa wasn't sure where anything was. With any luck the caterer and pianist would arrive soon. That would involve enough welcoming and organizing to keep Helen busy until it was time for the eleven o'clock ceremony to begin.

Now if only she had something to keep herself busy. Without Helen's bustling, the room suddenly seemed too quiet, too empty. There was only Lisa, all dressed up in her peach confection of a wedding dress, waiting.

She never knew if it was simply an idle impulse that led her to pick up the phone and try Roger Tillínghast's office one last time or some ever-vigilant instinct for self-preservation.

Since it was Saturday, she fully expected to hear his answering machine click on and was startled when instead a familiar gruff voice barked, "Roger Tillinghast here."

"Mr. Tillinghast," she responded, quickly gathering her thoughts. "This is Lisa Bennett. I'm sure you're very busy—"

"Me, busy?" he broke in. "I'd say it's the other way around. I gather congratulations are in order."

"Well, yes, thank you," she murmured, wondering how on earth the news of her small wedding had filtered to him so quickly. Evidently Jamestown was a typical small community. "You're right, today is a rather hectic day for me, but this is important, too. I was wondering if you could tell me who it was who hired you to locate me."

"What?" The word reached her on an incredulous chuckle. "This is a joke, right? Surely Sam told you—"

He broke off, and Lisa clenched the phone tighter without knowing exactly why.

"What does Sam have to do with this?" she asked in confusion.

"Uh. Whew. You know, Lisa, you've caught me off guard here. That is to say, without my notes. Didn't we discuss all this when I met with you in Chicago?"

"I'm sure we did, but you hit me with so many surprising revelations all at once that I'm a little hazy on some things. So maybe you wouldn't mind refreshing my memory on this one little point."

"All right," he agreed after a hesitation Lisa was certain she hadn't imagined. "As I told you, the neighbors were all very worried that the will would be enacted as written, the obvious result being the establishment of an unsightly paved lot blemishing their—"

"Please, stop," she ordered, interrupting his plunge into lawyer-speak. "Are you saying that the neighbors paid you to find me? That you are, in fact, working for them?"

Another, longer pause followed.

"Not exactly," he conceded finally.

"Then exactly who is paying you?" Lisa demanded. "And paying me, too, for that matter?"

"Lisa, I'm afraid I'm not at liberty to say." Roger Tillinghast's tone was quieter than it had been, but the note of implacability in it was unmistakable.

"I have a right to know who wanted me to come here badly enough to shell out good money for it," Lisa snapped.

Lisa kneaded her temple with her free hand, half wishing she hadn't followed the impulse to make this call today. Already she could feel her armpits dampening. Outside she heard the sound of Sam's bike roaring to a halt, and part of her wanted to hang up and rush across the room to catch a glimpse of him through the window. But she didn't, and right then something deep inside her recognized that what she wanted and didn't want to happen had ceased to matter. Just like in the old Mousetrap game she'd played as a kid, the silver ball had dropped, and events in her life had been set into motion. All she could do now was hang on tight.

"You may well have a right to know," Roger Tillinghast was droning in her ear. "But my professional obligation is to my client first, and to his right to remain anonymous if he chooses to do so. If you want to pursue your rights in this matter, I'm afraid you'll have to engage another attorney."

"You mentioned Sam a minute ago," Lisa countered. "Sam Ravenal. At least tell me what made you think he might have told me anything about this. Has he contacted you?"

It was the only explanation Lisa could think of, and it was like Sam to do such a thing, knowing how concerned she'd been about this lately. But then, why hadn't he told her whatever he'd found out?

"I did mention Sam, so I guess I should confirm that he's been in touch with me."

"And that's it?" she demanded. "You can't tell me what you told him?"

"I'm afraid not. Listen, Lisa," he added, a strange awkwardness in his tone, "off the record, I urge you to forget about this for a while. Especially today. I'm sure it's all going to work out for the best. Look at it this way: whoever hired me to find you did you a favor by putting you in touch with your past."

"That's not the point. I don't like being manipulated."

"I'm sorry you feel that you were."

"How else should I feel? Someone I don't even know has been paying me to live in this house and letting me believe I was doing it to help out a group of concerned neighbors—"

"Not to mention helping out yourself," Roger interjected. "Admit it, Lisa, you never made any secret about the fact that your motives in accepting my offer weren't exactly altruistic."

"At least I was honest about my motives!" Lisa exploded. "Which is more than I can say for you or your mystery client. Who knows what your motives really were?"

"They weren't sinister, if that's what's worrying you. The man involved had his reasons, and they really had nothing to do with you other than that your existence was a means to an end—namely, stalling any immediate demolition plans that might have arisen."

"So your client is a man," Lisa concluded triumphantly.

"Perhaps," he countered with no noticeable loss of composure at having made the verbal slip.

"Why can't you just tell me his name? You obviously were willing enough to discuss my business with Sam."

"And all I can do is suggest that you do the same, Lisa. Talk to Sam."

Suddenly Lisa felt numb. She slowly lowered the phone, wishing she could think of some way to misunderstand what had been written between the lines of Roger Tillinghast's evasive comments. Without knowing how she got there, she was across the room, frantically tugging the window open to get a breath of fresh air.

The truth was so obvious, Lisa wondered if it hadn't been lurking in her subconscious for days now, only to be smothered and submerged by the part of her that had its stubborn sights set on a happy ending. Of course, it had to be Sam. As she acknowledged it to herself, the muscles along her spine tightened almost painfully. Who else but Sam was interested enough in this house or the Bennett family history to go to so much trouble and expense? He had been interested from the moment they met. In fact, even before that, she thought, remembering how he'd immediately recognized the name on the house.

But even as her mind accepted the truth, another part of her fought to resist it. After all, if Sam was the obvious answer, he was also the most impossible, or at least the most illogical. There was simply no reason for him to have kept his involvement—if there was any—a secret from her. What could he possibly stand to gain?

Certainly not the house. He knew she didn't want the house even on the slim chance that she had some legal right to it. In fact, his support for the museum project, which would terminate any potential claim she might have on the property, had been instantaneous, and, Lisa was certain, genuine. And what else was there? At the time Roger Tillinghast had first approached her, she hadn't had enough in the way of cash or future prospects to catch a fortune hunter's eye.

She took another deep breath and found it came a little easier. No, there was absolutely no way that Sam could be the mystery man Roger Tillinghast was protecting. She was certain of that with her whole heart.

Yet she also knew her own insecurities, and she knew that she could not walk into that living room and promise to love and trust and be faithful to him for the rest of her life until she heard the words from his own mouth first.

She opened the bedroom door and stepped into the shadowy hallway. Of course her sudden, superstitious need for his personal reassurance was crazy. As crazy as walking into the park thinking that if she didn't look until she sat down, the Whittler and her other Muses would be there. Or that if she scratched the blocks on a lottery ticket in a certain order the ticket would be a winner. But she had a superstitious bent, and it told her that if she rummaged up the courage to go down and confront Sam right now, everything would be all right.

Carefully she held on to the rail as she descended the steps in the too-high heels the same shade of peach as her dress. She could already see the look Sam would give her when she asked him about this. His mouth would slant into that cocky smile, and his eyes would touch her with gentle sarcasm.

"Sure I hired him to fetch you, Lise," he would tell her. *"How else could a guy like me hope to find himself a wife? Now, you want to hustle back upstairs like a good girl and make a proper bride's entrance for me?"*

And she would. But first she had to hear him say it.

Everyone had already arrived, and Lisa was a little startled to see how crowded the house could feel with only seven people rushing around in it. Of course, the flowers easily took up as much room as the wedding cast. She smiled at the sight and smell of hundreds of red and white roses nestled amid untamed sprays of baby's breath. Leave it to Sam to turn her world into a fantasy.

A quick glimpse into the dining room showed the table cloaked in peach linen—Helen's influence, no doubt—and laden with silver and crystal. Candles had been lit, making the heavily draped rooms seem to glow, and Lisa's gaze instinctively sought and found the man who was the most beautiful part of the entire scene. He stood on the far side of the living room.

Against all his stubborn claims, Sam was wearing a tux.
The black trousers and jacket emphasized the lithe strength
of his body, and the pleated shirt was startlingly white
against his brown skin. It was the most gorgeous tux Lisa
had ever seen on the most gorgeous man she had ever seen,
and her heart ached with happiness when he glanced up and
saw her and smiled. Without hesitation he headed in her
direction, his eyes sweeping over her, gleaming with more
dark luster than the black satin of his lapels.

At the same time, Lisa felt frantic fingers plucking at her
lace sleeve and heard Helen's anxious voice. "Oh, my dear,
you can't come down here now. The groom must never see
the bride before the ceremony begins. It's bad luck."

Lisa didn't even attempt to explain to Helen that it might
have proved worse luck if she had stayed closeted in her
room, struggling to suppress this insane doubt about
whether the man to whom she was about to pledge her heart
and soul was a liar.

"Now you turn yourself around and march right back
upstairs," Helen chided.

"In a moment, Helen," Lisa promised without taking her
gaze off Sam, who was now only several feet away. "First I
need to ask Sam something about what Mr. Tillinghast told
me."

The instant the words were out, they ceased to be true.
Lisa watched the shadow flicker across Sam's face as he
heard what she said to Helen. She saw the stricken look he
quickly masked and realized that she no longer had to ask.
She knew now whom Roger was protecting, even if she still
didn't know why. And she knew that no matter what she
asked and he answered, she was never going to walk down
those stairs into Sam's arms for her happy ending.

She asked anyway, mostly because she didn't know how
to halt this chain reaction that suddenly seemed to have the
horsepower of a Mack truck hurtling directly at her. Her
mouth was dry, her palms slick as she tipped her chin up to
meet Sam's opaque emerald gaze.

"Did you hire Roger Tillinghast to find me?" she demanded.

"Yes."

"And you're the one who's been paying me to stay here?"

"Yes."

"And that first day, at the park, and then back here afterward..." Her voice caught, and she thought she saw a flicker of pain in Sam's eyes. But then, it was probably only annoyance at being found out. "All along, right from start, you knew who I was, didn't you?"

"Yes."

Yes and yes and yes. Three minuscule words. As if that were precisely the number of ax swings needed to send Lisa's world crashing, she felt it crumble around her.

"Get out," she ordered, momentarily stunned that such a feral-sounding growl had emanated from her. And then she felt nothing except cold, as if a giant wave of frigid emptiness had surged from deep inside, spreading to claim and insulate every part of her.

"Lisa, it's not what you think," Sam said, stepping toward her.

As desperately as if he were fire and she a bundle of TNT, Lisa lurched away from him until her back was up against the hallway wall. She put her hands up in front of her, beyond caring that she must appear demented to the others, who had clustered in a semicircle behind Sam. They looked bewildered and concerned.

"Lisa..."

Sam's voice had gone husky with emotion, but all Lisa saw was his hand lifting to cup her cheek. Involuntarily, she cowered closer to the wall. He stopped dead in his tracks. A shocked, almost horrified, expression appeared on his face. It was as if her instinctive shrinking from his touch had driven home to him how deep her mistrust and revulsion ran, and Lisa felt a bitter shot of satisfaction penetrate her numbness.

"I think Lisa and I need some time alone to talk," she heard Sam say to the others. "Maybe it would be better if the rest of you did leave."

"Not them," Lisa cried, "you! You're the one I want to get out of here and leave me alone! I'm not going to talk to you, and I'm certainly not going to listen to any more of your lies. Everyone else might as well stay and enjoy the party as planned...or rather, almost as planned. In case you haven't already guessed, folks, there isn't going to be any wedding."

But Helen had already shepherded the others off through the kitchen, and even before Lisa heard the back door close behind them, Sam was reaching for her. Sidestepping only succeeded in backing her into the corner by the stairs, and all she could do was swing her arms wildly as his closed around her.

"No! Get away from me!" she snarled, trying to kick out at him, only to discover that his body was as unyielding as a blanket of steel. "Don't touch me! You're never going to touch me again!"

"The hell I'm not," Sam growled, running his lips over her face, coming perilously close to her mouth. Lisa felt tears of frustration wash down her cheeks.

"I don't want this," she moaned. "I don't want you touching me."

"Then you'd better make a choice, pal," he warned in a soft, implacable tone. "Because I'm either going to talk to you or touch you. One way or another I'm going to break down this wall you're trying to put up between us."

"If there's a wall between us, it's a wall of lies!" cried Lisa. "And you put it there!"

Sam dropped his hands to his sides and stared at her. "You're absolutely right. And I've had to live with that and regret it every day since we met."

"Sure. You just never regretted it enough to do anything about it."

"I was doing something," Sam shot back. "The only thing I could do. In another hour you would have been mine. Then I could have told you the truth and made everything all right."

Lisa was caught off guard by the wistful catch in his gravelly voice. She glared at him, confusion mingling with her bitterness. "Are you out of your mind? You've been lying to me and manipulating me for weeks now, and you thought that if you waited until after we were married to tell me the truth, everything would magically be all right?"

"Not magically," Sam corrected in a suddenly weary voice.

"Well, believe me, *pal*," Lisa sneered, deriving great satisfaction from slamming her fist hard against his chest. "It would have taken magic to make this work once I found out what you'd done. Granted, you never made any false promises about loving me, but haven't you ever heard of another little thing most people consider basic to any kind of marriage—honesty? Or honor?"

"When push comes to shove, where you're concerned I guess I don't have much honor. I only have this great big need to have you in my life, and I would have done anything I had to do to keep you there."

"Anything?" Lisa echoed dazedly, stunned by the direction his defense was taking. She didn't know how she had expected him to react. Maybe with sarcasm or a glib denial, but certainly not with this uncharacteristic, almost heart-wrenching display of emotion.

"Yeah, anything," he confirmed, his smile a fleeting, self-mocking twist of his lips. "Anything short of violence, that is, and not very far short of it, at that."

Lisa rested her head back against the wall as the mindless rage of a few minutes ago seemed to drain from her body in a rush, and along with it all her energy. She had to take a few deep breaths to pull herself together enough to speak.

"I really don't understand what's happening," she revealed in a ragged whisper. "Or what any of this means."

"Don't you?" Sam countered. His smile was gentle, and any cynicism in it was directed at himself. "Funny how when it comes to the most important matters in my life, I seem to have trouble making myself clear to you. You didn't understand when I was proposing, and you still don't understand now that I love you."

Sam saw her reel with shock, and he was struck anew by how colossal a mess he'd made of all this. Could she truly not have guessed how much he loved her?

She gazed at him, her blue eyes wet and anguished. "What?"

"I said I love you."

"I know what you said," she shot back impatiently. "For your information, I even knew that you loved me. I just didn't think you knew it."

"Didn't know it? How could I not know it when I love you so damn much I ache all the time?" This time Lisa didn't flinch when he lifted his hand to touch her face, but she still stiffened, and Sam felt even that slight rejection like a blade in his heart.

"Then why did you say you *didn't* love me?" she demanded, her tone so injured it made Sam wince.

"So that you would believe me when I finally did tell you." He didn't blame her for narrowing her eyes and peering at him with cautious uncertainty. But he was determined to tell the absolute truth, no matter how twisted and asinine it made him sound.

"You told me you didn't love me so that I would believe you when you finally got around to telling me you did love me?" she repeated slowly.

Sam shrugged. "Yeah, right. I—"

"No," she interrupted, shaking her head and putting her palms up as if to push him away, even though he had already taken pains to move back to an unthreatening distance. "I don't want to hear it. I don't think I can handle any of this right now. I feel sick."

He grabbed her arm, pulling her into the living room despite her stiff attempt to free herself. "Then come sit down. Have a drink. But we have to talk."

"Why?" she demanded as he deposited her on the sofa and stepped into the dining room to get her a cup of coffee.

A shot of caffeine was probably the last thing her nerves needed right now, but it was either that or champagne, and somehow it struck Sam as an inappropriate time to pop a cork.

"Because talking—and listening—is the only way we're going to get this straightened out," he told her.

"Oh, no, hold on." The icy tinkle of her laugh made Sam's blood run cold. "Let's get that straight first; there is no way this will ever be 'straightened out,' as you so delicately put it. You can explain, you can apologize; the way I'm feeling right now, you can probably even force me to listen, but understand this..." Her eyes bore into his like blue-black icicles. "It is over for us."

"Never," Sam swore on a harsh breath. He'd been feeling remorseful, and plenty anxious, but now it was desperation biting at his soul. She laughed again, softly, and a trickle of nervous sweat ran along his spine beneath the fancy starched linen shirt. "Look, I know I was wrong, that I really screwed things up, but it will never be over between us. I love you, Lisa. And you love me."

Lisa's head moved back and forth, her expression growing more removed, more coolly controlled by the second, while inside, Sam felt all the threads of his logic and restraint snapping one by one.

"I *thought* I loved you," she corrected. "Just as I *thought* you loved me. When actually all that happened was that I made a mistake and you used me. End of story."

"Bull."

"Thanks for that insightful opinion. Now, if you don't mind, I think I'll go upstairs and change into something less depressing."

She made a move to get up, and Sam, a little more roughly than he intended, shoved her back against the cushions, then came down close beside her to see that she stayed put.

"I do mind."

"I guess so," she concurred coldly. "Well, I was right about one thing so far: you can indeed force me to sit here and listen. But then, that's your style, isn't it? Forcing people, manipulating them into doing what you want, using them."

"For what!" Sam shouted, feeling the whole situation slipping out of his control. "Just what the hell do you think I used you for, Lisa?"

She glared at him in silence.

"This house?" he suggested. "That would be the logical assumption, except that we both know that the house might never be yours legally. Besides, I've been pushing you to get going on the museum idea before the wedding precisely so there would be no question afterward that I was after the house."

Lisa's expression eased only slightly as she turned away from him, but it was enough to stop the frantic churning of Sam's guts. Now they simply churned slowly. He watched as she folded her arms across her chest and stared silently at the opposite wall.

"So what else could it be?" he continued in a quieter tone. "Money? Can we agree that it would have been an exercise in absurdity for me to pay you to come here so that I could steal your fortune?" Something resembling a smile flickered across her lips before they resumed their tightly drawn stance. "Agreed?"

"I suppose," she conceded without looking at him.

"Good. And along the same line, I swear to you, Lisa, that I had no idea you were working on a card proposal that might earn you a great deal of money in the future. All I knew was that you were the closest thing Miriam Bennett had to a legal heir and that your bank balance was low enough that Roger and I figured you could be persuaded to come here on a financial basis. I know you have no cause to take my word for it, so if you want I can show you my own bank statements, stock certificates, real estate deeds. I made all the money I'll ever need on that Florida Keys salvage job. I wasn't after your money, Lisa."

She shifted in her seat, shrugged and finally glanced at him with a quick nod of agreement. Sam's pulse slowed another beat.

"I guess that leaves sex," he announced softly.

Lisa's teeth caught her bottom lip, revealing that she wasn't as unmoved by all this as she was pretending to be.

"What can I say?" Sam asked. "I shouldn't have to say a damn thing, of course. You should know that I wasn't using you when we made love, that it was something so much more than sex. But if you don't know that, then just think about it. You're beautiful, Lisa, but do you really think I'd pay to bring a stranger all the way here from Chicago to have sex with her?"

Again that quick, encouraging smile, this time slanted a few degrees more his way. "I suppose not."

"And even if I were that desperate," he added, "wouldn't I have gone about things a little differently? Hell, I'm not a total misfit. If I'd wanted to seduce you, I would have brought you candy and flowers, not Italian cold cuts. The truth is, I was doing my damnedest not to seduce you, not to mislead you any more than I already had, not to lie to you."

"Then why did you!" Lisa cried, spinning in the seat to face him. "Why the hell did you?"

It required all of Sam's diminished self-control not to take her in his arms. He looked at the tear tracks down her cheeks and the trace of mascara they had carried to the bodice of the beautiful dress she'd worn to give herself to him, and his heart broke all over again. He'd thought it was safer to wait until her feelings were fully involved before telling her the truth, but he'd been wrong. Now, or an hour after the wedding had taken place, it wouldn't have mattered. This wasn't safer, it wasn't easier, it wasn't right. No explanation, no excuse would ever justify causing her this pain.

"Why, Sam?" she prodded. "Just tell me why."

"Because I was afraid."

Chapter Thirteen

Lisa eyed him with a mingling of surprise and suspicion. "Afraid of what?"

"Afraid of losing you," Sam answered truthfully, fully prepared for the skeptical arching of her brows. "Will you at least give me a chance to explain, and promise to listen with an open mind? And an open heart?"

"I'll listen," Lisa responded, both her tone and the delicate lift of her shoulder regally noncommittal.

That was still progress from a few minutes ago, and Sam decided not to press her on the small points.

"When Roger Tillinghast went to Chicago to see you," he said, feeling as if he were beginning to pick his way across a long mine field, "he may have created a false impression about who had sent him, but not the reason why. Miriam Bennett's will received quite a bit of attention in the local press, drawing a variety of comments and opinions from the American Civil Liberties Union and other legal hotshots, and all I wanted was the quickest, most foolproof way to block any misguided attempt to see the terms of the will ex-

ecuted. It was actually my mother's brainstorm to try to lo-
cate a legal heir in the hope that it might void the entire will.
I asked Roger to handle it because he was located here in
Rhode Island, and because he's an old friend."

"Your mother was involved in this?" Lisa groaned, covering her cheeks with her hands as he'd seen her do before
when she was embarrassed. "You mean even the other day
when we were in her office, your mother was aware that you
were using me in some grand scheme that I knew nothing
about?"

"No," countered Sam quickly. "She didn't. Unless she
made the connection with the name Bennett on her own,
which I doubt. For one thing, I'm not sure I even mentioned whose will it was during the brief phone conversation we had on the subject. And that was weeks before I met
you."

He dared to rest his fingertips on her shoulder, soothed
slightly by the soft, feminine feeling of the lace and the hint
of warmth beneath. "Lisa, this wasn't some grand scheme
in which everyone was in on the joke except you. Believe me,
I would never subject you to a thing like that for any reason."

Lisa's eyes flashed an accusing challenge as she drawled,
"Not even if you were afraid of losing me?"

Sam considered her question long and hard before shaking his head in denial. "No, not even then. If this hadn't
been such a private matter between you and me, I somehow
would have found the courage to tell you the truth earlier. I
only wish to God that's what I had done."

"That makes two of us," remarked Lisa. "So on your
mother's professional recommendation, you hired Roger
Tillinghast, and he found me and persuaded me to come to
Jamestown. The question is, why? I know you have an interest in history and all, but why would you take it upon
yourself to go to the trouble and expense of trying to save
this house?"

"On the off chance that tucked away in here somewhere
was a clue to the location of the *Black Star*."

"The *Black Star*?" A quizzical frown pulled the edges of Lisa's mouth down. "You mean the ship itself?"

Sam gave a reluctant nod. "Brace yourself, pal. I think this may be the part where it's going to get worse before it gets better. Lisa, I told you I'm doing some consulting for the university. What I didn't mention was that specifically I'm consultant to a team of graduate students from the Oceanography department trying to salvage the *Black Star*."

"You bastard," Lisa spat. "You couldn't have just told me that?"

"I could have, sure, right at the start. I told you, I wish I had. But I didn't. And then all of a sudden it was too late."

"But why didn't you?" she demanded, her usually soft voice taking on a clipped, angry cadence. "I'm not talking about the first day we met, either. I mean even before that. When I first arrived in Jamestown, why didn't you just knock on the door and introduce yourself instead of getting Roger to lie for you, and then setting up that elaborate farce at the park?"

"Because in the beginning I never planned to have so much personal contact with you. I figured the less you knew about the *Black Star*, the better. I didn't know who Lisa Bennett was or what she was like, and I was afraid she might start taking this heir business a little too seriously if she got it into her head that there might be more than a ramshackle old house at stake. Mention the word *treasure*, and some people start acting pretty weird."

"Yes," Lisa agreed, staring directly at him, "I've noticed."

"Ouch. I deserved that. Anyway, I didn't want anything to complicate the salvage attempt, so I decided that as long as you were already willing to stay here and keep the house standing, in case, as a last resort, we decided to search it for clues, I would just leave well enough alone."

"What do you mean, 'as a last resort'? I thought that was your reason for wanting the house standing in the first place."

"Right. *My* reason," Sam emphasized. "Not an official strategy by any means. Most of the others working on the search are pure scientists who have a lot more faith in their sonar readings than in any old scraps of paper I might turn up. Although they all agreed that those documents we found in the attic confirm our theory that she's nearby, probably resting beneath the sand only a few miles out."

He lifted his shoulders in a slightly apologetic shrug. "There was really no pressing need for me to come around here, except that I started to get this real itch to see what Elizabeth Bennett's descendant looked like. I hung around outside one day and followed you to the park. After that I couldn't stop myself. I had to get closer so I could hear your voice and see if you could possibly smell as good as I imagined you would." He slanted her a sheepish smile. "You smell even better, by the way."

"Thanks." The look accompanying the crisp rejoinder was about as friendly as barbed wire.

"Even though I thought you were uppity, all show and no heart, I was hooked. I started telling you about Alex and Elizabeth just to watch your reaction. I kept wondering if your facial expressions, your mannerisms, even that haughty-as-hell way you toss your hair back, were like hers."

"Quite the dedicated consultant, aren't you?" Lisa inquired in a taunting voice.

"I told you, this really had nothing to do with the salvage attempt."

"Then why the sudden fascination with a woman who's been dead for almost three centuries?"

"There was nothing sudden about it," Sam revealed. "I've been fascinated by the story of Elizabeth and Alex ever since my grandfather first told it to me when I was five."

She shook her head in a gesture of dismissal. "Really, Sam, I can see how a five-year-old, or even a ten-year-old, might be beguiled by the romantic tale of a pirate, but you're hardly—"

"Not just *any* pirate," Sam interjected. "Our own family pirate."

Lisa peered at him as if filtering that remark through her head. Then her eyes narrowed, and her head tilted to one side. "You can't be serious. You're not saying . . . no."

Sam grinned as she trailed off with another, more decisive shake of her head. He nodded. "I'm afraid so. My Great-Grandmother Costigan's maiden name was . . ."

"Brandon," Lisa said along with him, her tone soft, incredulous.

"You got it. I'm as much a descendant of Alexander Brandon as you are of Elizabeth Bennett."

"Unbelievable," she breathed.

"A twist of fate, I'd say."

"You mean twisted fate, don't you?" she countered sharply. "Twisted and manipulated, and all by you. You brought me here, you set me up, and then you didn't even have the basic decency to tell me what was going on."

"I've explained why. I had no idea what your reaction would be to the news about the *Black Star*."

"Oh, please, Sam. What could it be? The fact that some distant ancestor I didn't even know existed might have run off with the ship's captain hardly gives me any legal claim to whatever's on board."

"One would think not, but there are all kinds of greedy lawyers willing to bring all sorts of crazy claims for a quick buck. I didn't want to risk delaying the salvage project because I had indulged my . . . curiosity."

"I'll just bet you didn't. And I'll bet a potentially very profitable project it is."

"Not for me," Sam asserted quietly, using his most careless smile to conceal the disproportionate pain her accusation brought him. "The project is being funded by a combination of federal grant and private donation—including my own—with the stipulation that everything recovered be divided between the university and the Smithsonian Institute."

"Well..." Lisa shifted uncomfortably in the small amount of space he'd allowed her between him and the arm of the sofa. "I think that's very commendable. And you should have known that's what I would think."

"How could I have?" Sam shot back on a wave of exasperation. "I didn't even know you at the time. And you never made any bones about the fact that your reason for accepting the offer to come here was strictly mercenary. You kept insisting you had no interest in your past and no emotional attachments to anything remotely labeled *family*. How could I know for sure what you would or wouldn't do for money?"

She slanted him a withering glance before saying, "I meant after that, after you did get to know me better..." Her chin rose defiantly. "*Much* better. You still kept all this from me—who you were, what you were working on, the fact that it was you who had hired Roger... even this past week when you knew how much that was bothering me."

"I know, I know," he admitted, shoving his fingers through his hair. His head was beginning to throb. "I should have told you right after that first day, instead of wheedling my way further into your life by hanging around the place to do repairs." He sighed. "You're going to have to know sooner or later, so...the fact is, that was another piece of creative thinking. I never spoke to Fredericks about a job, never got paid for doing any of it."

He ought to be getting used to that partly injured, partly resentful look that turned Lisa's blue eyes almost black and made her soft mouth twitch slightly at the corners, but he wasn't. Sam knew that if he lived to be a hundred and was lucky enough to spend all those years with Lisa, he would never get used to hurting her, never stop feeling the reflection of her pain like daggers in his soul.

"I'd thought," he went on, breaking the awful silence between them, "that once we knew each other better it would be easier to tell you that I'd been less than honest with you up front. You see, I knew you were still raw from your marriage, ready to think the worst about any man who slipped up even a millimeter, and I hoped you'd gradually grow to trust me. But the more I learned about you, the more impossible it became to tell you. I came to understand just how much damage that bastard had done to you with his lies and his cheating."

Lisa turned away, anguish etched in each tightly drawn feature. If it was anything other than their future at stake, Sam would have backed off, shut up, done anything not to hurt her any more than he already had. But it wasn't anything else.

"I kept finding out bits and pieces about your childhood," he said quietly. "A little about your mother, and some of your experiences with men in college. I decided you didn't have a hell of a lot of reason to trust people's motives, and I didn't want you to think of me as just another user. Because I knew that if you thought that, you'd bolt, and no amount of talking or begging would ever get you back."

"You were right," she said.

"That's why I had to get you to marry me." He didn't pause long enough to let her deliver the scathing response her expression threatened. "The idea had been drifting around in my head for days, and I kept telling myself it was idiotic."

"Very astute of you."

"I tried not to let things happen between us, Lisa. I kept telling myself that being friends was better than nothing, that it couldn't be anything more for us, even when I knew deep down that it already was. Why the hell else would I be hanging around here fixing leaky faucets and cleaning out gutters just to be near you?"

"I wouldn't even venture a guess."

"There wasn't any other reason, Lise," he insisted. "That's why spending the day in Boston with you was the stupidest thing I could have done. But then, I guess I knew all along how it would end, and that's why I suggested it."

He reached out and caught her jaw in his cupped palm, applying gentle pressure to force her to meet his gaze. "After we made love, I realized that I was in this even deeper than I'd thought, in every way possible. That's why I left before you woke up. Because I knew that even I wasn't enough of a bastard to look you in the eye in the morning and go on lying to you after what we had shared.''

Suddenly restless, Sam got to his feet and paced across the room as he spoke. He wasn't sure if it was this stupid bow tie, or the snug cummerbund at his waist, or just the situation, but he felt chained, weighted down.

"Of course," he continued, "at the same time that my feelings for you were skyrocketing, so were the stakes. And the risks. I knew that if I told you everything then, you would conclude that I'd just wanted to get you into the sack. So I did some hard thinking, and suddenly that idiotic idea about marriage didn't seem so idiotic. In fact, it seemed like the only way out for us. I figured that if we were married, it would be a lot harder and more time-consuming for you to get rid of me, and just maybe I'd have long enough to make you understand that I never meant to hurt you, never meant for this to get so complicated.''

Moving back to where Lisa was sitting in unreadable silence, Sam crouched down in front of her and took both her hands firmly in his. "So I proposed, but I didn't tell you the complete truth even then, which is that I love you more than I ever thought it was possible to love someone. I held back because I never wanted you to think that I had said those words to you with less than my whole heart and total honesty. But I'm saying them now. I love you, Lisa. No matter what sort of machinations on my part brought us together and got us this far, I love you. And I want to spend the rest of my life with you.''

He shrugged, willing her to say something, to say *Yes, that's what I want, too.* His bag of tricks and explanations was empty. Now it was up to Lisa. He held her hands tighter, as if he could squeeze from her the response he craved.

"I know it's crazy, but does any of this make sense to you at all?'' he asked finally.

"I think so." She released a slow sigh, nodding. "Yes. Yes, it does. I can understand why you might have thought I'd overreact when I found out...."

Sam wanted to go on hearing that she understood and forgave him, but even more he wanted to take her in his arms and feel it. He stretched to his feet. Leaning over her, he reached for her with his hands and his mouth at the same time. Lisa's expression instantly turned panicked, and she plastered herself against the back of the sofa much as she had the hallway wall earlier, stopping Sam dead in his tracks.

"No, Sam, wait. I said I understood, but..."

"But what?" he demanded with sudden heat. The desperation that had started to recede was back, clawing at him more fiercely than ever. "But what?" he repeated. "Either you understand and you forgive me, or you don't."

"I do understand," Lisa insisted, her voice barely audible and strangely rough around the edges. "And I guess when I calm down a little, I'll be able to forgive you, too. But that doesn't change what I said earlier. It's over for us, Sam."

He eyed her in shocked disbelief, then laughed harshly. "And as I said earlier, bull. My mistake was trying to talk this out with you when you're obviously not in a rational state of mind. I should have followed my first instincts."

He had pulled back a minute ago when she'd told him to wait, but he hadn't stepped aside, and now he completed the move he had been about to make then. Bringing her down beneath him on the sofa, he stretched out on top of her, anchoring her with his weight and twisting his hands through her hair to hold her still for his kiss. Lisa whimpered as his mouth took possession of hers, and her body strained against his. Desperation made his tongue rough as it drove past her teeth, pumping into her mouth with a deliberately demanding rhythm, seeking the acquiescence of her body as if that would signal his reclaiming of her heart, as well.

The victory he sought came quickly, revealed in the sudden quieting of Lisa's struggles and the way her fingers clung lightly to his shoulders. But no matter how good he felt about the proof that he could still incite her passion, it was a hollow victory. It brought a bitter taste to his mouth even before he realized that the salty flavor of their kiss came from Lisa's tears. He tore his mouth from hers, pulling back to look at her.

"Ah, no, Lise, don't cry. Please."

"Why shouldn't I cry? Everything's ruined. It's over." She squeezed her eyes tightly shut, but tears still flowed down her cheeks faster than Sam's mouth could brush them away.

"Shh, baby, nothing's over. I'm going to see to that."

Lisa sniffled, pressing the back of her hand to her eyes, and then opening them to look up at him with a long, shuddering sigh.

"Sam, you asked me to understand the way you felt and what you thought you had to do," she said. "Now you have to do the same for me. Can't you see that there's no way I could marry you now?"

Sam arrowed to a sitting position, shaking his head the whole time. Lisa drew herself up stiffly beside him.

"No. No, I don't see why. You love me," he declared almost belligerently. The quiet certitude in her voice when she said she could never marry him had scared him more than her anger or cool scorn could have.

"Yes, I do."

"And I love you."

"Either me or Elizabeth."

"What!" he exclaimed, his expression part grin, part frown. "That's ridiculous!"

"Is it? I listened to you, Sam, and I think maybe I understood even more than you intended me to. All this talking and sparring we did about Elizabeth and Alexander the past few weeks—it wasn't simply a game to you. It's an obsession."

"That's—"

"Obvious," Lisa declared, overriding his protest. "You said yourself it started when you were a child—only five, for heaven's sake—and I can't help but think that one way or another it's driven you ever since."

"Lisa..."

"You did, after all, choose to become a marine archaeologist. Not a dentist, not a fireman, not a—" she threw up her hands "—skydiver."

"Maybe because the sight of blood makes me queasy, I'm allergic to smoke, and I'm afraid of heights. Besides which, I happen to love the ocean, the power and the mystery of it. That doesn't mean I can't love you. More."

Shimmying backward to avoid his caress, Lisa said, "No, it doesn't, provided you could separate the two. But in this case, I'm not sure you have. I can't help wondering if thoughts of me and Elizabeth aren't so entwined in your mind that what you love is a combination of us, or maybe just some nonexistent woman you made up long ago."

"That," Sam informed her, "is patently absurd."

And it was. Yet he had a gut-level fear that, simply because it was so absurd a suggestion, there was no way to effectively fight it. All he knew was that he had to try.

"Lisa, I admit that the legend of Alex and Elizabeth has always interested me. All right, all right," he conceded in the face of her quickly curled lip. "It fascinated me. Ever since I heard about the *Black Star* it's been my dream to find her... although I want you to know that my decision to become a marine archaeologist had as much to do with the fact that I was raised on the water as with the pirate hanging on my family tree. Anyway, no matter how fascinated I ever was, I'm not so romantic or irrational that I confuse fact with fantasy. It's you I fell in love with, Lisa, not my image of Elizabeth or some figment of my imagination. You have to believe that."

"I believe that you believe it," she said almost regretfully. "But it's something I have no way of being certain of. If we married, I would have to live every day wondering if your childhood fantasy wasn't a big part of your love for

me, and if you would someday outgrow the fantasy, or I
would fail to live up to it, or you would simply grow bored
and become fascinated with something else. Something I
wasn't a part of."

"Dammit, Lisa!" he exploded, lurching to his feet once
more. "There are a lot of things about love that you can't
ever be certain of. It's the nature of the beast. I can't rip out
my heart and offer it to you to examine the way I can my
bankbook. All I can do is tell you that *you* are more important to me than any stupid fantasy."

As she regarded him thoughtfully, her shoulders seemed
to square against the sofa back. Sam noticed the faint ripple of her throat as she swallowed hard. Almost, he thought,
as if she were waging some inner battle with herself. When
she finally spoke, his jaw dropped in disbelief.

"Then quit the *Black Star* project," she said.

"What?"

"You heard me. Quit. If I am more important to you than
solving the mystery of Alexander and Elizabeth, prove it.
Walk away from it. Prove to both of us that your love for
me is stronger than your need to fulfill some old quest."

"An ultimatum, Lisa?"

"No," she insisted. She stood, looking as miserable as he
felt. "It's just a possible solution. But not a very good one,
I realize now. Forget I ever said it. It really wouldn't prove
anything, would it?"

"No. Which is one reason I'd never agree to it. The other
is that I'll be damned if we'll start our life together with
either one of us jumping through the other's hoops. Love is
a risky venture, Lisa, just like the attempt to salvage a ship,"
he added, instinctively grasping for something familiar to
him. "Most of it is hidden beneath the surface. At best you
can only glimpse it for brief, shadowy moments that can be
so perfect they're almost otherworldly. Sometimes you can
go weeks, months, without anything to hold in your hand
to prove that it exists. You either believe it's there or you
don't. Faith, Lise," he concluded softly. "It takes faith."

Lisa folded her arms as if she were shivering. "Then maybe I don't have what it takes. Can't you see that I'm the kind of person who needs to be sure, Sam? And how could I ever be sure, knowing..."

"Knowing that I had already lied and misled you," he finished when she abandoned the statement with an awkward shrug. "That's really at the heart of this, isn't it, Lisa? No matter how much you claim to have understood and forgiven me, no matter how much you might really want to. You're just blowing smoke in my face with this talk about my being caught up in a fantasy."

"No. Yes, oh, I don't even know anymore."

She turned away from him, the set of her shoulders no longer rigid. She looked drained, spent, and Sam wished to hell she would permit him to get close enough to gather her in his arms and tell her everything was going to be all right. Because it was.

"It's all so complicated," she murmured in a small, broken voice. "And confusing."

"And irrational," added Sam, moving to stand as close behind her as he dared. "And I can't banish an irrational fear with rational arguments, can I, Lisa?" Her only answer was the slight lifting of her shoulders. "And all the pleading and apologizing in the world won't make your fears go away. It's all a waste of time. But don't worry, Lisa, I won't waste your time anymore."

If Lisa had known what Sam intended, she would have lurched away as she had every other time he'd attempted to touch her. But his hand lifted her hair quickly, without warning, and the caress of his warm lips on the back of her neck was over almost before she knew it was happening. Only the sensual thrill it sent speeding through her lingered. By the time she'd whirled to confront him, all there was to see was his back as he strode from the house, closing the door behind him with the most final-sounding click Lisa had ever heard.

She stood in the middle of the living room listening as the angry sound of his motorcycle gunned past the windows and faded in the distance. Still she stood there, desperately trying to recapture the feeling of cold paralysis she'd experienced earlier. That's what she wanted to go on feeling forever, a blissful nothingness. But it was impossible. Evidently her emotions had moved past that initial state of self-protection.

Now they were fully awake and warring with so many different, complex messages that Lisa couldn't have described exactly how she felt if her life depended on it. Bleakly she recognized the irony in the fact that, in a manner of speaking, it did. Would there ever again come a day in her life when she wouldn't feel Sam's betrayal like an open wound?

One feeling she did identify was the beam of hope that shot through her a few minutes later at the sound of the back doorbell. How was it possible that when fury was still so much an undercurrent of what she was feeling, she could want so badly to see him one more time? She started for the door in a run, then slowed, and once more her spirits touched rock bottom. If it was Sam at the door, surely she would have heard his motorcycle returning.

It was Helen, and Lisa tried not to show the aching disappointment that washed through her. Helen was still wearing her fancy blue dress, but like Lisa, her expression was better suited to a much more somber occasion than a wedding.

She reached out and patted Lisa's clenched hands. "Lisa, honey, I saw Sam leave, and I thought you might need someone to talk to."

Lisa's thoughts were so tangled that if Helen had merely said "How are you?" she would have had to struggle to compose an appropriate response. This matter was much tougher. She fought to harness her concentration and finally shook her head in a gentle refusal. Helen was a friend, a good one, but she wasn't what Lisa needed now. She needed Sam, and the sense of absolute connection and belonging that only he had ever made her feel. But she'd sent Sam away, and he had gone, promising not to waste her time

ever again. All she wanted now was to be alone to figure out
how in the world she was going to deal with that.

"Thanks, Helen, but I don't think I'm ready to talk to
anyone about this. Maybe later, tomorrow..." She
shrugged, trying to smile and failing. Her voice cracked as
she added, "I don't really know."

Mercifully the older woman didn't press her. "There,
there," she soothed instead. "I didn't come here to upset
you further, just to let you know I'm here if you need me."

"Thanks. I appreciate that, Helen. I really do."

"At the moment it looks to me as if what you could use
most is a nap."

"I don't know," Lisa demurred, not sure she was ready
to be that alone with her thoughts. She decided she would
prefer semblance of activity to distract her from the painful
process of coming to terms with all that had happened. She
glanced down at her dress. "Maybe I'll just go upstairs and
get rid of this outfit."

"That sounds like a good idea," Helen returned, maintaining her quietly cheerful tone in spite of the bitterness
that had crept into Lisa's. "And while you're doing that,
why don't I just slip in and straighten up the dining room for
you? I can put all that food away so that nothing spoils. I'll
be quick as a wink and out of here before you've finished
changing. Now run along," she directed, nudging Lisa toward the stairs. "I'm certain you'll feel better once you
snuggle into something more comfortable."

At the moment Lisa was just as certain she would never
feel better again. She headed upstairs anyway, silently giving thanks that Helen wasn't the sort to harangue her for a
detailed explanation of what had happened. While she was
at it, she tacked on a prayer that a little of her friend's op-
timism would rub off on her. Moving automatically, she
tugged off the dress and flung it onto the bed. With the same
distracted speed she pulled on her jeans and the old fisher-
man-knit sweater that was uppermost in the suitcase she'd
packed for her honeymoon aboard Sam's boat. It was just
what Helen had suggested, the sort of soft, comfortable

outfit you literally snuggled into. Today, however, it brought Lisa no comfort at all.

Helen had exaggerated her own efficiency and was still busy downstairs when Lisa finished dressing. Knowing Helen would understand her need for privacy, Lisa chose to linger in her bedroom until she was gone. Restlessly she crossed to the window, purposely avoiding the slightest glance at the crumpled peach lace reminder of what might have been.

The ocean was a sheet of dark blue, ruffled in white, constantly moving and changing. Watching it, a small, objective part of Lisa understood how Sam could find its mysteries so compelling. That only made things worse. She didn't want to understand. She wanted to find a thread of self-righteousness and cling to it like a lifeline.

Eventually she heard the back door close, signaling Helen's departure, and at last the house was blessedly silent. She considered going downstairs to make herself a cup of tea. If she tried all the old-fashioned remedies that she could think of for the blues, one was bound to work. Wasn't it? She made no move to leave her post by the window. *The blues* didn't come close to capturing the way she felt. She doubted any simple word or two could. Feeling more than betrayed, more than angry, she sagged against the wall, brought her cupped hands to her face and cried.

When she stopped, her eyes stung from the torrent of hot, bitter tears. She forced them open to face the same taunting glitter of the sea, which for hundreds of years had competed with women for the attentions of a few adventuresome men, and won. Lisa finally understood exactly what this smothering feeling overriding all the others inside her was. Fear. She was afraid.

When she'd discovered Ron was cheating on her, she'd felt humiliated and mad as hell. His lies and duplicity had torn fresh holes in her new pride and self-confidence, but she realized now that her heart had never truly been involved. If she had loved Ron half as much as she did Sam, she would have fought for him. In spite of all Sam had done, whatever his motives, she still loved him enough to fight, she realized. Unfortunately, she had no idea how to begin.

If her rival for Sam's heart had been another woman, she could have devised a strategy. But how did you compete with a man's fantasies? And how could you know for sure when you had won or lost? She had been right when she told Sam their situation was hopeless. Sure, her anger would eventually burn itself out, her wounded pride would heal, but could she live with the uncertainty of wondering whether he really loved *her* or the fanciful notion that she was the perfect choice to play lady to his pirate?

For want of anything better to do, Lisa decided to have that cup of tea after all. As she passed the dresser, she noticed the bundle of Miriam's letters resting against the mirror, where she had placed them the afternoon she and Sam had destroyed her bed. On impulse she picked them up and carried them downstairs with her. Several times since that day, she had been tempted to loosen the faded ribbon and read them, lured by what Sam had called a healthy curiosity.

Living in her great-aunt's house, dealing every day with the intimate details of her life, using the same china she had used, the same towels and linens, had made Lisa more than curious. It had made her care. Lately her feelings for Sam had distracted her, but she still longed to understand why Miriam had chosen to live as she had, and why she would leave such a legacy of destruction.

She was now willing to acknowledge that there was a link between her and Miriam that kept them from being strangers, despite the fact that they had never met. Today in particular she was grateful for the comfort of even that fragile link. True, it was a link Miriam had never known about and that Lisa once would have declared quite meaningless. Nonetheless, it existed, and for Lisa it sanctified her desire to learn what was in those old letters.

She waited until she was settled in her den with a strong cup of tea before opening the first one. The fine white stationery had grown crisp and yellow over the years, but the

words, written with impeccable penmanship, were still
clearly legible. Lisa had assumed the letters had been written to Miriam. She was surprised to discover that they were
penned by her instead, and all to the same man, a Mr.
Arthur Benoit, addressed to him at a post office box in
Buffalo, New York. And obviously never mailed, as the
opening paragraph of the very first letter predicted.

Miriam had written in her careful script.

Dear Arthur,

    I am writing to you to retract all the foolish things I
said yesterday when I refused your very moving proposal of marriage. Unfortunately, I know well that my
equally foolish fears will prevent me from ever mailing
this letter. Still I write, needing to put into words these
feelings that otherwise might explode from within.

Lisa looked up from the letter with a tremor of recognition. The words Miriam had written so long ago struck a
chord deep within her, and it was a few minutes before she
could read further, slowly working her way through the pile
of nine short letters written over a five-year period.

Arthur Benoit, Lisa discovered, was the traveling salesman Helen had heard about, the man Miriam had been involved with in her late twenties. Poor Miriam's predicament
came alive in the letters, and although it might seem ridiculous to a woman of that same age today, the pain and de-
spair conveyed by her stilted words brought tears to Lisa's
eyes all over again.

Miriam had loved Arthur Benoit but had bowed to her
mother's relentless insistence that he was beneath her. "Do
I want to live my whole life out of a suitcase, Mother asks
me over and over again. And truthfully, Arthur, I don't
know if I could bear the transience of it all." So Miriam had
sent Arthur on his way without her, six weeks before the
shocking realization that she was pregnant with his child.

In another letter she never mailed, she had eloquently told
him of her mother's infuriated reaction to the news of her

pregnancy, and of her own shame and fear, as well as confessing to a stubborn trace of wistfulness that they might yet have a life together. Likewise she wrote of the difficult birth of their son in the home of an aunt who lived in a neighboring state and who had been sworn to secrecy about the whole sordid matter. And she wrote of having to give the child away before she had even once been allowed to hold him in her arms.

The next several letters had been written on their son's early birthdays. Somehow Miriam had managed to find out where his adoptive family lived, and although she never so much as hinted that she might do anything about it, the knowledge alone seemed to bring her some small measure of comfort. Through the blur of her own tears, Lisa read the description of Miriam's feelings of loneliness and regret and helplessness.

The final letter in the pile was very brief and clipped in tone, as if whatever change of heart eventually led Miriam to leave such a bitter legacy had already taken place. Enclosed with the letter was a newspaper clipping, which Miriam suggested ought to be a matter of significant interest to Arthur. It was the notice of the death of a four-year-old boy due to a lengthy bout with tuberculosis.

Lisa closed her eyes. No wonder Miriam had been so bitter, especially toward children. The very sound of their laughter must have been like pouring vinegar on a never-healing sore. She hadn't hated children; she had hated herself.

For a long time after she had refolded the letters with shaky fingers and replaced each in its envelope, Lisa could think of nothing but the tragedy that had unfolded in this house, borne no doubt in silence except for the scant relief Miriam might have found in writing these letters.

If only Miriam had possessed the courage to defy her snob of a mother right from the start. So what if Arthur was *only* a traveling salesman? There were worse things in life than being mobile, for pity's sake.

And, a small voice pointed out, worse things than being uncertain.

Jarred by her own thought, Lisa reached for her tea. Cold. Replacing the cup on the table, she sat back in her chair and eyed the neatly retied packet of letters. A funny thing, fear, and evidently a quite common one. A half hour ago she would have sworn she was suffering the worst case of it in history. But there sat written proof that Miriam had been so fearful of taking a chance with the man she loved that she had let her entire life dry up around her.

Then there was Sam. He hadn't been ashamed to admit it was his fear of losing her that had made him make one stupid mistake after another. And Elizabeth. Whether she had gone willingly or bound and gagged to Alex's ship, she had to have been somewhat afraid to leave behind everything familiar to begin a dangerous new life.

The lesson was as clear to Lisa as the choice she had to make. There wasn't any doubt in her mind that, as reckless and uncertain as it may be, if history was bound to repeat itself, she would rather suffer Elizabeth's fate than Miriam's.

She was in the kitchen in a flash, dialing the phone number of Sam's houseboat. When she got no answer, she dialed his office at the university. While it rang, it occurred to her that the only other time she'd phoned him there was the day she'd learned that her proposal had sold. There was never any other need. Sam was always around when he said he would be. Reliable, that was Sam. And resourceful and compassionate and strong and sensitive and sexy. And, she could see now, honorable in his own fashion. And loving him was worth any risk she had to take. Somehow she was going to find the courage to make it work.

"Oceanography," said a giggly feminine voice on the other end of the line. "Oceanography...hold on." Another giggle and then, "I'm sorry. Oceanography department, Marcia speaking."

"Marcia, my name is Lisa Bennett, and I'm a friend of Sam Ravenal's. Is he there by any chance?"

"Oh, no, none of them are here now. They—" It sounded as if she had put her hand over the phone to say something to someone else. In the background Lisa could hear the kind of talking and laughter she associated more with a fraternity party than an office. "I'm sorry," the woman named Marcia said again. "You'll have to excuse me, there's a lot of excitement here today—a celebration, really. If you're a friend of Sam's, you'll be glad to hear they just radioed in a couple of hours ago with the news that they located the *Black Star*. We had a devil of a time finding Sam, but we finally did, and I'm sure he's on his way out to join them now."

"I see," Lisa responded, certain the excitement she felt at hearing the news must be minuscule compared to Sam's. Would he feel the same urgent need she had to share his triumph? "When do you expect Sa—I mean, them, back?"

"Who knows? A week...two. Maybe longer. They have plenty of provisions on board, and if I know Sam and Lewis, they won't put back in until they've secured her. I'll tell him you called, Leslie."

"No, it's...Lisa," she muttered into a suddenly dead line as the other woman quickly hung up. A week, Marcia had said, maybe longer. That was certainly plenty of time for second thoughts, and third and fourth. Lisa quietly replaced the receiver.

How the hell much courage could one woman be expected to have?

Chapter Fourteen

News of the discovery of a sunken pirate ship in coastal waters was reported on the six o'clock news of all three area television stations, complete with film taken by crews aboard hastily dispatched boats. Lisa flipped frantically from one station to another but never caught a glimpse of Sam among the horde of very excited scientists. Of course, between the jostling of the cameraman and all the exuberant champagne spraying on board, it was hard to see much clearly. Lisa had no doubt that he was there somewhere, though. And, she kept telling herself, she was happy for him.

Ecstatic. So happy, in fact, that she didn't know how she was going to make it through the rest of this first day without him, never mind the indeterminate length of time he would be gone. She wondered exactly what Marcia had meant when she said they had to "secure" the *Black Star*. And how long such a thing might take.

She resolved to submerge herself in work. Whatever progress she made now would leave her that much more time free to spend with Sam if—Lisa abruptly broke the thought. *When* Sam returned. She was going to rely on the power of positive thinking and refuse to approach this with any doubts whatsoever. *When* Sam came back, everything would be perfect.

Adopting that as sort of mantra, Lisa wandered outside after the news ended and did her best to concentrate on putting something on paper. It wasn't easy. Tonight every passing car and rustling leaf seemed more compelling than the ideas in her head.

Since she was constantly looking up and glancing over her shoulder, it had to be one more trick up fate's sleeve that she didn't see or hear anyone approaching until he was kneeling so closely behind her Lisa swore she could feel his heart pounding. His arms shot around to crisscross over her chest tightly, and his lips slid against the hair covering her ear.

"All right, lady," he whispered, his tone rough and deep and familiar, "you can either make this easy or hard."

The sudden ricocheting of Lisa's heart inside her chest had nothing to do with the burst of fear that hadn't lasted even a split second. She'd known almost immediately that the man who'd crept up on her was Sam. She had not only recognized his voice, but also his hands, his tanned forearms beneath the rolled-back cuffs of the formal white shirt he still wore, even the delicious, clean male scent of him.

Absently she noted that he didn't smell like a man who had spent the day either at sea or swilling champagne from a bottle. Just maybe, she thought, Marcia had been wrong. Maybe Sam had spent the day as alone and anguished as she had. Lisa felt a rush of tenderness and love for him and tried to turn in his arms to tell him so.

"Sam, you don't know—"

Immediately his arms tightened across her chest, not painfully exactly, but forcefully enough to choke off her words. "Uh-uh. No talking, no explaining, no debating. I'm through with that garbage. We're going to do this my way. Your only choice is whether you walk or go fireman style."

As he spoke, he drew her to her feet, keeping her body plastered intimately to the front of his.

"Walk where?" Lisa asked, confused.

"To my ship, of course," Sam drawled in response. "Tch, tch, Lisa, I thought you knew your role in this fantasy."

"What on earth ..."

"Time's up," he declared as the world fell from beneath her feet. "Fireman style it is."

Lisa quickly realized that the world hadn't fallen; rather, she'd been tipped head over heels and tossed over Sam's shoulder so that her feet hung in front of him and her head behind. It was an undignified position at best, and her neck arched as she anxiously glanced around to see if anyone was witnessing the scene.

"Let me go, Sam," she demanded, trying to lever off his shoulder to let him know that, even if he felt like kidding around, she didn't.

"Not on your life," he shot back. His slap on her backside was just as crisp as her demand had been, but much more effective. It quickly brought her wiggling to a halt.

"I mean it, Sam," she said, gritting her teeth and striving for an implacable tone that would bring him to his senses. "This isn't funny."

"Good. I wasn't aiming to amuse you. In fact, that would spoil the entire effect. You're supposed to feel indignant, vaguely threatened and slightly aroused although reluctant to admit it. Think you can handle all that?"

Beneath the faintly mocking note in his voice, Lisa detected the exact tone of implacability she'd been trying to project. He wasn't kidding, she realized belatedly. And he wasn't going to put her down. He was actually going to haul her off to his ship in some crazy reenactment of Elizabeth's abduction.

Already they were halfway across Helen's yard, heading, no doubt, for the dock between her property and the next. It was the only deep-water dock in the neighborhood, she recalled Helen saying once. She could only assume that's where Sam's boat was tied up. All she could actually see was what they were leaving behind, and that only if she lifted her face away from the flat surface of Sam's very nice butt.

"I'm just thankful this dock isn't any farther away," Sam grunted as he started down the shallow rocky incline leading to it. "You're not as light as you look. Of course, you're lucky the dock is here at all. The way you wiggle around, if I had to row you out to my boat, I'd probably have to bind and gag you to keep you from capsizing the damn thing."

"You just may have to do that anyway," she growled. "For your information, I don't like being carted off without any say in the matter."

"Suits me," he retorted, his shrug jostling her even more than his rapid stride already was. "Tying you up might add to the drama, don't you think?"

"What I think is that this is crazy."

"Of course it is. A totally irrational response to an irrational situation. I decided that if I was going to be condemned for being caught up in some romantic fantasy, I might as well enjoy living it. Only I've decided to make a few changes in mood, update it a little—from romantic to erotic."

"Oh, you have, have you?"

"Yep."

For the first time Lisa was a little thankful for her position, undignified as it was. At least her face was hidden from Sam's view. She wasn't sure she wanted him to see the small smile she was wearing. It had come to her along with a stirring of desire when he'd described his intentions as erotic.

Isn't this exactly what she wanted, for Sam to be with her, as eager as she was to put the pieces of their relationship back together? Lisa knew that it was, though she wasn't sure she liked the heavy-handed way he had taken absolute control of the situation.

Of course, she admitted to herself as the hand he was using to restrain her turned idly caressing on her bottom, releasing yet another ripple of desire, she wasn't altogether sure she didn't like it. True to his sardonic prediction of a moment ago, she was starting to feel more than indignant.

She felt vaguely threatened in an erotic way, and aroused. Actually, her indignation was fading fast.

"I hope you realize that Helen's probably watching this whole thing," she told him, more for appearance's sake than anything else. A heady feeling of anticipation was rapidly taking control of her senses as Sam's steps clattered on the wooden dock, finally stopping beside a long, sleek, gleaming redwood-hulled sailboat that looked, to Lisa's untrained eye, to be ready to fly. "She might even report you to the police for kidnapping...not to mention trespassing."

Sam tumbled her off his shoulder, but his hands were sure and steady on her hips, making sure that she touched down lightly. For the first time since he'd walked out of the house that morning, their eyes met.

"Hardly," he responded to her suggestion about Helen. "Not when she's the one who gave me permission to tie up here. In fact, I've been pacing around her kitchen for over an hour, waiting for you to show your face. I would have hated like hell to have to climb down the trellis outside your bedroom window with you squirming around on my back."

"Helen helped you?" Lisa murmured under her breath. "That traitor."

"Not at all. I had the devil's own time convincing her that everything I did—or was about to do—was because I love you." Self-disgust flickered in his dark eyes. "At least I succeeded in convincing *her* of that. She wants you to be happy, Lisa. Just like I do."

"And you two decided that being shanghaied this way will make me happy?"

"I decided it couldn't screw things up any more than I already had. Your only solution to this mess was telling me to get out of your life, and I can't do that. Maybe if we have some time alone..."

"How much time?"

Sam appeared oblivious to the hopeful catch in her question.

"As long as it takes," he told her gravely. His hand rose to briefly caress her cheek, but before Lisa could reach up to hold it there, as she longed to, he dropped it back to his side, and that grim, determined expression returned to his face.

"Get on board, Lisa," he ordered. When she hesitated, he added, "I don't want to have to force you."

"Oh, no, heaven forbid," she exclaimed, turning to step into the boat before he glimpsed the excitement sparkling in her eyes. Sometime soon now she was going to have to get around to telling him that he didn't have to force her to do anything he might have in mind. But not, she decided, before they had both had a chance to live their fantasy to the hilt.

"All right," she said, glancing around as he stepped on board behind her. "Where are the chains? Or do you seafaring types prefer to call them manacles?"

The lighthearted inquiry caused Sam to regard her quizzically. "I can see you have a lot to learn about pirates. We don't chain captured women, Lisa, we ravish them."

"You can certainly try," she snarled, whirling around to eye him challengingly.

Sam sighed, lowering his gaze as if resigning himself to the fact that he must have imagined any signs of softening on her part.

"Maybe a little later," he tossed back lightly, then pointed toward the open door behind her. "For now I want you to wait down in the cabin while I get us under way. I don't want to have to be distracted every minute worrying that you're going to jump overboard."

Lisa lifted her chin defiantly. "What an interesting suggestion. It's going to be pretty tough for you to drive this thing and baby-sit me at the same time, don't you think?"

His droll smile was fleeting. "*Navigate*, Lisa, not *drive*. And she was designed so that most of the navigating can be handled by computer once we're on open seas. That will leave me plenty of time for baby-sitting...and other things," he added. His gaze locked with hers, gently searching, vaguely hopeful.

That hopeful gleam was quickly extinguished as Lisa tossed her head with all the ferocious pride she'd inherited from Elizabeth.

"Don't count on it, pal," she advised with a sneer. "You dragged me here against my will, and we've already established that you're big and strong enough to force me to stay. But nothing in this world or the next will ever make me change my mind about you. Happy navigating."

Whipping around, she dashed down the stairs, but not before she caught sight of the shattered expression on Sam's face. She had decided to force him to play the scene out, figuring he deserved a bit of turnabout for daring to pull a stunt like this. Now she was wavering. It was a little cruel to make him go on suffering, thinking she was still angry with him.

The sound of the door closing above her, followed by the metallic click of a key in the lock, quickly stiffened Lisa's resolve. The nerve of him, thinking he could lock her up as if she really were some wench he had captured! Her first instinct had been right. Let him stew for as long as it took him to get them under way.

One hour and thirty-seven minutes. That's how long it took, Lisa discovered, to steer a boat safely out of Narragansett Harbor. Or maybe that's how long it took this particular man to steer it out and also to summon the courage to do what he thought he'd set out to do. In her heart Lisa knew that Sam wouldn't actually force her to anything she didn't want to. He could spout off all he wanted to about ravishing her; when push came to shove, Sam Ravenal was going to walk down those stairs with seduction, not force, on his mind. Only Lisa was going to beat him to it.

She didn't know the first thing about sailing a boat, but common sense told her she had plenty of time after that door locked to poke around and become familiar with Sam's cabin before preparing for him to join her. She ran her hand over the polished redwood paneling and perused the books neatly arranged at the back of his desk in the corner. Mostly they were marine archaeology textbooks, along with a dog-eared copy of *Moby Dick* and a few paperbacks of the international intrigue variety.

The bunk along the outside wall looked narrow, although Lisa surmised it was generously proportioned by nautical standards. At any rate, the bunk's size and the prospect of spending her nights aboard nestled close to Sam beneath its black plaid wool blanket didn't displease her in the least. Moving to the far end of the narrow cabin, she took her time admiring the beautifully crafted model ships securely bolted to their shelves. She smiled, thinking of her Whittler and of just how much of an inspiration he had indeed become to her. Only after she felt at home in the place that was so much a part of the man she loved did she slowly remove her sweater and jeans in anticipation of his arrival.

The sound of the key turning in the lock warned her Sam was coming, and as prepared as she had thought she was for this, the slow, steady thud of his footsteps on the stairs caused her to tremble against the dark blue sheets of his bunk. She had peeled back the blanket, thinking that the jewellike tone of the sheets made a more striking backdrop for the racy white-lace lingerie she had put on that morning and never bothered to remove.

It felt as if she'd lived a lifetime since then and had come full circle back to wanting to give herself to Sam fully, to please him in every way, to satisfy all his desires, fulfill his every fantasy. Lisa succumbed to a nervous smile, thinking how literally she was handling that last objective. Then her smile faded as Sam ducked his head to avoid banging the overhead panel at the bottom of the stairs and came fully into view.

Squinting as his eyes adjusted to the dim light below-deck, his gaze searched the cabin for her, growing a tad alarmed before eventually reaching the bunk. Evidently that was the very last place he'd expected to find her. As Lisa watched, the look of concern left his eyes, replaced by shock and finally burning intensity as he stared at the full curves of her breasts, generously exposed by the low-cut corset, then drifted down the trail of filmy white lace to the dark triangular shadow between her thighs.

"I thought..." His voice was raspy, as if his throat had gone dry in a hurry. He swallowed hard as he worked to force his gaze back to her face, and Lisa felt her confidence surge almost as high as her love for him. "I thought you said nothing would change your mind about me."

"I did." She calmly propped her head on her hand, turning slightly and drawing one knee up in a pose she knew would have been alluring even if she weren't dressed like one of the working girls in an Old West bordello. "I love you, Sam. And I want you. Nothing will ever change that."

Sam's heavy-lidded look of disbelief lasted all of two seconds—about the same length of time it took him to cross the cabin and fall to his knees beside the bunk. He touched her shoulder lightly, as if she might prove to be no more than a mirage. Then, with a hoarse groan, he bent his head and kissed the same spot, his mouth lingering on her skin.

"God, Lisa, I was so afraid I'd lost you forever," he breathed, still nuzzling her shoulder hungrily.

"Me, too," she confessed. "How could I have been stupid enough to tell you to leave the way I did? And how could you just walk out that way?" She dragged her fingers along his back, savoring the promise of strength in his bunched muscles.

"Hold on a minute." He lifted his head to regard her with a darkly ironic smile. "I didn't just walk out, lady. I died a little with each step. I had no idea where I was going or what I was going to do. Only that I had to get you back and that what I was doing wasn't working. I knew if I stayed, I'd keep hammering away at you, and end up driving you further and further from me."

"Probably. I was a little shell-shocked at the time."

"With damn good reason." He winced, remembering. "I can't believe I was so quick to call your ex-husband an idiot. It seems he and I are in the same league when it comes to mishandling women."

"Definitely not," Lisa declared. "There's at least one huge difference: I know you weren't ever motivated by greed the way Ron was, but by love." Her hands rose to frame his face, smiling as the hint of dark stubble on his jaw tickled her palms delightfully. "Sam, do you think it's possible to love someone too much for your own good? Or for theirs?"

"No," he answered without hesitation.

She giggled. "Me, either."

"I think what hurts is when you love someone so much and are so afraid you might lose them that you don't trust them. If I'd trusted you more from the beginning, we could have avoided all this pain."

"Or created even more," Lisa countered. "Your instincts were probably on target all along, Sam. You were right when you said you didn't even know me at the start. You had every right not to trust me with details of a project that was so important to you and to a lot of others. I, on the other hand, knew you by the time you tried to explain. I should have trusted you, Sam."

"I'd say the fact that you're lying here, like this—" his fingers reverently traced the edging of lace at her breasts "—is proof that you do trust me. You just needed a little time to work it out for yourself before you were able to accept that love means taking risks now and again."

As he pulled her close, Lisa thought of Miriam's letter, and her mouth curved in a smile against his hard, strong chest. After a few seconds she levered back to look at him. "Actually, I didn't work it out completely on my own. I had a little family help."

Sam's eyes turned to slits in his taut, handsome face, and his hands on her shoulders tightened possessively. "What family?"

Lisa chuckled, feeling very well protected. "Miriam. I read the letters, Sam. Miriam's letters." Briefly she explained about Miriam and Arthur and the baby.

"That's rough," he said softly when she finished. Gently his thumbs sponged the tears that had gathered at the corners of her eyes. "And with the rest of her life as empty as it was, she had plenty of time to brood over her loss."

Lisa nodded in agreement, then said, "Besides forcing me to face my feelings for you, reading those letters also served another good purpose. I'm finally satisfied that the children's museum is the right thing to do. And I think it should be named after Miriam."

Sam's eyes reflected his understanding. "That sounds fitting to me."

A contented sigh left Lisa as his fingers threaded through the thick, silky hair at her nape, sensuously kneading the muscles there. She was astonished by the purity of her happiness. It was the sort you wanted to share with the entire world. "Oh, Sam," she murmured, nestling closer to his warmth, "if only Miriam had had more backbone."

"Or Arthur had had a boat," he countered, his wry smile gentle.

"I'm awfully glad you have a boat," Lisa purred, sliding her hands along his throat to the buttons on his pleated shirt. His tough, masculine presence in the small cabin was growing more overwhelming by the moment. He stared at her from beneath dark brows, his eyes a smoldering forest green. She tipped her head back as his mouth dipped to claim hers, then her eyes opened wide with alarm.

"Boat!" she exclaimed against the damp heat of his open mouth. "How in the world could I have forgotten about the *Black Star*? Marcia told me you were headed out there hours ago... to stay for weeks maybe."

Sam lowered his brows quizzically, but at the edges of his mouth a smug smile had already started. "And just when did you talk to Marcia?"

Lisa said sheepishly, "When I called your office to tell you I'd made a big mistake sending you away."

"You mean this whole abduction scene was unnecessary?"

"Oh, I wouldn't say that," Lisa replied, slipping her hand inside his shirt to stroke his chest and pluck lightly at the dark hair covering it. "And I did try to tell you how sorry I was when you first grabbed me." She lowered her voice to a gruff imitation of his. "No talking, no debating, no explanations. Remember?"

"I remember," he groaned. "How is it possible for a man to screw up his own damn fantasy?"

"Why, Sam, you sound as if you think it's over," she drawled, slipping open the buttons on his shirt to reveal the sculptured beauty of his chest and the muscle-ridged flatness lower down. She touched him eagerly, daringly.

"One more mistake on my part," he murmured. "It's just beginning." Again his fingers found their way to the top edge of her lingerie, curling inside to brush her nipples to instant awareness. "I love this thing you have on, Lise. I just can't decide if I most want to make love to you wearing it or with only your skin touching mine."

"Does it have to be either/or?" she asked on a shuddering breath as his thumbs flicked across the aroused peaks of her breasts.

"How about first either, then or?" he suggested thickly as he nibbled his way up the side of her throat. His breath was like a storm in her ear.

"Whatever you say," she whispered. Then, unable to turn a deaf ear to her conscience, she angled her head, seeking his gaze, her own remorseful, imploring. "But first, please tell me you didn't listen to what I said about quitting the *Black Star* project. I'd never forgive myself if I made you give up on something so important to you. In fact," she forced herself to add miserably, "you probably ought to be there right now, instead of here with me."

Sam's strong hands bracketed her face. His expression was calm, without a trace of regret. His voice was soft but absolute in its conviction. "First of all, there is never anywhere I would rather be than with you. You are the most important thing in my life, Lisa, and you always will be. And yes, I quit the *Black Star* project, but not in the sort of self-sacrificing manner that should leave you feeling guilty."

With a reluctant sigh he eased himself onto the bunk, folding her close to his side before explaining further. "After I left your house, I rode around for hours, thinking. But I didn't definitely decide to quit until I got back to the boat and found the message that they'd located the *Black Star* early this morning and that the preliminary dives had showed no sign of the treasure she was supposed to have been carrying when she went down." He broke into that cocky grin Lisa adored. "One more bit of proof that Alex knew he was being set up—and that he outwitted them by unloading the booty ahead of time and hiding it somewhere. Then he sank the ship to leave the rest of the world guessing about it for almost three hundred years."

"Maybe your questions are answered," Lisa pointed out, "but isn't this when they'll need your expertise most?"

"I contacted a friend I've worked with before, and he was more than happy to fill in for me. And to Lewis—he's the director of the project—one marine archaeologist is as good as another. In fact, he took pains to tell me it would be a relief to have someone aboard who had an attention span longer than a minute and a half." With his teeth he drew one slender lace strap off her shoulder and caressed her shoulder blade with his tongue. "I've been sort of distracted lately."

Lisa shivered deliciously. "I know the feeling." She forced her eyes open, loving him too much not to ask one last question. "Sam, don't you at least want to go down and see the *Black Star* for yourself?"

He shrugged. "I'm sure I'll see her. We'll see her together. I'll like that even better."

He yanked on her, causing them both to roll to their sides at the same time, so close together that their noses bumped. They laughed softly.

"I'd like that, too," Lisa told him. "Sam, I was wrong about all this, as well. You're certainly entitled to your fantasies. God knows, I have a few of my own...."

"All you have to do is ask," he invited in a blatantly seductive tone.

Lisa smiled, amazed that she had been blessed with such a perfect man. "I never again want you to feel as if I'm fighting your fantasies, or competing with them. I want to share them, Sam.''

"Lisa, love," he murmured, running his hands over her breasts and hips, down to the smooth expanse of bare thigh between her panties and the tops of her pale stockings. There was a sudden hint of impatience in his touch. "Don't you know that you are my fantasy? Now and forever."

His lips found her, drowning her senses with a long, ardent kiss. She felt the hand caressing her thighs slip in between. He pressed. Lisa arched, and electricity danced along her nerve endings. She closed her eyes tighter, prepared to surrender everything, fully. If only...

Cursing her own need to be as certain as possible, she pulled back a little to say, "Sam? Just one more thing."

His mouth followed hers, wet, persistent. "What?"

"You know that I'm the sort of person who likes to be sure about things, one way or the other. And, well, I'm all for maintaining a little mystery in a relationship, but..."

"But?" The word was a damp caress of her lips, making her tremble.

"I was wondering...are you still planning to marry me?"

At last he lifted his head enough to look at her, his eyes almost black with passion. He smiled, and when he smiled that slow smile, Lisa knew she would love him forever.

"Of course I'm going to marry you," he assured her. "Right after the honeymoon."

* * * * *

Silhouette Special Edition

COMING NEXT MONTH

#487 A CRIME OF THE HEART—Cheryl Reavis
"Outsider" Quinn Tyler returned to Lancaster County, hoping the old scandal about her and Amishman Adam Sauder was forgotten. But to Adam and his people, one crime could never be forgiven....

#488 SMOKY'S BANDIT—Barbara Catlin
Holed up in a remote Texas cabin, Jerri aimed to kick two nasty addictions: cigarettes and Tyler Reynolds. Yet when the irresistible cowboy appeared, good intentions went up in smoke!

#489 THE LIEUTENANT'S WOMAN—Janice Kaiser
Anne-Marie was no longer a naive German girl in love with a dashing American lieutenant. But decades later, a savvy Californian, she found she still hadn't outgrown Royce Buchanan.

#490 GHOST OF A CHANCE—Andrea Edwards
Holly Carpenter reluctantly moved into a rickety old house, only to encounter a pesty poltergeist...and a dangerously tempting tenant. Could Zach Phillips mend Holly's broken heart?

#491 THE RIGHT MISTAKE—Janet Franklin
When a wilderness walk proved perilous, Jessica needed a hero...and Seth Cameron did just fine. Back on solid city pavement, however, she feared loving Seth was a mistake.

#492 THUNDER HIGH—Linda Shaw
Hired to buy off a senator's mistress, Brad Zacharias hadn't expected compassionate, spirited Catherine Holmes. He soon cursed his political ties, which threatened Cat's good works...and their thunderous attraction.

AVAILABLE NOW:

Silhouette Desire

TALES OF THE RISING MOON
A Desire trilogy by Joyce Thies

MOON OF THE RAVEN—June (#432)

Conlan Fox was part American Indian and as tough as the Montana land he rode, but it took fragile yet strong-willed Kerry Armstrong to make his dreams come true.

REACH FOR THE MOON—August (#444)

It would take a heart of stone for Steven Armstrong to evict the woman and children living on his land. But when Steven saw Samantha, eviction was the last thing on his mind!

GYPSY MOON—October (#456)

Robert Armstrong met Serena when he returned to his ancestral estate in Connecticut. Their fiery temperaments clashed from the start, but despite himself, Rob was falling under the Gypsy's spell.
